T0167255

The Twisted Fate

Thomas Blood

AuthorHouse™
1663 Liberty Drive
Bloomington, IN 47403
www.authorhouse.com
Phone: 1-800-839-8640

Published by AuthorHouse 3/30/2012

ISBN: 978-1-4685-7342-8 (sc)
ISBN: 978-1-4685-7343-5 (e)

Library of Congress Control Number: 2012905697

This book is printed on acid-free paper.

1

It is a painful world that we live in. How unfortunate that sometimes the world makes monsters of us. Even worse is that most if not all of us are already monsters, but only the worst get the title. I am one of those who not only took the title, but gave the world of monsters something to fear forever. I will never be caught and therefore live forever in the hearts of all. Perhaps, my story will change this world to a better one, even if I was the worst monster of them all.

As all lives begin, I was born into this world to be someone. The question was who was I to be, and what I was meant to do. My parents were told they couldn't have kids, but after so long trying, and several problems between them, I was born, I was their miracle child. I made them happy, and gave them a reason to stay together. Then, against all odds, they had three more kids. I went from miracle child to the one they had to work for. I can only assume things would have been better for me if I had been the only child, but who knows these things.

All of the others took their spots as thorns in my side. I got robbed of my crib as soon as I could walk. I got less attention then I wanted. In the end I was a loner and nothing else. Life went on, but compared to the others, I just wasn't the same. I showed signs of being devious among other talents that made me a danger to society, while the others behaved normal. I grew up showing no remorse or love for anyone or anything, but that would have been best left alone. I watched my parents fight with no sorrow in my heart. The others gathered around each other and cried. My grandmother died from cancer and I still felt nothing. My own brother grew to hate me for not being able to feel. For that reason, I wanted to feel. It was several years, but I got my wish.

I met someone, at church of all places, who I just couldn't resist. I had to know her, touch her, be with her. Even though she was my sister's friend, I asked her out, and for a reason I to this day can't explain, she said yes. It was because of her that I became emotionally alive. I was a kid who firmly believed in God, but thanks to that one girl, I knew God was there for me. I never missed a chance to sit next to her, or talk to her. I held her hand, whenever it was allowed. One night stands out more than any other. We were lying in the back of the church van, just cuddled up together. We never said a word, but in that moment, I fell in love with her, and I still can't forget that feeling, even though I wish I could. As all good things, my first love didn't last, and it sent me to a new level of madness. Even I didn't realize what damage I had endured, until years later.

I didn't know what I was becoming, but I do know that my mind went from fighting to torture. Characters in my stories didn't simply die. They suffered through terrible fates, before I killed them in disturbing ways. My villains went from bad guys, to demons and monster, which killed with no remorse. I lost touch with the world as I dove further and further into my own fantasies. My mind became more and more violent. I began to enjoy some level of pain and torment. Eventually, I began to enjoy seeing others in pain. I was a noble soul with a very twisted heart.

It wasn't until my junior year of high school that I started dating again. I was tired of being alone, and so I went out to find someone to keep me company. I dated one person that year, and it was nothing to me. The following year, however, I dated three people. One just kind of happened. It was something to do, but there wasn't a big connection. Then, the next one was interesting to say the least.

I started liking a girl on the bus that wasn't like anyone else. I talked to her, but never made any advances. But before I even tried to ask her out, I had the best and worst thing to ever happen to me, walk right into my life. I was working fast-food at the time. I always had to take care of myself. I did enjoy work a lot, gave me something to do. On two occasions, a girl walked in and took my breath away. The first was a girl I didn't know and never saw again. The second came in with a co-worker.

I was making sandwiches as always, when I looked up right at her walking across the front counter. I couldn't help but to stare the first few seconds, before I regained the control to look away. I stole every glance I could until she left. My partner in crime for the night noticed my behavior and asked if I liked her. I confessed. The next night, the co-worker she came in with, was informed of my attraction. He promised to help me meet her. He kept his promise and brought her back the following Friday. Instead of shying away, I made it a point to introduce myself. The next day I got her number and started talking to her. Her name was Kay.

Unfortunately for both of us, she had feelings for someone else, a guy who was engaged to be married to the first girl I loved. His name was Mike. I grew to hate him for playing with the emotions of both girls, who I cared for. It took me a month to get her to start letting go of him, so she could be with me, but he pulled a trick and convinced her that I was the source of the problems she was having, even though they started at least a month before I had ever known she existed. So since I lost her, I asked the other girl out. We dated for about three weeks, before her mother decided I was too old for her and made her break up with me.

While I was with the other girl, Kay came to realize that she had developed feelings for me. She missed me and soon realized that I was not the source of her problems. We started talking again, but this time Mike wasn't such an issue. We started dating shortly after. Mike on the other hand, had other plans. He invited Kay to hang out with him and some friends, one of which he brought over to take her from me. Kay couldn't say no, so she broke up with me to avoid cheating. I forgave her like the fool I was, and we got back together. This time Mike was removed from the picture. She became my first and I had decided that she would be the one. However, the summer came and she went on a college trip, where one of her friends decided to try to be with her. Once again, she broke up with me to avoid cheating.

The end of the summer came, and we couldn't stay apart. She cheated on the other guy with me, before breaking up with him to come back to me. We were happy for months before another incident occurred. I met someone while I was at work one day. I got her number, and somehow decided that I needed to give her a chance. I broke up with Kay for the first time, not to avoid cheating on her, but to see what else was out there. We didn't last long. So the day Kay and I decided to be back together, she went to sleep with someone else. Instead of getting back together, I decided she had to prove she loved me like she claimed for all the hell she had put me through. She did everything she could to prove it and in the end I took her back, just like I wanted to do the whole time.

I took a promotion to prepare for the family Kay and I wanted. Things were going great, and then Mike showed back up. He got a job where I worked and was a good employee for awhile, but just as I expected, he caused a scene and lost his job. Things started to go south for me and Kay. She had less to say and got mad at me for not saying much back. It went on until the start of October, when she decided I wasn't doing enough with my life. She left me in a broken heap and went straight to Mike. I watched as she stayed happy with a guy who bounced from job to job. He was no better than me and she knew that, but it was her choice. For the first time ever, I prayed and prayed and prayed for God to bring her back or ease my pain. I got neither.

It was a few months before I even tried to talk to a girl. Yes, one girl tried to get my attention, but I just didn't like her. I got drunk for the first time the same month Kay broke my heart. Halloween night, chilling with some of the best friends I had. A few more months went by and I started talking to one girl, but go figure, another shows up wanting my affection. On one hand, I had a girl who could lighten my mood and possibly bring me out of my cage. And on the other, a girl who wanted my love because she was Kay's friend and knew how I made Kay feel. One stood a chance of cheating on me, while the other showed signs of self-doubt on the highest level. My foolish choice would have been either one of them. I picked the one who wanted me to make her feel good even though she would never accept it.

We dated for two months, in which I showed her the kind of boyfriend I was. I was at her house almost every day. Kay was jealous and tried to split us up, but she didn't even need to try. We broke up after a month; because she thought I was cheating on her with the other girl I was talking to when I met her. We got back together, but after yet another month, she broke up with me again, saying I was after her fifteen year old friend. She said I made a move on her in a game of truth or dare. I asked a simple question as if I was playing with my friends, but held back. Little did I know that these two girls played truth or dare like five year olds. Instead of trying to win her back, I pushed her away and left it at that.

A few months later, my brother, his wife, and I moved into a trailer together. David was doing his best, but still needed some help, so I was the one that helped him. They stayed with me for two maybe three months, but eventually moved back to her grandmother's to figure things out. I kept the trailer and helped anyone who needed it. A friend of my dad's stayed for awhile. A little while after he left, the friends who did what they could to help me get over Kay moved in. Justin and Emily were two of my best friends. They got me out of my shell and partying whenever I got the chance. Partying with them may not have helped me find a girl, but it did help me relieve a lot of stress that was beginning to build up, and I can't thank them enough for that. As the summer reached its peak, I decided to move somewhere new, to see if there was someone out there for me. Unfortunately, it didn't last long. The guy I was staying with was a controlling asshole.

After I got back home, things felt different. I was back at my mother's helping her keep the house. I went back to my old job, but now I was a little more likely to go out and have fun. To some extent, I had a renewed vigor. I worked harder and lived better, but life has a way of dragging me down in the end. Life went back to the way it was before I left. I still partied, but only on the rarest occasion. I was twenty-one soon to be twenty-two and found that I was still utterly alone.

My mind was just as violent as ever. Anyone who pissed me off was tormented in my head, but only in my head. I held on to hope, and that saved me from becoming the monster that lay dormant inside me. I kept the hope alive by taking chances and asking girls out, even if they weren't my cup of tea. I didn't mean for any of them to be serious, just to hold me at bay until the right one came. How unfortunate it was that soon enough, everyone said no, and the monster started to rise. I had tried taking my own life once, and once alone, but discovered that my body simply could not harm itself. If God didn't give me the hope I needed, I would become a being of pure evil, the likes of which the world had never seen. I knew this and could do nothing to change it, for it was in God's hands to deliver my soul mate to me.

The more I was told that I was still young and had plenty of time to find that special someone only made me angry. None of them realized what I was. None of them knew what I was becoming. None of them could understand. Even with that said, I knew, somehow, that I would die young, one way or another. I could feel it in my bones, just as I felt the monster scratching at the surface. I hated everyone for telling to leave it to God and stop trying, fore I knew that if I gave up, I gave in to the monster and no one was safe if that happened.

There was only one person who I trusted without hesitation. She understood me and what I was going through, but she had so much more hope than I did. She was one of my best friends just like Justin and Emily, but for a different reason. She could calm me; help me hold on to what little hope I had left. She even vowed to stand by me, even if the monster took control. She was one of the few that the monster could not hurt. She was my anchor to this world in the event that I began to float away. Her name was Judy.

Every Spring I got lucky, and at the same time, not so lucky. I always met girls in pairs and this spring was no different. The problem was that one girl couldn't give me a family, while the other was still young. I talked to them both and felt a connection to both, but like a fool I picked the younger, because she could provide me with a family, and I felt that I could one day love her. To my horror, it was set up. A guy, who had claimed to be my friend, set it up so he could piss me off, which he did, but not enough to swing. He tried his best and failed, but only just. You see, he released the monster, and once I became the monster, a fight wasn't good enough.

I trained for a few months, perfecting my skills with various weapons. I turned my body from average and out of shape, to toned and lethal. I became the monster through and through. I started talking to Judy more and more as I prepared to take my revenge. I went to a few more parties; they were the last I would have with many of my friends. I quit my job the day I started my hunt for the perfect chance to destroy those who destroyed me. I found a job that would keep me on the move, making a lot more money than I needed, so I could easily invest in my kills. Judy had already set up a means to be my allay, for my personal kills as well as the kills I did for her.

The chance rose as I watched the girl and the so-called friend climb into the back of her car. I walked across the street and right up to his car, something he prized a little too much. It was a white camera with black racing strips. I slashed all four tires. I opened his gas tank and poured a whole bag of sugar into it. I opened the driver's side door and stabbed a knife into the ignition. With that done, this boy wasn't going anywhere. The fools didn't want to get caught, so they picked a secluded spot, where no one would find them. We were about ten minutes out of town on a rarely traveled road just inside the woods. What a mistake. I leaned against his car and waited for her car to stop rocking. I held a dagger ready to start the torment.

The guy got out first. He straightened his pants while the girl got out and grabbed her pants to put them on. He looked up and spotted me. Anger flared across his face as he realized who I was. She jumped as he swore, and quickly put on her pants. I didn't move as he started toward me.

"You come to get your ass kicked?" he asked in an arrogant tone.

I stood still as he closed the distance between us. The girl had finally finished getting her pants back on. She stood there with her arms crossed; looking as though she didn't want to be there anymore. It was too late for that. She was going to die, just like this pathetic piece of shit that was now just about two feet away from me. I turned my attention back to him as he made his last threat. No sooner were the words out of his mouth, than I pulled the dagger and sliced into his legs. The cut crossed both legs a few inches above his knees. The girl started to run away, ignoring her car, toward the woods. I launched two throwing stars at her. Each met there mark in the calf of each of her legs. She fell forward and screamed in agony.

"You're not going anywhere fast, so I'll take care of her first," I told him as I pushed him over and started toward her.

I approached her as if she was something of interest. I walked up and rolled her onto her back with my foot. She looked up at me with pleading eyes, but I ignored them and proceeded with the torment. I stepped on each of her legs to bury the other half of the throwing stars into the ground, so she couldn't try to get away. I crouched down over her trembling body and used knives to pin her hands to the ground. I took out another throwing knife and began carving into her face. It didn't matter what I carved so long as I destroyed her face before she drew her last breath. Once I finished with her face, I cut her from her neck bone to her belly button. I moved her shirt and carved a cross into each of her breasts. Her screams had faded by this point. The pain had trapped her inside of herself, so the only thing left to do was to let her die. I cut both of her wrists to give her death.

I turned to find him trying to get to his feet using his car. I launched the throwing knife, nailing one of his hands to his car. He put the other hand up as he tried to fight the pain, but I launched another throwing knife nailing that one to his door. I slowly walked over to him as he tried to move his hands. The harder he tried, the louder his cries of pain became. I took the last step quickly as I pushed a very thin knife in between his ribs and straight into his lung. I stepped back and did the same thing to the other side.

"You picked the place you would die. She cheated on

her boyfriend for you. She staged a relationship for you. She died because of you. You would have treated her worse than anyone, and she did all this for you," I said as I opened a five gallon bucket full of water and towels. "How does that make you feel? You thought you were an alpha dog, but you're just a mouthy pup. Now you get to slowly die by drowning on your own blood, but that's not all. I'm wrapping you in these towels so that when I start the fire, it doesn't spread anywhere I don't want it to."

I finished wrapping him in the towels, with the last one going over his mouth. I walked to my car and grabbed my gas can. I poured some between his legs, which was the only spot not covered by towels. I grabbed the lighter out of his car and struck it. I walked around and cherished the flame. I looked at him one last time as I dropped the lighter. The flame spread and caught his pants. I heard murderous mumbles that I knew would be horrific screams, if his mouth wasn't covered with a wet towel. I lingered for a moment to ensure the fire had the desired effect, before walking over to her car and grabbing her phone. I sent Judy a face from the girl's phone before putting it back in the car. Judy would send a picture of us together from her phone to make it look like I was with her when this all happened, that way I couldn't be charged with it. I walked back to my car and started toward Judy's house.

2

The monster within was alive. I couldn't help but to enjoy the feeling of power it gave me. No one even considered me to be a suspect in the unusual disappearance of the two unfortunate lovers. If memory serves correctly, it was several months before anyone found the bodies. By that point, the evidence was all but destroyed by nature, leaving me with absolutely nothing to worry about. Even with the knowledge that I had gotten away with my first kill, I didn't let it go to my head. I refused to get sloppy.

I made it to Judy's just as we had planned. It was the second time we got to meet face to face, but it was like the first time all over again. She wanted me to tell her all the details as we spent what time we could undisturbed. She gave me her hit list before her boyfriend showed up. We spent the rest of the night goofing off and being young adults. I stayed on the couch and left the next morning, heading for my first assignment. I was designing buildings for a large company based out of Alabama. They paid well and kept me on the road. It was the perfect cover for my new passion. It was on my first assignment that I met my third victim.

I was designing a home for a family in California.

They had been married for twenty years and had two girls, Jessy and Beth. The oldest, Beth, had just turned eighteen, while the youngest, Jessy, was about to turn sixteen. Both of their parents were in marketing, so neither had much time at home. I ended up talking to their daughters more than them. Beth had a twenty year old boyfriend named Derek. I noticed the first time I met Derek, that his eyes always shifted toward Jessy when she entered the room. However, when I was paying attention to her while he was there, she always seemed troubled and distant. This wasn't like her at all. It took me about two weeks to gain her trust. Jessy confined in me, and informed me that Derek had raped her on her fifteenth birthday, but she had been too scared to ruin Beth's relationship, so she never told anyone. I promised her that she would be okay and finished my job. After our talk, Jessy didn't seem afraid of Derek anymore. I was glad she was over her fear, but I wasn't happy with pushing her fears away. Derek had to pay for what he had done to her, and I knew how to get it done.

I waited until I was in the middle of my next job, about three hours away, before returning to take care of Derek. When I came across him, he was harassing a girl who couldn't have been more than fourteen years old. I drove by slowly to scare him away from her long enough for her to run. He stared after me until I rounded a corner. I parked about a block down the street. I walked to the corner and used the store windows to figure out where Derek was. He started in my direction. There was an alley right between us. I rounded the corner with the intent of meeting him at the alley. He was a few steps ahead of me, but it wasn't enough to stop me from pushing him into the alley. I threw him into a dumpster. I slammed into him, planting my knee into his chest. I grabbed his head and spun, throwing him further into the alley. He caught his balance and put his hand up, pleading for me to stop. I pulled my dagger and took his hand off.

"Little girls aren't for grown men. How many have you defiled?" I demanded.

"Please man, I won't do it again, I promise," Derek vowed.

"You got that right," I spat.

"I don't want to die. I've got a kid on the way. She's four months pregnant," He tried. I had been keeping in touch with Jessy and she would have told me if Beth was pregnant.

"Really? Is it one of these little girls you've been assaulting?" I inquired.

"No, she's twenty-one. Her name is Lisa. I love her man, but I just can't help myself," Derek begged.

"And now we add cheating to the list," I stated as I pulled my hood back.

Some level of understanding entered Derek's mind as he realized who I was. I watched to fight leave his eyes as he understood why I was punishing him. I could only guess that he accepted his fate, but still, that wasn't good enough. I handcuffed his last hand to a pole, and started the torment. I pulled a hammer out of my back pocket and smashed each of his remaining fingers. Every time he screamed, I gave him a quick tap on his forehead with the hammer. By the time I smashed the fourth finger, he had stopped screaming. I made him drop to his knees as if he was begging for forgiveness. I used the hammer to break all the ribs on his right side, until I knew one went into his lung. As he began gasping for air, I planted the claw from the hammer into his gut. I smiled at him as I pulled my hood back over my head and walked away to let him die alone.

I got a phone call about a week later. Jessy was sad, but full of joy. They had found Derek dead in an alley. Beth was very upset until she learned that he had two other girlfriends, one of which was pregnant. Jessy told me that she told the police what Derek had done to her and that ten other teen girls came forward and with the same story on him. One of them was the younger sister of Lisa, his pregnant girlfriend. She was pregnant with his kid just like her sister. Jessy thanked me for letting her know that everything would be okay, because it was the first time that anyone ever told her that without it being a lie. She begged me to come visit whenever I could. I told her I couldn't make any promises, but that I would do my best to be there when I could. I also promised to see her on all of her birthdays. She was overjoyed with my promise and was expecting me to be there in two weeks for her sixteenth birthday.

I showed up just as I promised. The officer that took Jessy's statement was there too. He made it a point to thank me for giving Jessy the courage to step forward. I had to insist that it wasn't soon enough; otherwise, Derek would have been behind bars instead of dead. The officer agreed, but didn't have time to say anything more, because Jessy ran and jumped into my arms. I hugged her and set her back down. She grabbed my hand and pulled me across the room to meet all of her friends. I didn't have to play a part that day; I actually had a lot of fun thanks to Jessy. The best memory I have of that day was when Judy texted me, and Jessy saw the name and got very jealous. It took me an hour to convince her that Judy was just a friend and that the text was to inform me that she was getting married and wanted me to be there. Jessy begged me to take her, but I had to set her right because she had school to attend to. That was one of the fondest days I can remember. Jessy wasn't the first young girl to have a crush on me, but she was the first to actually get my attention, even if it wasn't the kind of attention she wanted.

I left out the next day. Judy was waiting for me at the airport with a wicked grin. She had left her fiancé somewhere which meant she had business to discuss with me. I loaded the luggage I brought into the back of her car and got in. It was about a thirty minute drive to her house so we had time to discuss the matter that left her fiancé at home. I waited for her to bring it up since it was her hit.

"Have you guessed why I came alone?" Judy asked.

"You have a mark you want me to take care of, probably before the wedding," I answered.

"Yes, if she isn't eliminated before the wedding, she will ruin it. I can't let that happen, not when this is what I've wanted for so long," Judy started to explain.

"I understand. I'm in a similar boat. Do have a picture?" I stopped her before she got too far.

"Yes," She answered as she slipped me a picture of a young blonde. Her name was Heather, it was written on the back.

"Has she done anything so far?" I had to ask.

"She keeps calling me, telling me that Jason is her man, and that she will have him back. She keeps showing up at his work making advances. He keeps turning her down, of course, but it is still getting on my nerves," Judy explained.

The rest of the ride was spent talking about how we

were doing, how excited Judy was, and the normal things people talk about. I spent most of it with half of my mind wondering why I would kill Heather, when she is simply being foolish. The fact was, I struck a deal with Judy. She would help me as long as I killed for her. I don't break my deals or my promises, so I was bond to kill Heather for that fact alone.

I laid on Judy's couch that night, trying to figure out the best way to kill Heather. This wasn't like the other kills I had preformed. Heather was for the most part innocent. I didn't want her to suffer like the others. I found Heather the next day. She lived a fairly simple life, lots of routines to work with. She went to the gym everyday at six. Got home just after seven and cooked supper. She worked the seven to five shifts. On her lunch she went to visit Jason, and sure enough, she made several advances. Lucky for Jason, he turned them all down. Heather was in bed by nine. The simplest way to kill her would have been to cut her breaks before work, because there was a hill that rounded a curve that just dropped at the curve. Unfortunately, she parked her car in a garage.

It was the second day of watching her that the only way to do this dawned on me. Heather decided to go out and eat. I made it a point to bump into her. I quickly apologized and bought her a new meal. We sat and talked for about an hour before she realized what time it was. I asked if I could have her number and maybe take her out the next night. She gave me her number and said she would see me the next night.

The next night arrived. Heather gave me directions to pick her up from her house in my rental. I let her pick the restaurant and the movie we rented. Then, as I hoped and planned, we went back to her place. We didn't even make it through the movie before we were in the bedroom. We went at it for several hours, before she fell asleep. I slowly got out of bed and went down to the garage. I slid under her car and put a slit in her break line. I crept back upstairs and into the bathroom to avoid suspicion. Heather stirred when I got back in bed, but didn't bother asking. The next morning I kissed her goodbye and waited to follow her to make sure my plan worked. It did. Her car flipped when it hit the railing and went over. I wasn't the only person on the road, so I played my part and stopped. I ran to the rail where she went over as her car blew up. I had done my job, and fate took care of the evidence. I stayed and made my statement, letting them know that I had just spent the night with her. The officer gave me his condolences and let me go home.

Judy was thrilled to hear that she was dead. She wanted all the details, so I gave them to her. Shock and something else flashed across her face when I told her that I had slept with Heather. Her mood dropped a little, but as soon as Jason got home, it picked right back up. Later that night, Judy pulled me over to the side, wanting to take a ride. I just nodded and followed her out to her car. She drove in a direction I wasn't familiar with and stopped when we were basically in the woods. She got out and walked to the edge of the woods. She stared into the woods as she waited for me to join her. The moment I was at her side, she broke the silence.

"Why didn't you torture her?" Judy demanded.

"She wasn't a bad person, just foolish. I could have made her forget Jason, but I held no feelings for her," I answered. I noticed Judy's body relax as what I said set in.

"I'm glad you didn't care, but I wanted you to make her pay for trying to ruin my life," Judy scolded.

"She paid, but she wasn't aiming to ruin your life, just fix hers," I informed her.

"Please tell me that you will never love anyone," Judy whispered.

"Judy? Why would you ask me that? We both want the same thing, and will be there for each other no matter who we bring into our lives," I told her.

"Cause I want you all to myself. Selfish, I know, but I got jealous when you told me that you slept with her. I don't understand this," Judy explained.

"We are very much alike, and very close, but your heart belongs to Jason. You don't love me. You covet me as a prized possession. I just need you to remember that no one will separate us. We are the closest of friends, and the darkest of teams," I reassured her.

"You've got that right," Judy laughed as she gave me a hug and went back to the car. I took one last look into the woods before joining her.

Judy's wedding was everything I had hoped it would be. She seemed happier than I had ever known her to be. He daughter was the flower girl. As I requested, I sat in the back during the ceremony, but I was at their table during the reception. It was the only wedding I enjoyed, even though I had only been to two before this one. At the end of the wedding I said my goodbye to Judy and Jason before heading back to the airport to go back to work.

3

My next assignment took me to New York. I was helping them remodel two levels of offices. This is where I found my next set of victims. The manager of these two levels made it a point to hire females into his department, because he used all of them and they all knew it. He had ten women working for him, all of which pleased him at some point during the week. He was using his job to get laid, even though he had a wife and three kids at home. His name was Stan and the girls were nothing more than numbers to me.

I decided to be on safe side and kill a few of them in accidents, before killing the others all in one night. The last kill had to be Stan and the last girl, while they were in the act, so his wife would know that her husband was a piece of shit. I was going to be on this job for a month, so I decided to use the whole month to take care of business. I watched all of them as I made the plans, so I wasn't out of place watching them. I decided the first victim would be the one who seemed ashamed of what she was doing to keep her job.

She was allergic to peanuts. All I did was sprinkle crushed peanuts onto everyone's lunch when I picked it up, which I so generously offered to do. While everyone was grabbing their food, I grabbed her antibiotic and moved it to her coat pocket to avoid too much thought. The swelling was slow and almost unnoticeable at first, but then it took hold. Panic filled her eyes as her throat began to close. She gasped and ran to her booth while I made the nine one one call. She scrabbled looking for her antibiotics, but slowly feel to the ground, suffocating from her closed wind pipe. She was dead by the time the medics arrived. Her neighbor found her antibiotics right after the medics arrived. She blamed herself for not moving faster, and made herself my next victim.

This one was the newest member of the team. From what I could gather, she got down on her hands and knees to get the job. She obsessed over her looks and always carried makeup. It was some what difficult deciding how to kill her, but I finally found my opening. She jogged when she didn't stay over to take care of Stan, so that night when she went jogging, so did I. I made it a point to jog the opposite direction so that when I passed her, I could bump right into her. I timed it perfectly and ran her off of a small drop. I jumped down behind her and clocked her with a piece of the rail I had removed the night before. The gashes in her head was bleeding badly and as soon as I made sure no one saw what I had done, I set up the scene to look like she accidently fell over the railing because the top bar was lose. It looked as though she landed on the bar and cracked her head open. She bled out before she was found the next morning.

The office was buzzing about their department being cursed. Two of the girls got transferred out, which made me decided to kill them after I was done with the clean up. This left six girls and Stan. I did run into two set backs.

Both dealt with the same girl. Her name was Kelly. She asked me out to dinner about a week after I killed number two. This made me think that number three was up, but what she told me over dinner was the second set back, which made me take her off the list.

"You're a great guy, but I'm sure you noticed something odd at the office," Kelly stated after we finished eating.

"Do you mean the so-called curse?" I asked.

"No the fact that all of us sleep with Stan," Kelly corrected.

"Yes, that's why this is quite a surprise," I admitted.

"The truth is that Abby is the only one that enjoys it. None of us want to do it, but with the economy being what it is, we all did what we had to do to get the job," Kelly explained.

"But to defile yourselves for him or a job, is beneath all of you," I stated firmly, but without judgment.

"I agree, that's why I filed a police report. They are going to open investigations within the week. By Friday they should have everyone's statements, but Stan's and Abby's. The only reason I took this job was to get my son back, but until I see Stan behind bars, I don't deserve him," Kelly stated.

"Having the courage to stand up to Stan the way you are, that is why you deserve your son. Don't let anyone take that fact away from you," I told her.

Kelly was happy that I thought highly of her. She insisted on me staying with her until I got sent somewhere else for work. That night was passionate, but not what I wanted. The only reason I entertained her was because she needed it. I stayed focused on my task, but I gave her a pardon. She was a great girl and I wanted to help her get her son and find her place in the world, but I was a monster that had no place with her. That was the way it was and had to stay.

With the police getting involved, I had to move my plans up. Friday was the last day for me to kill those who were left. I rigged the exit of the building to give the other four girls a green light even though it wasn't safe. Since they carpooled, it would happen all in one shoot. Luck was on my side for this plan, because the vehicle that hit them was a semi. All four of them were killed with no other casualties. I waited in the building until just about everyone else had gone home for the day, before setting up to kill Stan and Abby. Abby stayed behind to take care of Stan, just as I expected. I let him have his last little bit of fun before I barged into his office. Abby was bent over putting her shoe back on, while Stan was zipping up his pants. Abby's right hand was on the wall, which made it easy to do what I wanted to. I pulled out a nail gun that I had rigged and shot her hand, nailing it to the wall. Before Stan could react, I shot one through his foot, nailing him to the floor.

"What the hell!" Stan screamed.

"You've been a very naughty boy. And we can't leave your slutty ass out of this now can we, Abby," I stated calmly.

"That's right; you and Kelly have a thing going on now. What did you find out about the hit I put on her?" Stan questioned.

"You what?" I demanded taking a step forward.

"You heard him. Kelly will be dead by nine tonight," Abby spat.

I turned toward the clock on the wall behind me. It was only seven. It would take me around twenty-five minutes to get to Kelly's apartment with traffic. I wanted to be there before eight-thirty, to be on the safe side. That left me around an hour to take care of these two. A smile crawled across my face.

"I've got time then," I stated coolly.

I placed my palm on the chest of a very confused Stan, and pushed him into his chair, ripping the nail through his foot. A cry of horror and pain filled the room, one from Stan and the other from Abby. I nailed each of Stan's hands to his chair, and then turned my attention toward Abby. I grabbed her hand and held it to the wall. I put the nail gun right to her hand and pulled the trigger. She screamed in agony as her second hand was nailed to the wall. Her knees started to buckle, but once she started to fall she realized that the pain would get worse, so she forced herself to stand up. I wanted her to die looking like the slut she was. She was already in a short skirt so I ripped the front of her shirt open to give the final touch. I gagged her like she was a toy. This muffled her screams as I shot a nail into each of her ass cheeks.

"Haven't you tortured her enough?" Stan yelled. I back handed him for silence.

"You'll get your turn, and your pain will be far worse," I informed him.

Stan didn't say a word after that, so I went back to work on Abby. I shot a nail through each of her breasts. Tears rolled down her eyes as I pulled the trigger putting another nail in her stomach. Her legs were trembling. I knew she wanted to just fall, but the pain was more than she was willing to bare. I looked her over for a moment, deciding what to do next. I shot one more nail into her stomach to see if she would collapse. She didn't. She wanted the pain to stop and I was out of ideas for her, so I put the nail gun to her head and pulled the trigger. This time she fell, but there were no screams, just a quiet thud.

With Abby dead, I turned my attention toward Stan. I smiled as I shot a nail into his gut. He didn't scream or moan in pain, he was trying to show me that he wasn't scared of anything I had in store for him. I couldn't let that stand, so I shot him in the crouch. This time he squealed like a little bitch. I stepped forward and back handed him to shut him up. Instead of shutting up, he got louder. I grabbed his stapler and stapled his mouth shut. His head drooped down as he started to lose hope. I put a nail in each of his knees, just to loosen him up. His head shot back in agony. I looked up at the time to make sure I wasn't losing track. It was just barely seven-thirty. I shot him in each of his shoulders, matching the number of nails I shot Abby with. I wanted him to have at least two more, but I didn't know where I wanted to put them. I went ahead and shot him in the other foot to make it even, and then it dawned on me, one in the heart followed by one in the head to finish him off. I put the nail gun to his chest and pulled the trigger. I quickly moved the nail gun and put another one through his forehead. I was done here, now it was time to go save Kelly.

I took the route out of the building that kept me out of camera view. I made my way through the streets as fast as I could. I could only hope that the hit man wasn't someone who liked to get things done early. If she died, I had to admit, I wouldn't lose any sleep over it, but she was trying to be a better person, and I wanted to see her succeed. I stopped by a payphone and made an anonymous call to the police tipping them off to the murder attempt. I made it to her building at eight-ten. I ran up all the stairs and came to her door. I adjusted my appearance and knocked on the door. Kelly answered with a surprised look on her face. She relaxed and stepped to the side to let me in.

"Why do you look so surprised to see me?" I inquired.

"You said you had a few things to take care of, so I thought you wouldn't be back until tomorrow," Kelly answered, starting to become happy because of my arrival.

"So what would you like to do tonight?" I asked as I walked up behind her and wrapped my arms around her waist.

"What ever you want," she answered as she leaned her head against my shoulder and kissed me.

In one quick movement, I swept her off her feet and carried her toward the bedroom. A knock on the door stopped me in my tracks. I gave her a puzzled look, which she returned. I set her down and followed her toward the door. She turned toward me and grabbed my hand before grabbing the doorknob. My heart slowed and my body prepared to do what ever it had to as she opened the door. A man holding a shotgun kicked the door as soon as she turned the knob. I caught Kelly before she fell and looked up at the intruder. He went for a kick to my face, but I swatted it out of the way, rolling Kelly onto the floor and out of the way. While the intruder was turned to the side from my block, I charged him. We both slammed into the wall in the hallway. His shotgun went off. I caught him with a knee to the gut and used the opening to throw his gun down the hall. It worked, but he came back with a punch that caught me in the right eye. He used the opening he just created to throw me back into the apartment.

"Stop! Police!" I heard as I hit the ground.

Next thing I heard was gunfire. The intruder landed on me and rolled toward where I left Kelly. I grabbed his arm and rolled him back toward me, landing a right to his face. He pulled me into his roll and elbowed me in the face as I got closer. I wrapped my arm under his and pinned him on his gut until the police pulled us apart. The intruder spit blood as the police took him away, while I had blood running down my nose and a black eye starting to form. The police informed me later that I cracked his lower ribs on his right side with my knee shot. They discovered that Stan had hired the intruder to kill Kelly, but when they went to his home, he hadn't returned from work. When they got to the office building, they found his body as well as Abby's. The police had stumbled onto an ironclad case against Stan, but it seemed that someone else had beaten them to him.

I spent the next three weeks with Kelly, while the traces of the fight faded. The company deemed it unwise to send me to the next client looking like I had gotten into a brawl. The first impression would have been very bad, until they heard the story. That's what I told them, but they didn't want to chance it. I enjoyed my three weeks of vacation. It was the first vacation I got to spend with a woman I had grown to care about. Too bad she wasn't the one for me and vice versa. The other two girls from the department where mugged two weeks after Stan was found dead. The mugger took all their money and then put a knife in each of their hearts. A fitting end if you ask me. With them dead, Kelly was the last surviving member of their department, which would have put her on the suspect list, if she wasn't being attacked at the time of Stan's death.

4

The next contract was cancelled before I left Kelly's. Christmas was less than a month away, and I was already receiving calls asking if I was going home for the holidays. I was going to find a place to hide for the holidays, but Kelly overheard a conversation between David and me. It took her a week, but she convinced me to go home for the holidays and let everyone see me. I did it on one condition, which she met. I insisted on having company in my misfortune, so I made her come with me. She seemed more thrilled than scared. I wasn't sure bringing her was the best idea I ever had, but it made her happy, which was something I loved to do.

I swung by Judy's on the way in. She was delighted to meet Kelly, which surprised me. Judy took Kelly shopping before I even had time to tell her that we weren't staying long. I looked at Jason, who just shrugged and took a seat. I looked after the girls one last time before joining him. He was watching Criminal Minds, which happened to be one of my favorite shows. I thought it was going to be quiet until the girls came back, but I was very wrong.

"I wonder what it would be like to be a serial killer." Jason pondered out loud.

"I imagine, it would be annoying," I stated blankly.

"How do you figure? The thrill of the kill. The power of life and death in your hands. How can that be anything but exciting?" Jason questioned.

"Everyone dies, but it isn't our choice that decides when they die. If we are to be the tool, then so be it, but we are not the ones in control of life and death. We are barely in control of our own lives. Only a fool would believe he or she had control over someone else. Besides, having to avoid detection just to stay alive would kill the thrill," I answered both of Jason's questions.

"I see your point, but I still think it would be exciting," Jason stated.

"If you want excitement, then join BAU. They get to be the hunters. Nothing is more thrilling than a hunt," I insisted.

"But killers are always on the hunt," Jason pointed out.

"And for the reason they hunt, they are hunted. Why not be at the top of the food chain, with backup. For a man who has people that he holds dear, needs help when on a hunt, or his family will be fed to the dogs. That is the way the world works. Only loners should turn into the kind of killers you refer to," I explained, putting an end to the subject.

The girls arrived about three hours after they left with a few bags each. Even Judy's daughter was carrying a bag or two of her own. It was getting far too late for Kelly and I to finish the trip. Judy had convinced Kelly to stay the night while they were gone, so it all worked out. I made a pallet for Kelly and me in the living room floor. Thanks to Judy, we were all up until almost two in the morning.

Kelly and I went to sleep so we could finish the trip by noon the next day.

When I woke up, Judy was getting ready for work. Jason had already gone, and Judy's mother was coming to babysit. Kelly was keeping Judy's daughter entertained until her grandmother arrived. I stepped into the bathroom to get changed so we could leave. It was then that I found the note Judy slipped into my clean pants. It was the next target she wanted me to take care of. She included the marks name, address, work address as well as his phone number. The reason was explained in a picture. The picture held nothing more than a young girl covered in bruises. The girl looked familiar, but I couldn't place her. When I walked out of the bathroom, I nodded to Judy to let her know that I would handle it. She nodded back with a wicked smile as she opened the door to let her mother in. Judy, Kelly, and I all piled out the door and headed our separate ways.

We made it to my home town in under an hour, which meant I was flying like a bat out of hell, but I do that. My mother was at work, so I just let Kelly and myself in. I showed Kelly the house, and we settled in. Kelly decided we just had to have a shower, so we took one. It was one of the best showers I had ever had, but it was interrupted by yelling. My youngest sister was there. She noticed that I had arrived and was trying to get my attention. I yelled that I was in the shower and would be out when I was done, but she kept on. Finally, I got out of the shower, leaving Kelly to finish the shower by herself. I quickly dried off and got dressed. I stepped out of the bathroom and shut the door behind me. My sister was there with one of her friends, one I didn't know.

"Charles, this is Shea," she introduced immediately.

"Hi Shea. Rockie, what the hell is all the fuss about?" I demanded.

"I wanted you to meet Shea. Why did you leave the shower on?" Rockie asked.

"It's still on because my girlfriend, Kelly, is in there," I stated guessing that Rockie was trying to hook me up with Shea. Shock took hold of both of them as they realized what I said.

"Did you say girlfriend?" Shea asked.

"Yes. I met her in New York about two months back. It was her idea for me to come home for Christmas, so I made her come too," I explained.

"And you didn't tell us?" Rockie stated with a very stern face.

"Don't do that. Your face will get stuck," I joked.

"You butt," Rockie said as she stuck her tongue out at me.

The shower cut off. Both Rockie and Shea turned and went into the living room. I leaned against the wall and waited for Kelly to walk out. When the door opened and I saw Kelly walk out, I was taken by surprise. She looked better than I ever saw her. I could only guess that she was trying her best to look great for when she met my family. I could only hope she was ready to meet such a strange bunch. I smiled as I took her hand and brought her close.

"Do you think they will like it?" Kelly asked.

"It doesn't matter what they think, but let's find out," I said as I pulled her toward the living room.

Kelly seemed to be a little slow to follow, but I had hold of her hand, so she had no choice but to keep up. We walked into the living room and blocked the television. I pulled Kelly to my side and smiled at my sister, who was looking over Kelly. I caught Shea out of the corner of my eye with a jealous look on her face. A wicked smile reached across my face.

"This is Kelly. That's my sister Rockie and her friend Shea," I introduced.

"God, Charles, she's too pretty for you," Rockie stated quickly with an evil grin on her face.

"Thank you," Kelly said before I could open my mouth.

"I'm just being honest. I was going to hook my brother up with Shea as a Christmas present, but it seems that he's been holding out," Rockie joked. I glanced over at Shea who wasn't amused.

We all sat there talking until mom came home. Then I had to go through the introductions again. Mom seemed a little wary of her at first, but she was always like that. David tried to keep me out of fights, while mom tried to guard my heart. Mom was only home for about twenty minutes, before David, his wife, and two kids showed up. I had to do introductions again, but this time it was a little more comical and adorable. Kelly took to my youngest nephew quickly as he wasn't even a year old yet. Plus, Aiden, the oldest, kind of shied away from her. Shea took that as her queue to leave, so she told Rockie that she would catch up with her later and left.

I helped mom cook spaghetti for super that night, so we could feed everybody. After we were done eating, the others went home. Rockie had to go pick up her husband. David and his bunch had an early day ahead of them. I pulled Kelly off to the side and asked her if she wanted to go out for a bit. She did, so I grabbed my keys and my wallet. I took her to the nature trail at the park. It was my favorite spot. I could always clear my head as I walked the trail. Kelly and I walked the trail hand-in-hand for almost an hour just talking and enjoying each others company. Finally, I pulled her in front of me and wrapped my arms around her. I stared up at the sky as she seemed to melt in my arms. It seemed so wrong to hold her this way, knowing that it wouldn't last and that she was the one who would get hurt. I wished that there was a way that I wouldn't hurt her when it was time for me to let her go, but I couldn't see any way for that to happen at this point.

I took her back to my mom's and for the first time, I showed my mother the respect she asked of my when I was younger and didn't have sex with Kelly in her house. Kelly understood, so we just laid there and fell asleep together. The next morning, when I woke up, Kelly was already out of bed. I got up and walked out of the room to find her cooking. She was talking to mom and who might as well be mom's boyfriend. Kelly was cooking a grand breakfast with eggs, bacon, sausage, biscuits, gravy, and ham. I was surprised, because Kelly always wanted to go out for breakfast, so I assumed she couldn't cook breakfast. We all sat at the kitchen table and ate. This was rare for two reasons. We didn't eat together a lot after my parents got divorced and we never ate at the table. It was nice, but very out of place.

After we got done eating, Kelly washed the dishes while I jumped in the shower. When I got out, she was wiping down the stove. I got dressed and helped her finish. When we got done, we decided to let mom and her friend have the house so we could get the Christmas shopping done. Thanks to my job, I had over three thousand dollars sitting in the bank after paying Kelly's bills. The shopping went great. It took us close to three hours to take care of everyone, including Kelly's daughter. I promised Kelly that we would take her daughter's present to her when we got back, which made her very happy. When we got back to my mom's, Kelly took charge of the wrapping, which turned out to be a good thing.

Less than an hour after we got back, David called me. He was meeting a guy a little later to handle an issue and wanted me to come help. He said that he wouldn't have asked, but everyone else was too scared to help and he knew I wasn't scared of anyone or anything. I told him I was on my way. I let Kelly know what was happening as I got ready. I kissed Kelly and went to meet David.

When I pulled up, there were five people gathered around one guy on the ground. There were two guys sprawled out on the ground a few feet away. There were two more standing there watching and one leaning against a car. I got out and walked up behind one of the two watching. I put my foot in the back of his knee as I grabbed his throat with my right hand and threw him down hard enough to crack his skull on the concert. I shifted my weight and threw a knee shot into the other watcher's ribs before he reacted to my presence. He stumbled back as I planted myself and did a flying punch to his chest. He fell backwards and shriveled up in pain.

Three of the five assaulting David turned their attention toward me. I walked right up to them. The first threw a punch which I stopped just outside of the swing radius. The one on my right charged with a flying punch. I avoided his punch, grabbed his head, and flipped him over my shoulder. I did jump, turning in mid air, and landed on his chest. The one, who was on my left, caught me with a kick to the chest that sent me off of his friend. The one was down for the count, but the other two were still coming. I regained my balance and waited for the next strike. The one on my right threw a kick, which I caught. The other one kicked me in the head just a second after. I used the momentum from the kick to my head to flip over, while still holding the other one's leg. As I hit the ground, I pulled hard, breaking his leg. I let go and rolled to my feet just in time to see David throw a haymaker at the last guy, knocking him out.

"When and where in the hell did you learn to fight like that?" David demanded.

"Self training in my spare time. I'm very good with throwing weapons and bows," I informed him.

"How many bones did you break?" David wondered out loud.

"The first guy's leg. This guy's leg in two spots. Those two's ribs," I recollected.

"Impressive, but your brother owes me a debt," the only one standing stated.

"I believe I just gave you ample reason to drop that debt. I didn't use any weapons, but I'm not afraid to kill. Drop the debt or face me on a whole other level," I warned.

"This won't soon be forgotten," the man pointed out.

"I should think not," I stated.

With that said the man got into his car and left without his men. I accessed the damage for a moment, then called the cops to inform them that nine men where injured trying to assault me and my brother. They bought it and were on their way. I checked the side of my head to see how much damage they had done, but it didn't look as though they succeeded in doing any. I looked over at David who had two black eyes, a bloody nose, and bruises everywhere I could see skin. The police arrived quickly, and once they took our statements, let us go home. I started toward my car when David stopped me.

"I shouldn't have done it, but I borrowed money to better myself. Thanks to the man who set this all up, I failed. I don't know what has changed in you, but it is good and very bad. Please don't do anything foolish," David explained to me.

I nodded my head and continued to my car. I got in and went back to my mother's. Kelly looked at me when I walked into the room. She scanned over me very quickly, but I knew what she was doing. I climbed into the bed next to her and kissed her softly. She melted into my arms and seemed to forget every worry she had. I was glad to have saved my brother and to help Kelly relax, but David was right. The change was very bad. I was a monster, a stealer of lives. Even if their lives weren't worth saving, they weren't mine to take. I had at least one more to take, as I promised I would.

The next day I left Kelly at the mercy of my two sisters. She seemed scared, but my sisters weren't going to bite. I took a trip up to see my next target. I stood on the building opposite of his. I held my bow ready for his appearance. He stepped out of his house and locked the door. As soon as he started to put his keys away, I took the shot. The arrow went through his right shoulder. He dropped his keys and hit the door. He turned around to run for cover, but I was too quick. My second arrow went through his left shoulder. The man stumbled and tried to run through the pain, but I put another arrow through his right leg. He stopped and started as weakness started to overcome him. I shot his left leg and he fell to his knees. Slowly, he looked up, and as his eye gazed upon my form, I put one last arrow through his throat. The last one was on fire, to burn away the evidence. I watched as fire engulfed his body, then left. To the neighbors, I was never there, to me, I was death and nothing more.

I went back to my mom's to find Kelly and my sisters goofy off watching a movie. I winked at Kelly as I walked through. I went straight to the room and grabbed a change of clothes. I made it to the bathroom door before Kelly was at my side. She joined me in the shower as she so often did. I enjoyed her company more than usual. I could only guess that with the killing behind me, I saw life in a new way, and took it in stride.

When we got out of the shower, I asked Kelly if she wanted to go someplace. She, of course, nodded in agreement. I took her out to my grandparent's old place. It hadn't been touched since the house burned down around three years before. My great aunt reclaimed the land after my grandfather, her brother, died. My brother would have loved to be the one to get the land, but he knew he would never see it as his. I may not have cared about my grandparents as much as he did, but this place was the last piece of my childhood. I treasured it almost as much as he did, but I would give it to him in a heart beat.

I gave Kelly a quick tour as I explained the place and its values. I told her stories of my childhood, and pointed out the spots that held the most worth to me. I enjoyed myself a lot more than I had and didn't worry about putting up a shield. I let it all go as I spent time with Kelly. When we made it back to the car, Kelly climbed in the back seat. I gave her a funny look and walked over to the open door. Kelly grabbed me and pulled me inside. We made love for the first time since we left her apartment in New York, but to me, it felt like the first time I had ever made love. It made me feel as though I had a reason to live, to try, to love again.

When we got back to my mom's, everyone was there. I got a message from Jessy. She was just letting me know that Beth was pregnant and that she was doing great and hoped I would visit soon. I messaged her back and asked her to congratulate Beth and that I would visit first chance I got. I also had a message from Judy, thanking me for the favor. That night the whole family was together until we all went over to my dad's. Mom stayed behind which was nothing unusual. David told dad the war story and how I was untouchable, even though I got hit twice. We stayed at my dad's late into Christmas Eve, but eventually went back to our own beds, promising to return the next day.

Christmas was better than ever for me. I didn't get much, but to me, it was more than ever before. Kelly was at my side the whole day and I wasn't letting her go anywhere. I had decided that this was how I wanted to live, and Kelly was the first step. The day was over before I knew it. Early the next morning, Kelly and I started packing. We had to leave before noon if we were going to make our plane. We barely got there, but we did. Before we went back to Kelly's apartment, we stopped by to see her daughter. Kelly's ex-husband, insisted on me waiting outside, and I honored his request. Kelly was there for about twenty minutes, before he rushed her out the door. Tears filled her eyes, but when I stepped forward, she put her hand on my chest. I stepped back and opened the door for her. We got back to Kelly's and spent the rest of the day just lying on the couch. I wanted to make her life so much better, but I could only give her support. I decided right then to help her get her daughter back, and raise her.

5

I got sent off to work the second week of January. I was promised two weeks off for my birthday in April. So I worked none stop until then. I finished four designs in that time, all of which brought me a lot of joy and money. I made it to where Kelly had access to my account, so she could pay her bills until she could find a job. I talked to her every night until she did find a job that had her working nights. After that, I called her before I went to work every morning. My life seemed like it was becoming perfect. Only one thing could make things better, but it wasn't time yet.

The week that I was set to go back home, Kelly told me that she had a surprise for me. I begged her to tell me, but she refused. I couldn't wait to see her. The plane ride seemed to take forever. When I finally got back to New York, traffic kept me for close to an hour before I was standing in front of Kelly's apartment building. I half ran up the stairs to get to her faster. I walked in the apartment to find Kelly on the couch. She looked back at me and smiled. She slowly stood up showing me my surprise as she did.

"Charles, I'm pregnant. We're going to have a baby," Kelly announced.

The bags fell out of my hands as the shock set in. I rushed over to Kelly and pulled her into my arms. I said it was too soon, but I would take it. I kissed her softly as tears of joy rolled down my face. This was everything I had ever wanted and always been denied. Now I knew I could finally be happy. My birthday seemed to be forgotten due to all the excitement, but Kelly still managed to get me something to make sure that I didn't forget it.

Kelly and I moved back to my home town, so she had someone close at hand while I was at work. My whole family was there for her. They all knew what this meant to me and were happy for me. My sisters were treating her like she was part of the family, which in my eyes, she was.

The baby was due in October. I had already made arrangements to take a few months off starting the last week of September. I wouldn't go back until after the holidays. It was only June, but I was buzzing with excitement. Kelly and I talked every chance we got. I missed being with her and missing the baby's first kick. I wasn't there, but I was the fifth person, including the doctor and nurse, to find out that I was having a son. My life was coming together, and in a few months time, it would be perfect.

I went back to California in July. I stopped to see Jessy and Beth. Beth was due in August. I told them my great news and both of them seemed to jump for joy, Beth more that Jessy, but Beth informed me that Jessy had developed a crush on me. I spent a few hours with them and got to know Beth's new boyfriend. He was a good man; I could see it in his eyes. I promised to bring the baby with me as soon as I could so they could meet him. That seemed to make Jessy's day. I was glad to see her smile the way she did. I left as the sun set, just like a cowboy or something.

As soon as my last job was done, I went into the nicest jewelry store I found while in California. It took me almost three hours to pick out the perfect ring. I had decided to propose the moment I got home. We would wait until after the baby was born to have the wedding so we could do it right. I couldn't wait to get home and have her answer. We decided to wait until I got home to pick out a name for our son. Yet another reason I couldn't wait to be home. The plane ride was about ten hours, but to me, it felt like twenty or thirty. I touched down and swung by Judy's to give her all the good news and show her the ring. She wished me the best and demanded that I keep in touch. I promised to stay in touch as I walked back out the door. I only had another hour to reach my destination.

I busted into my house hoping to surprise Kelly, but I was the one in for shock. Kelly was on the floor, lying in a pool of her own blood. Her stomach was cut open and our son was lying, dead, in the floor next to her. Kelly's head was turned toward him, her eyes filled with a mix of horror and immense sorrow as she looked at our dead son. The house was trashed as if she had fought back. The clock was broken set an hour earlier. I was an hour too late to save my family.

My knees gave out from underneath me. I hit the floor and fell face first as it all sank in. The monster not only stirred, but came to full power as my humanity seemed to die. My mind processed everything as I lay there, unable to move. I could see nothing that told me who had done such a thing. My brother found me some time after I got home. He called the cops and tried to get me to a hospital, but the moment he touched me, I couldn't lie still anymore. I got up and regained my composure. I walked through the house, as I waited for the police to arrive, looking for anything that would lead me to the man who killed my family. I picked up Kelly's camera and started looking through it. That was where I found my evidence. There was a picture of the front door as an arm swung through it. There was a tattoo on the forearm. I recognized it from the hit man back in New York. I had Judy look him up while I dealt with the police. He had escaped, while they were transferring him to prison, two days ago. He was the man who took my family from me. His name was Richard and I had to kill him.

When I tracked him down, he and four other men had entered an airport together, but boarded five different planes. I followed Richard back to New York. He would give me the names of the other four as I took his life. I tracked him to an apartment in the northern side of Brooklyn. He never knew I was behind him, but I could tell he was always on watch for anyone that could be following him.

I followed him to a warehouse on the south side. This seemed to be where he stored all his weapons and information on his targets. I followed him in and watched as he crossed off Kelly's name. My name was right below hers, followed by four more. I walked out of the shadows with a knife in each hand. I stood there waiting for him to turn and face me. It was several minutes before he stopped messing with a scrapbook. When he turned to see me standing there, shock and delight entered his eyes. He went for the gun in his side holster which brought his arm across his chest. I launched the knife in my left hand and caught his gun hand as it drew across his heart. He dropped his gun, but didn't seem too worried about it. He pulled the knife out of his hand with his left and positioned it with the blade going out the back of his hand.

He shifted to cover his injured right hand as he prepared to fight me.

I stepped forward as he advanced. He went for a quick jab, hoping to catch me with the knife, but I caught his arm. I stabbed him just below the elbow and took my knife from him. I pulled my knife out of his arm and broke his arm, making him cringe in pain. I took a step back and waited for him to make a move. He started trying to inch back, as if he planned to run. With the flick of my wrist, I launched the knife in my left hand, logging it just below his knee cap. He fell on that knee, burying the knife deeper into his leg. He fell onto his side trying to ease the pain. I walked over to him and crouched down beside him.

"I want the other four," I insisted.

"What other four?" Richard tried playing dumb.

"The four you entered the airport with. The four that helped you kill Kelly. I want their names," I explained as I slowly cut into his side, twisting the blade to make my point.

"You can go to hell. I can handle the pain," Richard claimed, but I could see that he was starting to break.

I ripped the knife out of his side, cutting him open. I reached over him and grabbed my other knife and ripped it out, making sure to slice all of the tendons to his knee cap. He bit back a slight cry of pain, trying to prove himself to me. I started going through Richard's things. I found a canister of gun powder. It gave me one hell of an idea. I poured it on his leg and made a line leading to his side then to the open wound on his left arm. I branched off on his chest, heading for his wounded right hand. He kept looking at me like I was crazy. I just smiled and kept pouring. I buried his right hand in what was left of the gun powder. I grabbed his light and smiled.

"Are you sure that you can handle the pain?" I asked him as I sparked the fire.

Richard gritted his teeth and refused to answer. I lite the gun powder on his leg. His body started to tremble as the powder burn his skin until it hit his wound. He let out a scream of agony as the powder burned the open wound. It progressed up his leg, across his stomach, to his side. Tears began rolling down his face as the burns hit his side wound. He was crying, but it was too late to stop the powder from running its course. As it branched apart, he screamed, promising to tell me. It hit the wound on his left arm first. He screamed again, but not like he did when it reached the pile of powder at the end. There was so much gun powder on his right hand that I heard small bang, as it blew his hand off.

"Names!" I demanded.

"There is a book underneath my scrapbook. It has the name of every hit man in the association. The ones with stars are the ones I will work with and I called all four of them in on this hit," Richard confessed.

"Thank-you, Richard. Now was that so hard?" I asked as I ran my knife between his ribs, piercing his lung.

I got up just as he started coughing up blood. I slid the scrapbook over and grabbed my prize. I started to turn, but curiosity got the better of me. I opened the scrapbook and flipped through each page. It had pictures of all his victims. It looked as though he took pictures after he killed them. I got to the last page to find that he had added two new pictures. My son and Kelly were the last victims he would ever have. I poured a little gun powder on that page and set it on fire. I turned just in time to see Richard take his last breath.

I went back to Judy's to enlist her aid. I offered to train her, just incase something happened to me. She seemed excited that she was going to learn how to kill in the worst possible ways. I trained her for two weeks before I had to go back to work. I insisted that she kept working while I was gone, which she promised to do.

My next job took me to Nebraska, which just so happened to be the home state of one of the four hit men I had to track down. His name was Michael. He was a gambler, but since he was so good at killing, no one made him pay up. He stayed about two hundred miles from where I would be working, so finding him wouldn't be too difficult. I arrived on a Monday and was scheduled to complete the design in four weeks. I would be here all the way through Halloween, which didn't bother me. In fact, I planned to use the holiday to my advantage.

As I worked and gathered information on my target, I discovered a problem. One of the men helping with construction had a son. I saw his son everyday waiting on him, but I also saw the bruises on his arms. I watched the man work one day, and it was obvious that he was the dominant type. I followed him home one day and watched as he got drunk and started beating his son. He had a truck and a motorcycle, which gave me an idea.

The day before Halloween, the man let his son go stay with his grandparents on his mother's side. I asked the man if he would take me to a bar, but as soon as we got in the truck, I hit him with a temple shot. He was out cold. I loaded up his bike, and tied him up. I climbed in the driver's seat and we were on our way. The man woke up about halfway there. I had to pull over to silence him, because he was getting on my nerves with all the thrashing around he was doing. I pulled up next to the biker bar that Michael preferred. I got out and looked for his bike. The moment I saw it, I decided that this was the time to kill him and everyone else in there.

I walked into the bar and was the immediate center of attention. Michael was at the poker table with about five other guys. There were four guys at the bar, the bartender, and one waitress. I wasted no time heading to the bar to have a seat. I waited for the bartender to approach me, but he didn't. Instead, he eye-balled me with intense curiosity. I looked over at he and his gaze fell else where.

"I need a shot of Jack," I stated as he started away from me.

"Money first," the bartender demanded.

I slapped a twenty on the bar and waited for my drink. The bartender nodded and grabbed a shot glass. He set it down in front of me and filled it. I nodded and he walked off. I stared at the glass for a second, before taking it. A moment later the bartender refilled my glass. Just as before, I stared at it, but this time, I didn't take it after a second or two. Michael caught my attention.

"Do I know you, stranger? You aren't from these parts, but I know I've seen you before," Michael called from across the room.

I hesitated for a second and took a deep breathe. I picked up the glass and drink it. I turned toward him and looked him over really quick. I cocked my head to the side and squinted like I was trying to think. I shrugged and stood up. I took a few steps toward the poker table, putting myself in the middle of the room. For the first time

I realized that everyone, except the waitress, was armed. I took another breathe, before doing anything else.

"I'm not too sure. Have you been to Alabama recently?" I asked.

"I had some business with a friend down there, not two months ago.......," Michael said as it started to sink in.

Michael stood up as it hit him. A smile crossed my face as my hands wrapped around my throwing stars. Everyone went for their guns all at once. The waitress ran behind the counter as the bartender grabbed the shotgun he had hidden under the bar. I launched my throwing stars before anyone could pull the trigger. I hit two of the guys at the table, one at the bar, and the bartender. In the same motion, I pushed myself back onto the pool table, rolling over it to land behind it. Gunfire filled the air as I ducked out of the line of fire. I jumped toward the bar and threw four more throwing stars. I shifted back to my feet not worrying about which I may or may not have hit. One of the guys from the table started to round the pool table. With an underhanded flick, I caught his gun hand with one star and his throat with the other.

"I think this is the second time I've seen a knife do more damage than a gun in a gun fight. My friend Pedro would love to meet someone as gifted with knives as he is," Michael called to me.

"Don't worry, he's next," I retorted as I spotted one of the guys that was sitting at the bar trying to creep up on me from behind the bar.

I flung my hand up and released three more throwing stars over the counter. I watched as the one trying to creep up on me fell with a thud. I shifted so that I could see the rest of the room in the mirror. Besides Michael, there were two guys left, both of which were at the poker table with him. They were inching toward the door when Michael turned and shot them both. I took a deep breathe and stood up. I launched two throwing knives at Michael, who took his shot at me. His bullet grazed my right arm, while one knife sliced his hand between the knuckles and the other cut the tendon of his thumb on his other hand. He dropped his gun and went to grab his other, but couldn't grab it now that the tendon was cut. I pulled out three throwing knives between the knuckles on my right hand and approached him.

"Not bad tough guy. Never thought Richard would get me killed like this," Michael laughed as I put my left hand on his right shoulder.

I punched him in the gut, putting all three of my throwing knives in him. I pulled all three out and hit him again. This time I left them all in. I pushed him into his seat and walked back to the bar. I tapped the bar to get the waitress's attention. She slowly stood up and approached me. I looked at her for a few minutes as Michael slowly died. I saw tracks on the waitress's arm, a sign that she was a drug addict. I held out my hand for her. She stared at it for a minute or two before putting her hand in mine. I pulled her over the bar and searched her pockets. I found the drugs she was using and set them on the bar. I tied her to a chair and grabbed the needle. I filled it to the brim, more than enough to kill her. I injected it into her arm and watched as it took her. She shook violently for close to fifteen minutes before her body shut down.

I went outside to grab the man out of his truck. He was awake again, but this time I needed him to stay awake. I grabbed the plastic glove I brought with me and put it on. I pulled the man out of his truck and pushed him into the bar. He panicked when he saw all thc bodies lying around the room. I pulled the gag off and cut the wire tie I used to bind his hands. I pushed him toward the pool table and grabbed Michael's gun.

"What the hell is this?" he yelled.

"I saw what you did to your son," I stated calmly.

"What? Beating him?" he asked.

"What else have you been doing to your son that would warrant this reaction?" I asked as I examined the gun.

"Nothing. My dad beat me and it made me tough. I'm doing the same for my boy. I bet your dad beat you when you were a kid. Bet that's why you're a cold killer," he spat.

"My dad punished me when I was bad, but he never beat me. As for why I kill, society made me this way by deciding that I was an outcast who shouldn't be loved. God made me this way by denying me a family of my own. You made me this way by making me necessary," I said as I cocked the gun.

I unloaded three rounds into his chest. I tossed the gun into the floor next to where Michael was sitting. I kicked the waitress over as I walked out of the room. I pulled the bike off the back of the truck. I climbed on and started it. It felt good to have the wind caressing my body as I rode back to his house to drop off his bike. I went back to work the next day, and showed just as much concern as the rest of the crew when he didn't show up to work, but his son showed up to go home with him. The police told his son that his dad got mixed up in a drug deal gone bad and was killed in the cross-fire. His son didn't shed any tears as he watched his father get lowered into the ground. I didn't blame him, but I don't think anyone did.

I returned to Alabama to continue Judy's training between jobs. Her accuracy had improved greatly. She could hit a stop sign at just over fifty feet. I poked fun at her so she challenged me to do better. I went another fifty feet out. She shook her head as I grinned at her. Before she even realized what I was doing the blade was slicing through the air. Not only did I hit the sign, I got my exact mark. Center of the O. I jogged to catch up with Judy who was running toward the sign. She pulled it out and eye-balled me.

"Yes, I aimed for the O," I admitted.

"When are you going to show me how to be that accurate?" Judy asked with a sly smile.

"That's nothing. I can hit a man across a football field," I boasted.

"Not possible," Judy challenged.

"I'll show you sometime," I promised.

6

I trained Judy for a week this time, before I got called with my next job. It was in Texas. Judy had always wanted to go to Texas for some strange reason. She had some time off so I invited her to come along. Jason and Judy's mother promised to watch her daughter while we were gone. So in turn, I promised Jason that I would take care of Judy for him. We were driving since we could make it in under a day if we took turns. Judy's car wouldn't make it so we took mine. It was a truck, never really paid attention to what model cause I had to leave it in Alabama most of the time and I was never there.

It took us about eighteen hours to get there. It was a small town called Andrews. To be honest, it wasn't small to me or Judy, just to Texas. It had more residents than the county I was from. We found a hotel, but it was a one room, one bed deal. I let Judy have to bed because to some extent I liked the floor. The first day I went to work, Judy went to the park to train. She couldn't do any weapons training, but she could train her body to handle excessive amounts of pain. While she trained, I worked and found out about a guy who shot at his wife and infant child a few years back. The wife took him back, but the kids just never accepted him after that. I decided to take care of him before I left town.

When I got back to the hotel room, Judy was in the shower. I got some clothes ready so I could take a shower after she was done. I turned the television on to keep me entertained until it was my turn to shower. An hour went by, but Judy never came out. Finally, I decided to check on her. I knocked on the door, but got no answer. Slowly, I opened the door. Judy was sitting on the toilet, crying. I took a knee next to her and turned the water off. I got her to look at me so she would tell me what was wrong.

"What happened?" I asked staying as calm as I could.

"She's here," Judy whispered.

"Who?" I inquired.

"I want her dead. Please help me kill her. I owe her," Judy whispered as she started to straighten up.

"Tell me a story," I requested.

"We were friends once, but she wanted more. She wanted me, but not just as a friend or lover. She wanted me like I was her property. I need to kill her. Please help me," Judy explained.

"Have I ever turned you down?" I asked Judy, implying my assistance.

The next day, Judy tracked the target, while I was at work. When I got back that night, Judy was pacing around the room. I looked at her for moment, before stepping in front of her to bring her to a stop. She simply walked around me and kept going. I got annoyed, grabbed her and walked her over to the bed, where I sat her down. She stared up at me so I knelt down to make it easier for her to meet my gaze. We looked into each other's eye for a while before she decided to speak.

"She works at a gas station over night, alone. That is the best chance to take her," Judy stated.

"Good. You can take care of her. I'll watch your back and let you handle it. Taking a life is very different from dreaming about it," I stated.

"I know, but I won't fail," Judy stated.

That night, Judy and I walked to the gas station. We saw maybe two other people out driving, but other than that, it was dead. Judy held off going in until after I was in. The girl in question wasn't someone I would give a second look to, but I did what I could to get her attention. Instead of standing behind the counter, she was sitting in a booth reading the newspaper. There were two cameras, one of which just barely caught her in its frame. I sent Judy a message telling her to lure the girl to the bathroom. A minute after the message was sent, Judy walked in. I checked out and left, hiding around the corner.

I took a quick look inside, spotting the girl walking toward the bathroom. Judy was out of sight, so she had to be in the bathroom already. I waited until I knew the door had shut before walking in. I made it impossible for the camera to identify me as I made my way to the bathroom. I cracked the door to hear Judy and the girl arguing. I slowly opened the door until I could see them both. I slowly closed the door to avoid being heard. The girl pushed Judy into the stall door and held her there. I didn't wait for Judy to make a move before I did. I grabbed the girl's wrist and twisted. Then I pulled her wrist toward her and twisted again, breaking her wrist. She screamed in pain as I let her go. Judy punched her, dropping her to her knees.

"I don't belong to anyone," Judy spat as she drew out her knife.

Judy stabbed the girl in her left shoulder and twisted the blade. The girl began crying as the pain seeped in. Judy pulled the blade out and back-handed her. I took a step back to let Judy work as she carved a line across the girl's forehead. Judy carved into her arms and stomach. To some extent, this reminded me of my first kill. After what had to be an hour of torturing the girl, Judy slit her throat and wiped the blood on the girl's shirt. Judy looked at me with thrill in her eyes. She was like me now, a killer of those who should be killed.

I let Judy walk out first, so we were never seen together. I waited five minutes before following her. When I walked out, there was a guy lying in a pool of his own blood. He was by the counter, most likely a customer who was waiting for someone to check him out. Judy must have killed him to cover her tracks. I walked over to the counter and picked up the phone. I dialed nine-one-one and told them to come to the gas station. I walked out the door and met up with Judy about a block down. I pulled her into an alley to hide until the police were all on the scene. We watched four police cars go by before taking our leave.

We made our way through any side roads we could find. It took us twice as long to get to the hotel as it did for us to get to the gas station. Judy went in first, and just fell onto her bed, beaming as she hit the covers. I slammed the door and walked into the bathroom. I turned the water on and started washing my face. I washed it several times before grabbing a towel and covering my face. When I moved the towel, Judy was standing behind me looking me over. I stared at her long and hard in the mirror, deciding what to do.

"You were foolish and put us at risk," I stated coolly.

"How do you mean?" Judy asked.

"You killed an innocent," I spat.

"No one is innocent," Judy returned.

"But not everyone deserves to die. You killed a man because he was at the wrong place. You killed him for nothing," I explained.

"What was I suppose to do?" Judy questioned.

"Smile and walk out the door," I answered.

"And if he told the police who we were?" Judy demanded.

"I would have taken care of him as if I were the cashier. Then I would have destroyed the cameras and records of our presence. He wouldn't have been there as far as the cops were concerned," I explained.

"There is a way to do everything, isn't there?" Judy asked.

"Not everything. Take a second to consider what your options are before acting upon them. It could save a life as well as your own," I told her.

"You are something else. No one could be anything like you. You know that don't you?" Judy pointed out.

"It sets me apart, but in the same token, it makes me a monster. How I am, makes me better and worse than everyone else, because I have better ways of thinking, but for that, I'm alone. And because I'm alone, I wish to hurt those who have destroyed the man I should have become. In my own twisted way, I am Fear for those who prey upon everyone else. I am the one who will scare everyone into being better people. I guess that regardless of how I turned out, I will have impacted the world for the better," I said blankly.

"That is true, and I am so sorry that it has to be this way," Judy apologized.

"You didn't make me this way. People, God, and the world did this to me. The blame is shared by all," I stated.

With that said, I turned and went to my pallet. Sleep tried my patience, but eventually took hold. My alarm brought me back from a dream of blood. It was the first time I had a dream in quite some time. It would have been a nightmare to anyone else, but I wasn't anyone else. I watched Kelly die as if I was there. As the alarm slowly brought me back into reality, I realized that it was my fault that my own child was dead, but I didn't care. I knew what I was and what I would do.

I had the next two days off, so Judy and I went exploring the town. We ran into my target while he was gassing up his truck. I made sure he couldn't see me as we watched him. Judy was over eager for her next kill, which did bother me, but I understood her well enough to know I wouldn't be able to stop her. I decided that the best approach was a straight forward approach at his home. Judy and I went to the park to goof off while we waited for him to get off.

The time to confront him came. Judy and I walked down the road from the church we parked at, to his house. He pulled up as we reached the driveway. He stepped out of his truck and gave me one hell of a look. I stopped a few feet away from where he was standing. Judy stopped just behind me. He looked us both over before taking a step forward.

"You've got some nerve coming here, boy," he stated.

"You should talk. Pulling a gun on your wife and newborn. You should have never come back," I countered.

"So you know. Big deal. You couldn't hash it here, so you left," he chuckled.

"I saved your ass. One of the other two would have swung at you. I trust you understand that you couldn't take James," I pointed out.

"I have a gun," he sneered.

"And before you even pulled the trigger, I would have put a knife through your heart. I saved a lot of blood that day, but I'm here to correct that mistake," I explained.

"Boy, you ain't no fighter. You can't take me," he laughed.

"You're right. I'm no fighter, but I am a killer," I spat.

"You ain't killed nobody," he challenged.

"The counts up to twenty-seven," I stated. "About to be twenty-eight."

Before he could even move, I launched a throwing star at him. I angled it off to go between his ribs. It lodged itself against the back of his ribcage. The throwing star was sitting in his lung. He grabbed his chest as he backed into his truck. I turned and looked at Judy. She nodded and started back toward the car. I turned back just in time to see him cough up the first bit of blood. I smiled at him as he slid down the front of his truck. I pulled out a can of hairspray and a lighter. I took aim and shot fire at him. As he began to roast in the flames, I stopped spraying the flames. I tossed the can at his feet and walked away. I made it twenty feet down the road, before the can ignited, blowing up at his feet.

I walked right up to the car and got in. Judy was in the driver's seat waiting for me. She pulled out and took us to the store across the main road so we could pick up some snacks, since we didn't have a kitchen at the hotel. We heard the sirens all the way in the store. We both looked out the window with a confused look on our faces to avoid attention. We finished up our shopping and went to leave when the cashier stopped me. She smiled as she slipped a piece of paper into my hand. I looked at it as we walked out the door and put it in my pocket as we got to the car. Judy didn't say a word on the drive back to the apartment. She helped me unload the snacks and shut the door behind us.

"Are you going to get laid tonight?" Judy asked as soon as the door was shut.

I took the piece of paper out of my pocket and threw it in the trash. I started to put the snacks up as Judy stared at me with utter amazement. I picked up the bags and threw them in the trash covering up the number. Judy walked up to me and smacked me in the back of my head. She sifted the bags out of the way and grabbed the number.

"Why not?" Judy asked as she held it in my face.

"If I was meant to love, Kelly would have lived," I stated as I pulled the paper out of her hand and ripped it in half before returning it to the trash can.

"You didn't love Kelly," Judy pointed out.

"But I would have loved our child," I informed her.

"I'm sorry, but you keep pushing any chance you get away. It's like you've given up," Judy explained.

"I basically have. I allowed myself to be happy with Kelly, whether I loved her or not. My happiness was denied and now I realize what I am, and what I will be doing. It's not fair, but it's out of my hands," I explained.

"I'm sorry," Judy apologized.

"It's ok. I understand. I wish I didn't have to give up hope, but loves not in my cards,' I stated.

"Hey let's go to the park for the game," Judy suggested randomly.

"Ok?" I agreed with a puzzled look on my face.

We each took a shower before we walked out the door to walk to the park. It didn't take us long to get there, but there were a few police looking everybody over as they walked in. It was a good thing that Judy and I were wearing hoods when we killed those two. The police stopped us for a second, but let us pass because they had no real leads. It was starting to get dark as the baseball game kicked off. Judy and I just kind of chilled in the back as it went. The cashier from the store walked up to me.

"Hey there," she said once she got my attention.

"Hey," I returned.

"Hi, I'm Judy," Judy interjected.

"Oh, hi. I'm sorry, I didn't realize you were taken," she apologized.

"Karen, isn't it?" I stopped her.

"How did you know my name?" Karen asked.

"You stood out, so your name stuck," I informed her.

"He's good like that, and he is single. I'm one of his good friends," Judy explained.

"But your ring?" Karen pointed out.

"I am married. I'm just here hanging with one of my best friends," Judy explained.

"Do you want to go for a walk, before she confuses you?" I asked Karen.

"Sure," Karen answered as her face turned a bright red.

We made our way away from the baseball field so we could hear each other over the roar of the crowd. Karen kept as close to me as she could without tripping me or tripping over me. We made it to what seemed to be the darkest part of the park. She turned to face me and leaned against a tree. She smiled as she reached for my hand.

"So what's your name?" Karen asked as she slid her hand into mine.

"It's Charles," I answered.

"I haven't seen you around before today," Karen hinted.

"I'm here on business. I design buildings," I informed her.

"I want to go to school for nursing. I know a lot of people say that, but my mom's a nurse and I want to follow in her footsteps," Karen shared.

"You're only seventeen, aren't you?" I asked calmly. Karen's face turned red as she heard what I asked.

"How did you know my exact age?" Karen asked as she turned away from me.

"A good guess. You know there can't be anything between us, right?" I asked to be sure.

Before she got a chance to answer, her body went rigged. Her hand slipped out of mine as she began falling toward the ground. I dogged a knife and moved to catch her. I slowly set her on the ground and pulled the knife out of her chest. I looked up in time to shift my head to avoid another knife. I jabbed the knife I pulled out of Karen into the ground next to her and stood up. There was a man standing about forty yards away in the shadows.

"Impressive. You don't seem to be scared. That can't be easy after what I just did. Even more impressive is the fact that you didn't lose control after I killed your partner," the man in the shadows stated as he stepped into the light.

"You must be Pedro," I guessed.

"Indeed," he confirmed.

"Well, that wasn't my partner. She was an innocent little girl with a crush. I must admit, I never expected one of you to track me down. I must say, I am unprepared to kill you properly," I pointed out.

"A true killer is never unarmed," Pedro stated.

"I said unprepared, not unarmed," I corrected.

I waited for Pedro to make his move. He stared me down, looking for an opening. After what seemed like an hour, Pedro started launching his knives at me. I retaliated by snatching them out of the air and throwing them at the ground just as fast as he could launch them. I did have to dodge two of them while my hands were full. Pedro seemed to run out of throwing knives after he launched about twenty at me. He looked me over and smiled.

"You caught eighteen and dodged two. I barely learned how to catch a knife, but I could never catch one at the speeds I throw them. You're even more impressive than I expected," Pedro congratulated.

"You aren't too shabby, but you have nothing on me," I mocked.

"Let's see about that," Pedro challenged as he pulled a machete out of its sheath.

I dropped the last two knives. I put my hands in my pockets, Pedro watching me like a hawk, and pulled out a pencil in each hand. Pedro started laughing when he saw my weapon of choice. The moment he stopped laughing was the moment he charged toward me. I ducked beneath the first swing and blocked the back swing forearm to forearm. I punched Pedro with my left, forcing him to step away from me. I moved my left foot to the back and waited for Pedro to make his next move. Pedro looked me over for a minute before charging me again. This time he went for a thrust. I stepped to my right to avoid the attack. Pedro stopped the attack and swung at me, attempting to catch me off guard. I stepped toward him and blocked his swing. I head-butted him and as he took a step back, I planted one of the pencils in his right side. Pedro tried to pull it out when he backed away, but I had pushed it in as far as I could, making it impossible. Pedro stumbled as his lung started to fill with blood. I started toward him. He swung wildly trying to stop me. I moved my left hand to stop him and stabbed him with the other pencil in his weapon arm, all in one move. Pedro dropped his machete and fell to his knees.

"I told you I was armed," I stated as I bent over to pick up his machete.

"That you did. That you did. I'm glad you were the one to kill me," Pedro said as he began spitting up blood.

I ran him through with his machete and left it there. I looked back at Karen and sighed. She wanted to save lives, but lost her life before it had truly begun. It was sad, but part of reality. I turned and walked away. Judy was waiting for me at the edge of the crowd. She looked confused when she realized that I was alone. I walked past her before she could even ask, and headed for the hotel room. She followed in silence. It wasn't until Judy shut the door behind us that she broke the silence.

"What happened?" Judy demanded.

"One of the hit men found me. He killed Karen thinking it was you, my partner. She didn't stand a chance, let alone see it coming. The hit man failed to kill me. Don't worry. He's dead," I assured her.

"I'm sorry," Judy began.

"I didn't know her. You have no need to apologize to me," I interrupted.

"But you don't get to have anyone to love," Judy blurted.

"It's my punishment," I stated simply.

"For what? You've been in this situation since before you started killing. Hell, that's part of the reason you started," Judy pointed out.

"I don't know what I'm being punished for, but I am. That's all I know. It's because I'm alone that I lost my respect for God. I acknowledge him, but I can never love him. I won't bow before a being that makes my life a living hell. So it gets worse as time goes by. That's all I know," I explained.

"But look at the good you're doing," Judy stated.

"I'm killing. That isn't good no matter how you view it. I'm a monster, plain and simple," I informed her.

"You have saved people from death by stopping those who would have killed them. You have given some people hope. That is a great thing. It isn't going to be an easy life, but it isn't a curse and you aren't a monster," Judy tried, but I wasn't convinced.

7

The next two weeks went by without any excitement. All I did was work and sleep. I wasn't in the mood to actually live my life, but I had no choice. Judy continued to practice while I was working. She was getting pretty good. At the end of the two weeks, I sent Judy back on a bus so I could go visit Jessy. She was on the verge of turning eighteen and wanted me to come she her. Her parents were out of town and Beth had moved out a few months before she had her baby. That left Jessy in the house by herself.

"How does it feel to have the house all to yourself?" I asked.

"I'm scared half the time. I hate being alone," Jessy answered.

"Because of Derek?" I asked. She nodded in reply. "He won't bother you ever again. You should feel safe, because any who would wrong you should realize that you have someone watching over you."

"Like a guardian angel?" Jessy asked.

"Not quite. Angels only kill when ordered by God," I corrected.

"Then what about you?" Jessy asked.

"What do you mean?" I asked with a puzzled look on my face.

"Don't you have someone watching over you?" Jessy reworded her question.

"No. I have a helper when I need her, but no one watches over me. I'm not innocent like you," I informed her.

"I'm sorry about your son. I couldn't wait to meet him," Jessy apologized.

"Me either. He was to be my way of redemption," I said as a tear ran down my face.

"Don't count yourself out yet," Jessy stated as she walked up behind me and wrapped her arms around me.

"You know, don't you?" I guessed.

"I had a feeling. It wasn't until you came into my life that good things happened to me. It's thanks to you, that I can walk around without fear even if its only in daylight or when you're close," Jessy explained as she slide under my arm so her face was right in front of mine.

"This can't be. I am a monster. You don't know what I've done. To tell you could ruin you," I stated.

"Then I won't ask you to tell me. That way it can be," Jessy whispered in my ear just before she kissed me.

I stopped her. I wanted this so badly, but after what happened to Kelly for being with me and Karen for just wanting to, I couldn't put Jessy in harms way. Everyone I let get to this point died. I wouldn't allow Jessy to die for loving me. I wrapped my arm around her and pulled her close so I could whisper the one thing she had to know without being heard by anyone, hopefully not even God.

"Everyone who gets close to me dies. I won't let that happen to you. We can't be for your safety, but I will always be here to protect you from any and all harm. That I promise," I whispered.

Jessy laid her head on my shoulder. She was about six inches shorter than I was, but I hunched over to make it easy for her. I picked her up and carried her to the couch. I sat her down and grabbed the TV remote. I sat down next to her and she shifted over to where she was curled up next to me. She pulled my arm around her and laid her head against my chest. We didn't even make it through the movie before she fell asleep. I picked her up and carried her to her room. I went to set her in her bed, but she woke up and grabbed hold of me. She refused to let go so I had to climb into the bed next to her so she would go to sleep. She wrapped her arms around me so I couldn't leave after sleep took her. It didn't matter though, because I fell asleep very shortly after she did.

The next morning, Jessy was up before me. I could smell eggs and bacon so I got up and went to the kitchen. When I got to the living room I managed to catch the news. It said that there was an earthquake about fifty miles north of here. I couldn't help but to hope that it took out every fiend up there so I didn't have to kill so many people. As I entered the kitchen, Jessy was hard at work making breakfast. It looked as though she was trying to make it perfect. I leaned against the door and watched her for a minute before she realized I was there.

"Why couldn't you stay asleep another twenty minutes?" Jessy demanded.

"I have no idea, but I smelled eggs and bacon and came to eat," I said with a grin. Jessy blushed as I spoke.

"I was trying to surprise you with breakfast in bed. I had hoped that you had never had it before," Jessy admitted.

"Are you kidding? The way I live, I keep a box of pop tarts next to my bed. I have breakfast in bed every morning," I joked, but Jessy's smile started to fade. "Now what I don't get often is a home cooked meal."

"Then today is your lucky day," Jessy said as her smile got bigger.

We joked around as we ate. I felt younger, more alive than ever, but I didn't let myself fall into something that wouldn't be healthy. It wasn't easy, but I stopped Jessy's advances without hurting her feelings. I was saved by the bell, literally. The door bell rang so Jessy had to put her advances on hold to go see who was at the door. It was Beth, her soon to be husband, and their adorable baby girl. I kind of got quiet when I saw the baby. It didn't sit well with me, I guess.

"Charles! How are you?" Beth asked as she walked into the kitchen carrying her baby.

"I'm alright," I said obviously not as happy as I was before. "Steve, nice to see you again."

"Oh my God. I am so sorry. I didn't even think about it when I asked you that," Beth spilled.

"Beth relax. I'm fine. Just makes me wonder," I lied.

"So is there anything we can do?" Steve asked with a great deal of concern.

"You could let me hold her," I shrugged.

No sooner did I have the words out of my mouth, than Beth was setting the little girl into my arms. She was asleep, but still I smiled. This helped a little, even though I didn't think it would. Jessy walked up next to me and looked down at her niece. Beth looked at me, and then looked at her sister. I caught her look and shook my head to assure her that nothing had happened. Jessy caught my motion and looked at her sister who pretended like nothing happened.

"She's beautiful, but I still don't know her name," I commented.

"It's Jane," Beth informed me.

"That was my grandmother's middle name," I mused out loud.

It was a great day for me. I hung out with Jessy and the others until it was time to head home and visit my family. My dad was in a wreck so I wanted to check on him. I left as the sun began to set. Jessy followed me out to my truck. I turned to give her a hug, but instead she kissed me. I took a step back and gave her one of those "you know better" looks, before getting in my truck and leaving. It took me a day and a half to get back to Alabama. I made it to my dad's just after five that evening. He was happy to see me. Even after being in the hospital for a week, he was a damn good cook. I decided to stay the night there to catch up with him. Nothing special had happened since the last time I was home, so we just ended up watching sports and the news.

The next day I headed out. I stopped at a gas station to fill up when I spotted Mike, Kay, and their son. They were over by the self car wash behind the gas station. They weren't alone. There was a guy sitting there harassing them. Mike stood between the guy and his family. I guess he did change after all. The guy's hand went toward his waist as if he had a gun. I hit my horn one good time to scare him into realizing that he was being watched. The guy looked at Mike and then Kay and the kid. He nodded and walked away. I watched him get into a blue neon and start toward me. I glanced at him as he stared me down in his passing. I finished filling my truck and paid with a card.

I followed that guy for an hour. He seemed to work for the man that was hassling my little brother. I walked right into the house before anyone spotted me. It was one of the guys I took down that night with David. He stopped dead in his tracks and stared at me as he realized who I was. He threw his hands up and started to back away. I snapped my fingers and pointed to the spot right in front of me. He obeyed and stepped forward.

"The guy in the blue neon. Where will he be around seven?" I demanded.

"He is a drop guy. He'll be dropping off a stash at the park about that time," the thug answered.

"What part of the park?" I asked.

"Nature trail," the thug replied.

"You never saw me," I stated.

"They'd kill me if they knew what just happened," he informed me.

I turned and went back to my truck. I visited with the family until just after six. Then I went to the gas station closest to the park. I parked my truck and started heading for the park. I got there with about ten minutes to spare. I picked the best spot to watch the trail to surprise him when he came. I watched the blue neon cross the park. He parked it by the trail entrance. The park was empty as it was suppose to close after dark. He got out and started into the trail. I left my hiding spot and waited for him to get back to his car. That's when I saw another set of headlights head my direction. I slide behind a tree and watched as another blue neon, an exact match of the other, pulled in. The driver got out and got into the other neon. He drove away as if nothing had happened. It dawned on me that I had just witnessed the drop. It was more of an exchange.

I walked up to the new neon and waited for the guy to walk this way. It took him a little while to get all the way around the track, most likely making sure he never saw the other guy. As started back toward the entrance he spotted me. He pulled his gun and pointed it at me. I gave him a funny look.

"You've got some nerve following me like that. Get in the car," he spat.

I did as he said. He got in the driver's seat. He left the park and headed for the football field. He parked right in front of it and made me get out. He handed me a key and told me to undo the lock. I continued to obey as he led me into the dark football field. He walked me all the way to the other side so there was no real escape. He had me turn to face him, but he was right behind me so as I turned, I grabbed his gun and pulled it from him. He took a few steps back as I dismantled the gun right in front of him.

"What the hell!" he cried.

"I prefer knives," I stated bluntly.

He turned and started to run. He was making good time, but I had a good arm. I grabbed a knife and waited for him to reach the fifty yard line. I launched it at a slightly upward angle. I started walking back across the field as his body fell in the end zone. As I approached his lifeless body I realized that Judy should have seen that throw. I pulled my knife out of his back. It had hit him right between the shoulder blades; at the very least it would have paralyzed him. I launched the knife into the cemetery next to the football field and walked away. The football field was closer to where I parked than the park was so it took me half the time to get back.

I didn't go straight back to my mom's for the night. I detoured to the apartment complex that Mike and Kay lived in. I slipped in through their son's window. I couldn't help but to watch him sleep. It was something I would never get the chance to do. The light flipped on and Kay was standing at the door to the room.

"Don't scream. Mike's in no condition to fight, and I'm not here to do anyone any harm," I announced before she completely realized what she was seeing.

"Then what do you want?" she snapped.

"To help," I answered as I tossed an envelope on the floor in front of her. "That will help with the debt and the treatment. You can tell Mike what I have done, but please tell no one else. I'm no saint."

"Why are you doing this?" Kay asked as I stood up to leave.

"Cause family is precious. I'm helping keep yours together," I answered.

"I heard about your wife and unborn child. Mike and I were both very sorry. We visited the grave after the funeral to pay our respects," Kay informed me.

"Thank you," I said as I started out the window.

I made it to my truck before Mike made it to the door. I was driving past as he started out the door. I simply nodded and kept going. I looked in my rearview mirror to see Kay walk up behind him and hug his waist. He wrapped his arm around her and looked down. There was a part of me worth saving, but for the most part, I was forsaken, a monster who needed to die. I crashed at my mom's house that night, but the next morning I was gone. I had two weeks before my next job so I planned on using the time to get further on with my revenge for the death of my son. One of the hit man was close and I planned on finishing it.

8

According to the information I had gathered, the hit man had a mark in Birmingham. I had pulled the target's name and address, so all I had to do was follow him to finish getting my revenge. The mark was a rather strange man, who seemed to be good at nothing. I watched him for a few days, but there was no sign of the hit man or the reason he was being targeted. It dawned on me that this wasn't an ordinary hit. The target wasn't real. It was a setup to lure me to my death. The only question I had was who was playing what part. Was the fake mark the hit man or an innocent bystander? Was there someone watching me from the shadows deeper than those I was using? I decided it was time to pull back, but that was out of the question.

"You've been following me these past few days," the fake mark stated as I past him heading to my truck. I stopped and glanced back at him, but he was standing right behind me with a knife drawn. I quickly spun around, redirecting his attack and putting my palm into his chest to knock him back a few feet.

"So you are the last hit man on my list," I guessed.

"Nope," the man retorted.

"What do you mean?" I demanded.

"Your last mark has no name or face. He is a phantom in the night and has many who serve his wishes," the man mused.

"So you're his little bitch," I tempted.

"I am the one given the glory of removing you from his sight! You have become a thorn in his side by killing his friends! I will take his vengeance for him!" the man yelled.

"So he doesn't even know you're here," I reasoned.

"He knows everything, including your real name. I don't know why, but he refused to tell me. He told me not to come after you, but I had to defend his honor. You must die by a hand that suits you," the man claimed.

"You couldn't kill me if you tried," I challenged.

The fool did just as I expected and charged. I side stepped and grabbed his knife hand to avert the attack away from me. I stepped in and stabbed him in the side with a pencil. I pulled the pencil out and stepped back as I planted my knee into his gut. The man fell back, but managed to roll back to his feet. He grabbed his side and looked at the blood that spilled onto the ground in front of him. He looked at the blood that was already staining his hand.

"Damn. Who know you could do that much damage with a pencil," he said as he straightened up.

"I....," I began.

I stopped as the man went ridded. I watched as he dropped to his knees in front of me. I didn't drop my gaze so I could see the shooter. It wasn't hard to see him. He was standing close to a hundred and fifty feet away from me with a handgun outstretched. I shifted to the side just in time to dodge the second bullet. Realizing that I was the real target, I rolled behind a tree and looked for a way out of this predicament. It was a forty yard dash to the best cover to get to my truck, but after seeing how well the shooter could aim, I didn't like my chances. He was just out of range for my projectiles to be of any use. I looked down to see my salvation. It was a sheet of metal lying on the ground two feet in front of me. I grabbed the metal sheet and slide it up the back of my shirt. I didn't wait to find out if he had gotten closer before I took off running. I felt two tings in my back, both of which hurt like hell, but I didn't stop running until I was at my truck. I jumped in and took off.

I didn't stop for an hour, trying to make sure I wasn't being followed. This guy was on a whole different level from the others. Pedro was good, but this guy was at my level at the very least. I had no doubt that he had some kind of military back round, mostly likely Special Forces. I pulled over behind a rundown warehouse. I got out and pulled the metal sheet out. I took off my shirt to see where he hit me. One shot would have hit me right between the shoulder blades. The other would have been a heart shot. Why he didn't go for a head shot is beyond me, but I was glad he didn't. This was no longer a simple case of revenge, this was a showdown.

I grabbed another shirt out of my truck. I set the shot up shirt on the metal and pulled out my lighter. I set the shirt on fire to eliminate evidence. I put on my hoodie and went back to the scene to look for evidence. I didn't want to be noticed by the police, but the hoodie would make it hard for the hit man to know it was me, just incase he was still there waiting.

As predicted the scene was swarming with cops. None of them were anywhere near where the hit man was shooting from, which made my job a little easier. I walked around the area he was standing for second, looking for a shell casing, but I had no luck. He was good at covering his tracks, which meant the only reason I even knew he existed was because the others weren't as careful as they should have been. It dawned on me that this hit man could actually kill me. Good thing I had started training Judy to replace me.

I sat down and looked over the park. I didn't see anything at first, but then I spotted him. He was sitting on the back of a truck just staring at me. He was maybe seventy yards away, but with all the cops in the area he didn't try to shoot me. We sat there just watching each other. He seemed to be sizing me up, which was fine because I was doing the same. Physically, he was similar to me in so many ways it was scary. Dark hair, large frame with an average build, just like me. His gaze was different from mine. He had no compassion for anyone and I could see it in his eyes. He lived to kill while I lived to help by destroying. I got up and started toward him. He jumped off the back of his truck to meet me halfway. We stopped with ten feet between us.

"Find what you were looking for?" he mocked.

"Something better," I retorted.

"You were gone for over an hour, which means you're smart, but at the same time, you fell for Han's trap," he stated.

"I didn't fall for his trap. He wasn't someone who

would be on a hit list. So either he was the hit man or the bait," I corrected.

"You followed him for three days. Sounds like you got duped," he tried.

"Either way, hit man or bait, he could lead me to my revenge," I spat.

"I never touched her. I just cleaned up the evidence. That reminds me. How did you find the others? I never leave a trace," he questioned.

"The woman you killed took a picture that caught the tattoo on you're partner's arm. I recognized it from the tussle in New York. I found a video of the five of you walking into the airport together. I went after him first. Got your names from him. I hunted two of the others down. Pedro, on the other hand, found me before I even went looking for him," I explained.

"Impressive. Pedro was the only one of the other four that could ever find me. He never could sneak up on me though. I hear you like knives. What kind of range do you get on those? Pedro could be deadly accurate at seventy yards," he said.

"I'll let you figure that one out. I can guess that you can hit your mark from close to two hundred yards with a handgun," I guessed. The hit man smiled at the guess, probably because I was right.

"And you can't guarantee a hit at a hundred and fifty yards out," he guessed.

"But the question is can I kill you before you can kill me," I pointed out as we continued to size each other up.

"Good point. I like to know the names of the people I kill, so I give you mine. Thomas," he introduced.

"I am Charles," I said with a slight bow which he returned.

"Until next time when we aren't so crowded," Thomas suggested.

"I agree," I said as I took a step back and walked away.

No one in their right mind would turn their back on a hit man who intended to kill them, but I wasn't exactly in my right mind. To me it showed Thomas that I believed that I could take him and had no reason to be afraid of him. Whether or not he got the message is beyond me, because when I got to a spot that gave me a side view of him, he was already gone. I went the long way around the park to avoid the cops and get to my truck. I went to the nearest hotel and checked in. I had no idea how long this showdown was going to take so I told them to hold the room until I told them I was ready to check out. The room had only one window, which had an open shoot to the bed, so I slept on the floor on the other side of the bed. It gave me cover just incase he tried to snipe me in my sleep.

I stayed up late that night, looking over the city on the computer. I was looking for a good place to have a showdown that closed us just enough for me to be able to hit him. There were three locations that were about a football field's length. They were all warehouses which meant there had to be some cover, which worked in both of our favors. I decided to scout them out in the morning, but the night was half over and I needed to get some sleep before the sun woke me up.

The next day I went to each of the locations I marked on the map. They were all perfect for the fight, but one of them was too close to a suburb, so I had to rule it out. The other two were too perfect for me to pick between the two, so I set them both up. It worked out better this way cause it gave me two options just incase one was harder to get to than the other. It took me all day to set them up and thankfully, Thomas didn't show up anywhere. I went back to my hotel for the night.

The next morning was something else. When I went to get up, I put my hand on the bed. When I pulled myself to eye level, I spotted a bullet hole on the other side of the bed. I looked up the bed and found another hole just over a foot away from where I was laying. Apparently, sleeping next to the bed wasn't as good an idea as I had originally believed. I adjusted the bedding to make the hole less apparent. I took it as a good reason to go ahead and check out and find someplace else to sleep. The lady behind the counter looked some what concerned when I walked up to the counter.

"Is everything ok?" I asked as I pulled out my cash.

"The person in the room below you was killed last night. They can't figure out where the bullet came from," she informed me.

"That's odd. What was he or she doing?" I inquired.

"We don't know. The police say that if they knew that, they could figure out where the bullet came from," she stated.

"It's a terrible thing when people are killed in their own rooms, far from home," I commented.

"The housekeeping noticed that you didn't sleep in the bed the night before. Was it not to your liking?" she inquired as I put my money back.

"I have a back problem and sleeping in the floor helps. I never touched the bed," I stated to cover my tracks.

"Oh ok. Well have a nice day, sir," she said as I turned to walk away.

"You too, Mary," I returned, no doubt getting a double take from her for saying her name.

When I left the hotel, I went back to the park. As expected, Thomas was there waiting for me. This time I saw him, but he didn't see me. He was watching all the kids playing in the park. For the first time, I saw something besides killer instincts behind his eyes. He regarded the children as something valuable, not like money, but as humans. I tied a note with the address of one of the warehouses I had set up and launched at his seat. I watched as it made for its target, but I didn't stay to watch it land. I had to start moving before he did in order to keep an advantage.

I pulled up to the warehouse and ran inside. I ran up to an upper floor to watch for him out one of the windows. Oddly, he never came, or so I thought. I heard a click somewhere behind me and dropped just in time to dodge a bullet aimed at my head. He had found a back door and used it to get the drop on me, but it wasn't good enough to take me. I rolled until I fell off the ledge and landed on the catwalk below me. I ran down the catwalk and stopped once, which was a perfect guess, because a bullet crossed my path where my head would have been. I jumped over the rail and rolled behind a piece of machinery when I hit the ground, just barely avoiding a shot that bounced off the ground where I had landed. I grabbed a knife in each hand and waited for my turn to strike. I heard a piece of metal scrap the floor about thirty yards away on the other side of the machine. I jumped out and launched both blades. I fell just in time to dodge another bullet, but not before I saw where my blades went. Thomas managed to dodge one all together, while the other niched his right sleeve. I rolled behind another piece of equipment as he unloaded another shot.

"I have never had to use as many bullets on any target in my life. Three tops and I've already fired more than that in this building alone. I've shot at you six times since we got here and haven't hit you once. I shot at you four times at the park and have no idea how you survived. And why did I miss you at the hotel?" Thomas pondered.

"I used a piece of metal like a bulletproof vest at the park. You hit me twice, both were kill shots. As for the hotel, I didn't feel like getting sniped in my sleep so I didn't sleep in the bed. Don't worry, you did kill somebody. Which brings a question to mind. How many people have you killed?" I explained.

"While I was in the military, about a hundred. After that, including the fool at the park and the bystander at the hotel, thirty. What about you?" Thomas returned.

"I've killed thirty people," I answered.

"In how long?" Thomas asked. "You don't seem to be very old."

"I'll be twenty-four in about two months," I answered. "I started killing right after I turned twenty-two."

"Damn, well you are a worthy opponent, I'll give you that much, and one more thing. I had a hit on the last man on your list. He's already dead. Kill me to complete your revenge," Thomas informed me.

Anger festered inside of me. It was my right to kill these men and no one else's. He had robbed me of what

I had to do, and he would pay dearly for it. I pulled out two more knives and prepared to attack, but something wasn't right. I felt a change in the wind that told me that something behind me had moved. I turned just in time to see his gun round the corner. I launched the blade in my left hand as I darted out from behind the equipment and across the warehouse. I heard the shot he took when my blade hit him. I slide behind another piece on machinery as he fired another shot. This one grazed my right arm, which I retaliated by launching my other knife at him. I didn't stay in the open long enough to see if it hit its mark or not. I pulled out two more knives and ran down the wall. I ran up a piece of equipment and launched the blades at Thomas as I leapt through the air. He, of course, returned fire with two shots. One stopped the blade he couldn't dodge, while the other grazed my leg. One good thing came from my air assault. I saw that my blade from when he tried to sneak up behind me had hit his shoulder while the other was lodged in his stomach. He had fired ten shots without reloading, and if memory served me correctly, that meant he was using a twelve round clip. He had two maybe three shots left if he kept one in the chamber. I had six knives left so I kinda figured I was in the lead. I started around, trying to avoid being caught in the open, but got shot at once during a sprint. I ducked behind a crate and pulled out two knives. I turned and stood fast, launching both of them to the best of my abilities. I dropped back down just in time to avoid the bullet that answered my assault. I heard the clip hit the floor and relaxed, waiting to hear another clip being loaded. The sound never came.

"This is new. I never carry extra ammo. Never needed it. I'm empty," Thomas claimed as I moved to another spot.

I stood up and dodge the last shot he had. Thomas dropped his gun in some form of amazement, but at the same time he seemed to be excited. I couldn't blame him. Even though I had been wounded, I was having the time of my life. I guess to some extent, all of us destroyers were the same. It was the reason that we were who we were that made us stand apart. I walked around the equipment and started toward Thomas with the look of victory on my face.

"You knew I had one in the chamber to start with. Not bad for a knife guy," Thomas complimented.

"You look as though you've had the time of your life," I pointed out.

"Indeed I have," Thomas agreed.

"Too bad there won't be a second time," I said as I pulled another knife out to finish the job.

It didn't dawn on me that he might have other guns on him until he shot me. He had two one shot guns slide up his sleeves. I couldn't avoid the shots so I shifted to minimize the damage, which meant I got shot in both arms, which made them useless. Thomas smiled as if he had just won, but I had a trick to play too. I shifted my foot to release the six inch blade I had hidden in my shoe. When Thomas took a step forward, I flung one of my arms, slugging him in the face hard enough to make him bend over. Then I kicked him in the throat, putting the knife right into his windpipe. He fell with my foot and almost tripped me when I tried to pull the knife back out. I shifted my foot to retract the blade and walked out to my truck. I used voice command to call Judy to come help me out. Jason dropped her off close to an hour later.

"You're a mess," Judy pointed out when she got a clear view of me.

"Just got into a fight with an ex special forces hit man. Do you honestly think I would pull off an easy victory?" I asked her with my worst smartass tone.

"I would expect you not to get shot up enough to not be able to drive away," Judy retorted.

"I was close, but he had hidden guns that I simply didn't think about. You're lucky that trick didn't kill me," I informed her as she started looking over my injuries.

"I wonder what kind of damage the last one will be able to pull," Judy wondered out loud.

"That one killed him already. My revenge is over, so it's back to business as usual," I informed her.

"Usual. You are so far from normal, you shouldn't use that word at all," Judy joked.

"Look who's talking," I laughed.

I had Judy burn my wounds shut after she pulled the bullets out of the two, so they wouldn't get infected. It took me most of the day and hurt like hell, but I pushed myself to use my arms so I could drive instead of Judy. I was in recovery most of the following week before I returned to work. Judy told me to skip work and finish healing, but I had to maintain the illusion that nothing had happened. It was the only way to keep me from being caught, so no matter how much it hurt, I had to press on. The only draw back was that I was in no condition to kill anyone who deserved to die. That part hurt more than the gun shots did.

9

I was out of killing condition for two months. I decided to go stay with Jessy for my birthday. She was thrilled to see me, and I had to admit that I was happy to see her as well. Her parents were gone, as usual. She didn't take as long as I thought to discover my injuries even though they were almost fully healed. She took this opportunity to make me sit on the couch and rest while she "took care" of me. I didn't like this idea, but in the end, I enjoyed it very much.

"How are your arms?" Jessy asked after we got done eating.

"They're fine, Jessy. You really didn't have to do all of this," I tried, but to no avail.

"None sense. I want to help you as you have helped me. It's only fair," Jessy pointed out.

"Shouldn't matter," I stated.

"To you maybe, but to me, it does," Jessy insisted. She was the only person that could win an argument with me and I had no idea how.

"How is it you can win every argument without breaking a sweat when no one else can even win an argument to begin with?" I asked as I usually did.

"I have no idea. Guess I have power over you," Jessy replied.

"Well, I don't mind that too much," I commented.

"Good, cause I plan on using my power to get everything I want from you," Jessy stated as she sat in my lap.

"Jessy, I already told....," I began, but she stopped me with a kiss.

I couldn't help but to fall into her kiss. It seemed like it was out of my power to fall deeper into her arms as she pulled me in. I picked her up and carried her into her room. I set her on her bed without breaking the kiss. Jessy's hands slide up my shirt as my hand slide down her leg. She started tugging at my shirt, so I stopped kissing her to let her take my shirt off. I went back to kissing her as if I had never stopped. I slide my hands up her shirt and undid her bra. She pushed me back and pulled her shirt and bra off. I started kissing her stomach, working my up to each of her breasts. I sucked on her breast softly making her moan with pleasure. She pulled my hair until she got me to kiss her lips again. She undid my pants and pulled back so she could take her pants off. She pulled me tight as I slipped inside her. We made love until the sun came up that morning. We laid there quietly as if we were still taking in what had just happened. The day seemed to slip away, but we never left the bed.

The next morning I woke to find Jessy cooking me breakfast again. I gave her a "you shouldn't have" look, but was too hungry to argue with her. We sat next to each other and ate while we talked about Jessy's dream to be a psychiatrist. She wanted to help people who had been hurt the way she had. I thought it was a noble idea, but not something I could ever do.

As always, Beth and her family came by for Sunday lunch. It was a tradition they had since their parents weren't there enough. I felt that I needed to leave, but they ganged up on me and made me stay. It was a good day, but the day before was one that shouldn't have happened. I had no intention of letting Jessy get caught up in my world, nor forfeit her future for me. She may have felt that it was her decision, but in truth it was mine. I decided whose fate I would seal, but hers wasn't one of them.

"So what brings you here this time?" Beth asked.

"My birthday was Thursday," I informed her.

"And what did Jessy give you for your birthday?" Beth asked with a wicked grin on her face.

"The week off," Jessy intervened.

"Was that all?" Beth toyed.

"Yea. I haven't done any cleaning or cooking or anything since I got here. Jessy will make someone a great wife one day," I stated.

"Alright, I'll drop it," Beth said as if she knew what we had done.

That night after Beth and her family left, Jessy kissed me. It took everything I had to pull her back. She looked at me with confusion in her eyes. I let her go and went to the couch. I sat down and put my head in my hands. Jessy followed me and curled up next to me. She tried to look at my face, but I had buried it too deeply for her to see my eyes.

"What's wrong?" Jessy asked in a concerned voice that ripped through the ice on my heart.

"I told you that this couldn't be. I shouldn't have let it go so far. I don't want you hurt because of me," I explained.

"Charles, I made the decision to love you and no one else. I don't care what dangers may wait for me. And I don't care to wait until you have done what you believe is necessary to make the world a better place. I'll do whatever you want me to do," Jessy explained.

"Go be with someone else. I'm damaged beyond repair. I've lost far too much to a good man for you. Please move on," I begged.

It hurt her for me to ask that, but I could see that she understood what I was trying to avoid. She curled up next to me and went to sleep. Tears rolled from her eyes that night as she slept. My heart called to her, but I couldn't let it have what it wanted. I was beyond salvation and the more I let myself believe otherwise, the more I would suffer and the more those I did care for would suffer. It was best for me to be alone. I knew this better now than ever before. I waited until after she went to school the next day before I left, heading to my next job. I was healed and more than able to kill any who deserved that fate.

My next job took me to Florida. I hated it when I got there for one reason. The sun seemed to be too bright. I enjoyed the fact that there were parties every night, but I just couldn't get past the sun. This job had me working all week seven in the morning to seven at night. So I didn't party until the weekend. My first Friday night, I went to a club. To everyone else, I was looking to have a good time, but I was there for other reasons. I hadn't killed anybody in over two months. I needed another victim. The club seemed like the best place to start, plus I needed a drink.

I went up to the bar and ordered a shot of Jack. The bartender gave me my drink and went back to what she was doing. I took the shot and toyed with the glass for a second. I set it down and nodded to her to get another.

She refilled my glass without a word. I took that shot and paid her. She smiled meekly which made me think she didn't like her job, but I was wrong. A guy at the other end of the bar called to her and her facial expression changed to disgust before she turned to face him. He slapped the table and ordered a round, informing her that she had to take a shot with him and his buddies, who were looking her over. I watched them poke and prod her until after one in the morning. The bouncer decided that they had too much to drink and made them leave. It was almost closing time. So I caught up my bill.

"Bet you wished that people weren't such assholes," I commented when she came to collect. I noticed the bouncer take a step toward me, but the bartender shook her head to let him know it was ok.

"Those jerks are in here every weekend buying me shots, thinking they can get with me. How come you didn't say anything earlier?" she explained.

"I'm not like them, so I decided to wait until they were gone so you wouldn't put me in the same league as those drunks," I answered.

"I don't think I would have put you in there with them. They just want in my pants. You seem to want something else," she guessed.

"I can't say I wouldn't mind trying, but I'd go a different way about it and wait until next weekend when I've been in here a bit more. That or I wouldn't try at all because I'm here on business and won't be here more than a few weeks," I explained truthfully.

"Honesty is good. Maybe I wouldn't mind having some fun with you before you leave," she informed me as she slipped me her number.

I smiled and put her number in my pocket and kept talking. I stayed all the way up to closing. She asked me to wait with the bouncer so I could walk her to her car. The group of guys that had been harassing her was standing on the far end of the parking lot. The bouncer pointed them out when the bartender walked out. He decided it was best to walk with us to her car. He stopped a few feet away to give us some privacy. She unlocked her door and turned to look at me.

"I didn't catch your name," she pointed out.

"Charles and yours?" I returned.

"Everyone calls me Ally," she answered as she stepped forward and kissed me.

I opened the door for her and let her drive away. I turned and the bouncer nodded and walked back to the door. I took a deep breath and started toward my truck which was continently located right in front of the group of idiots. I walked right up to the door without a word, but they just couldn't keep their mouths shut.

"Hey, bitch, she's our trophy so leave her to us and go get your own," the one who seemed to be the leader of the pack called.

"Forgive me for believing that women aren't trophies to be won," I replied, gazing over at them. I could see the bouncer watching from the corner of my eye.

"I'm not gonna warn you again," he retorted.

"You're drunk and in no condition to be throwing threats. Now go home to your wives, and for the two of you who aren't married, your hands," I insisted.

One of them popped off and started toward me, cussing away and thrusting his finger in the air. He walked right up to me and pushed me into my truck. I looked him right in the eyes and smiled as he continued to cuss me out. The bouncer started toward us. Three of the other guys moved to intercept him. The one cussing me moved to swing. I stepped in and head-butted him, sending him tumbling to the ground. The others started toward me. One ran over and threw a punch, which I swatted away and close lined him. The other two stopped and put their fists up. I faked a shot at the one to my right and did a spin kick, catching the one on my left in the chest. The other one got over the shock and tried to tackle me. I shifted fast enough to catch him and fling him into the car behind me. He bounced off and hit the ground rolling. None of them were sober enough to get back up, so the fight was over. I turned around to see the bouncer throw the last one that went to oppose him against a wall. The other two were sprawled out on the ground. I smiled and got in my truck. I didn't think they would be worth the effort in the long run so there was no point in trying to find out who they were.

The next night I went back to the club to meet Ally. I had called her when I got back to the hotel. She wanted me to come back the next night so we could go out afterward. I didn't ask where we would go because I had an idea. I spent the whole night at the bar talking to her when she had a minute. While she was on break she took me to the dance floor and basically had to teach me how to dance. She only had an hour, but I think she was satisfied with the end result of my dance moves. That night since we were going the same place and I was kind of drunk, we just took her car. She decided to take me to her place. I could only guess what she had planned and I was for the most part right.

We had very passionate sex for hours. Some things I knew how to do better than she did, while others, I never tried or heard of. It was an interesting experience, but there was no real emotion behind it, which meant it was just sex. At this point in time, it bothered me, but I couldn't let that one reason be, so I did it anyway. It must have been almost seven before we fell asleep. It was a great night's sleep, but not as good as the sleep I had at Jessy's. I had to get her out of my head so when I woke up, I wrapped my arm around Ally who was awake enough to roll on top of me and start having sex again.

This time we were interrupted, but not by thoughts of Jessy. This time, Ally's phone started ringing. She sighed in aggravation and climbed off. She walked out of the room and answered her house phone. She didn't come back for some time, and when she did, she was crying. I sat up and put my pants on. I followed her into her walk-in closet to see what was wrong.

"What's going on?" I asked.

"My brother was killed last night. He got into street fighting. The police say he must have lost, but they have no idea where to start looking for his killer. I have to go identify the body. I'll drop you off at your truck on the way," Ally informed me.

"Alright, call me when you want," I told her.

After she dropped me off, I started going around looking for information on the street fights. I found out that nobody knew when or where until about an hour before the fight and that they got your information there, but you had to be brought in by someone else. I found someone who was willing to bring me in if I could fight. I was glad to help because that's what I planned on doing. I had to wait until the following weekend to actually fight, but he promised me a way in. I told Ally that I had to take care of something and that I'd swing by as often as I could so she wouldn't worry, but she figured out what I was up to and wanted in. I refused to let her, promising to take care of everything. She submitted, but not without a fight.

That Friday, after work, my new friend was waiting on me. He took me to a pier that we had to get underneath. That was the location of the event for the night. It was an open fight night for new fighters to get in on the action. Your objective was to knock out your opponent. Killing was supposed to be for a championship fight only, but if you couldn't take your opponent down by any other means, they made an exception. Ally's brother died in a championship fight against a man named Orion. He was currently undefeated and had held the tittle for just over a year now. He made it a point to kill every challenger, so few made the attempt anymore.

As it was my first night, I had to fight another trying to get in. My opponent had about a hundred pounds on my, but I wasn't worried. He looked slow and as soon as he started swinging, I knew he didn't have a chance. His first swing was meant to be a jab to the face. I grabbed his arm and pulled him into me. Then I planted my knee in his side. I shifted and launched him over my shoulder. I landed a heel kick to his face to finish the match. The cheering stopped almost as fast as it had begun. No one seemed to be satisfied with the fight, because it didn't last very long at all.

The next fight took a few minutes, because nobody else finished as fast as I did. I could only guess that my best bet was to let the fight drag out a little bit. As it turned out, I didn't have to. My next opponent came in and planted a kick to my chest before I even knew he was coming. I rolled back and dropped just in time to dodge his next kick. He spun around and launched another kick, but this time I countered. I stepped in and put my knee into his back. He fell forward and rolled back to his feet. He came at me with a flying kick. I side stepped and elbowed him in the face, which backfired. As he started to fall, he shifted his leg and kicked me in the head. I stumbled back giving him enough time to get back to his feet. He changed his stance and went for a flying punch. I diverted the attack and planted my knee in his gut. I stepped in and wrapped my arm around his neck. I choked him out to win the fight.

Only four of us had showed up to get into the fight circuit so he was the last one I had to fight for the night. I took a seat next to my new friend, who patted me on the back. I wiped blood off of my mouth and shook my head as I looked around. While I was in the second fight, the guy running things had collected my information from my new friend so I didn't see him until he decided he could trust me. I watched the fights that had been called for that night. I picked one of the winners and asked my friend to set up the fight, but it was too late. Someone else had already challenged me. It was one of the guys from the parking lot at the club. Apparently, he wanted to get payback, so he asked for the match to be that night. I didn't care because I knew he couldn't beat me.

I got up and approached him. He had a huge smile on his face. Without warning he took a swing. I dropped and landed a blow in his gut. He hesitated for just a second before elbowing me in the side of my head. The blow pushed me to put my hand on the ground. I retaliated with an elbow to the side of his knee. He dropped to his knees.

I recoiled my arm and backhanded him with it. He hit the ground hard. I stood up and waited for him to get up. He didn't, the fight was over. Two of his friends from the other night came and took him to their car for treatment.

That was the last fight for the night. Everyone started leaving after that. I walked over to get my new friend, but he had company. A guy standing about six, four was standing over him have a pleasant conversation. True, my new friend looked intimidated, but he was a mouse compared to this guy. The conversation stopped when they realized that I was coming. This didn't sit well with me.

"Ah Charles, it's a pleasure to meet you. My boss looks forward to your next match," the big man greeted.

"That's good to hear," I said plainly.

"My boss is the champ. He has been watching every fight with hope for a worthy opponent and he thinks you might give him a decent fight, if you aren't afraid," the big man explained.

"I don't get scared, just pissed," I stated.

"Very good. Then once you have beaten four more fighters, giving you the right to challenge, Cecil will come find me to let me know you are ready," the big man said with way too much enthusiasm.

I was a bit more beat up than I anticipated I would be, but I played it off like I was just fine. Oddly, no one asked which had to mean that everyone knew. That night when I got off, Ally was at my hotel waiting for me. She looked me over in the elevator, but never said a word. When we got to my room, she shut the door behind us and locked it. I took off my shirt and turned to face her. What happened next was something I never would have expected. She pushed me onto my bed, which I expected the pushing. Then she undid my pants, pulled up her skirt, and climbed on top of me. Before I knew it we were having some of the most heated sex that we ever had together, not that we had much to go on. We went at it for three hours. When she was too tired to continue, she simply got off, kissed me, and left without a word. It was as if she was just rewarding me for what I was doing for her.

My new friend was waiting for me the next night. I went to face off against two more opponents. One was the guy I picked two days before. The other one was challenging me just as I had challenged the other. I took on the challenger first since he lost the match he was in. He tired and failed to put up a fight. His swings were too wild so I just side-stepped and hit him until he fell. The guy I challenged was a different story altogether. He was trained in some form of martial arts, but I couldn't put my finger on it. In order to bring him down, I had to plant my knee in his gut and then to his temple. He didn't get up, but I was fine with that. The big guy that worked for the champ looked impressed with my fight, but I didn't care. I wasn't fighting him, his opinion didn't matter.

The next night, Ally was waiting in the lobby again. It was the same as the other night. We had great sex, without a word, and then she left as if she had nothing more for me. The next night, my new friend was nowhere to be seen so I knew I didn't have another fight. Ally was waiting for me in the lobby again. She followed me up to room, but this time when she went to push me down, I grabbed her and pinned her against the wall. I can't say that I wasn't enjoying the sex, but I had to know what was going on with her.

"What's going on with you?" I demanded.

"I'm rewarding you for trying to avenge my brother, before you die," Ally informed me.

"Then why won't you do anything more than fuck me. What is keeping you from saying something?" I questioned.

"You're going to die and leave me in pain again," Ally admitted.

"Ally, I'm not going to die. That I can promise. But as for any feelings that you are starting to develop, I told you that I wouldn't be here long. I was going to have to leave sooner or latter anyway," I pointed out to her.

"I know, but I don't get why you're doing this if you don't care," Ally snapped back.

"I was stepped on until I reached my breaking point and now I take care of those who believe they have the right to step on others. That's why I'm doing this. Because I have become an avenger," I explained and with that said I let her go.

Ally kissed me softly. I took a step back to give her some room to breath. She followed me every step I took. I backed all the way to the bed with her still kissing me. I fell onto the bed and she fell with me. The kiss broke for a second while she laughed. I simply smiled as she kissed me again. I rolled her over, putting me on top of her. I pulled back to stop her from kissing me anymore. I couldn't do this with her. Jessy's face was there every time I closed my eyes. Not to mention, the fact that the only reason Ally was doing this was because I was trying to avenge her brother. Ally's confused face fell back in a submissive manner. I stood up and took a step back. Ally sat up, more puzzled than before.

"I can't. It would be taking advantage of you," I answered her unspoken question.

"No you wouldn't," Ally tried.

"You came here to thank me for what I am doing," I pointed out.

"And if my brother was still alive, would we not still be doing this?" Ally asked a very good question.

"Probably just on the weekends. Ally, you need to find a good man who will take care of you, and isn't afraid to fight. I'm not a good man. I'm more or less a monster. Don't worry. I will avenge your brother, but we can't do this again," I explained while leaving out the part where I was actually in love with Jessy. It was bad enough that I knew it, but it would have been too much for me to admit.

Ally stood up right in front of me. She looked me in the eye before nodding. She kissed me on the cheek and started toward the door. I could feel her turn to look at me before walking out the door. In truth, she could have never been more than what Kelly was to me, and it was apparent that she would die if I allowed it.

My phone started vibrating in my pocket. It was my new friend with some directions to my next fight. It started in an hour so I moved quickly. It took me about forty-five minutes to get there, but when I arrived, something wasn't right. The crowd was all gathered around a ring made of stones. There was a guy just taller than me sitting in what looked to be a throne. The guy that worked for the champ was standing right next to him, which told me that he had to be the champ. My new friend was waiting for me just outside of the crowd. He had a black eye and was scared shitless. I walked right up to him as if nothing was wrong.

"You get a crack at the champ," my new friend said with fear backing his words.

"So you came after all. Ladies and gentlemen, this is my next victim. This man, Charles isn't it, came here to avenge my last victim. He came here to kill me. He doesn't belong here with us, so I decided to challenge him now instead of letting him destroy our world," the champ announced as he entered the circle of stones.

"And yet I only needed to find to kill you. I came here to humiliate you in front of your fans. You think you can win against me, well that remains to be seen," I countered. I pushed through the crowd that no longer wanted me there. I entered to stone circle ready to complete the kill I set out for.

"But I can and will kill you. Anytime you're ready, sunshine," the champ challenged.

I stood there checking for weak spots, trying to find my opening for a kill shot. There wasn't one. He had too much muscle for me to deliver an effective kill shot, so I had to improvise. Before I decided to act, I noticed that the champ was slowly getting madder. He was impatient and that gave me an idea. I held out just a little longer and then made my move. I stopped just short of his arm's reach which allowed me to avoid his first attack. I did a spin kick to his ribs. He took a step forward and tried to catch me with a back swing, but I ducked beneath it. Unfortunately, I didn't see his other hand move in until he had his hand around my throat. He picked me up with his one arm and tried choking me out. It was a good idea, but I had a better one. I pulled my knees into my chest and kicked him with both legs in the chest. I toppled to the ground as he stumbled back. I used the momentum from the fall to roll back to my feet avoiding too much damage. The champ recovered and gave me one hell of a look as he charged toward me. I charged him and dropped at the last moment, elbowing the top of his knee in the process. I rolled out of the way and dived into the same knee trying to finish it off with my shoulder. I wasn't sure if it worked, but the champ elbowed me in the face for my troubles.

I refocused and prepared for his next attack. When the champ moved to stand, his knee gave, causing him to drop back to his knees. I used this opening and moved behind him. I charged, this time pulling both knees up just in time to ram them into the back of his head. I went down with him, but I was able to roll back to my feet. I turned to see what damage had been done, but it took a second for the champ to pull his head out of the dirt. His moves were clumsy and slow, which meant he was almost done. I walked up to him to deliver the finishing blow, but I was caught in his monstrous grip. He was faking to catch me, so I reacted as fast as I could. I wrapped my hands around his neck, putting one knuckle in his windpipe, cutting off all airflow. Now it was just a matter of waiting to see which of us could hold out longer. I held my breath and began counting. Every time I hit thirty I would take a breathe and start over. I did this six times before his grip started to loosen. I did it twice more and he let go of me altogether. I counted it four more times before I let him go. I snapped his neck to be on the safe side and stood up. The crowd was quiet for what seemed like an hour, but after it set in, they started to disperse. I walked back to my truck and went back to the hotel to get some sleep before I had to go to work.

After work I went back to the bar. I sat down and nodded to Ally, who started crying and walked away to hide it. The group of guys from the first night was sitting in their normal spot. I looked over at them and they all left. I had become to well known on this one. It was best if I finished my job quickly and got out of town for good.

10

The next few weeks were kind of dull for me. Jessy had called a few times. She was doing well, found a boyfriend that left her when she found out she was pregnant. I asked if she needed me to come help, but she just told me that Beth had her back. Judy was busy too. She had just found out that she was pregnant too. She took herself off of killer duties until this child was able to walk, which was a good idea. I worked away and found very little entertainment. That was until I got to my next job at the end of the summer.

My next job took me to Louisiana. I thought it would be a completely uneventful job until the locals started talking to me. They kept warning me about the night. As a matter of fact, the town had a curfew due to some recent incidents. Most were cattle mutilations, but the last few were people coming up missing. I didn't pay them much mind until my first day of work. I arrived at the time my employer had requested, but the police were all over. My employer was standing there talking to them. I approached, curious as to what was going on.

"Ah Charles, sorry for the mess. I'm sure you've heard

about the missing people, well they all turned up," my employer informed me.

"Well, that's good news, isn't it?" I inquired.

"Not quite. They all turned up dead here at the site. Most of their blood is missing," the Sherriff interrupted.

"They weren't here yesterday, that I can assure you Sherriff Hamilton," my employer defended himself.

"That's not what I'm saying, Mr. Dufton. I'm simply pointing out the facts," Sherriff Hamilton clarified.

"Can we calm down for a second?" I asked getting everyone's attention. "I'm sure we need to let the Sherriff do his job. Then we can do ours."

"You are right, so if you please, Mr. Dufton, I have work to do," Sherriff Hamilton confirmed.

I scanned the area as Mr. Dufton demanded to be allowed to do some work. The Sherriff allowed us to get a scope of the land from outside of the yellow tape. I accepted before Mr. Dufton made an even bigger fool of himself. I did the best I could to gather information from beyond the yellow tape, but I did find something the police failed to. Some of the grass was parted, heading toward the woods. I got the best view I could to find a spot to start tracking, but I was going to have to hike at least a mile to stay out of sight as far as the police were concerned.

That night, after curfew, I snuck out and made my way into the woods. I decided that I didn't have the means to follow the trail until we had full access to the site. Instead, I decided to watch the town for anyone out past curfew. They were either in on what was going on or they would be targets. Either way, they would help me get to the bottom of what was going on. It was an hour before I saw any sign of someone breaking curfew. It was a couple, no doubt, out on a date just trying to get home. Unfortunately for them, I wasn't the only one waiting in the shadows.

From out of no where four cloaked figures surrounded the couple. They were quickly over taken and subdued. Four more figures calmly crept into the light. There were a total of eight cloaked figures hovering over the couple. What happened next was far beyond even my twisted ways. Each of the figures took out tubes with needles on the end. They stabbed them into the couple and put the other end into their mouths. I watched as the tube went from clear to a blood red. I tensed as I realized what I was witnessing, but something forced my attention.

I was flanked from both side, but these fools were unprepared to take me on. I blocked to first, exposing my back to the other, and threw the figure over my shoulder. The other figure nimbly dodged the one I tossed, and pressed the attack. I caught the figure's knife hand with my left and its throat with my right. I stepped forward, pushing the figure into a tree. The other got back up with incredible speed. I shifted the one I was holding between the other and myself, but it did not good. The one I was holding dropped to its knees, exposing me to the other. With no other options, I let the figure go and kneed it in the face, sending its head into the other's gut. They both fell back. I pulled a knife out to finish them off, but the others caught my attention. They were heading toward me. I did the only smart thing and ran into the woods. I only had six knives with me, and these figures were not normal by any means. I climbed a tree and sat there as still as I could, watching the woods around me, trying to see if they were near. I waited until it was almost four in the morning to come down. I slipped through the trees without a sound.

I made it back to town without any trouble, but was in for a surprise. The bodies were gone. I started out of the woods when I was jumped from behind. It was one of the figures. I hit the ground and rolled throwing my elbow into the side of the figure's head. It rolled off of me and back onto its feet. I rolled the other way, back to my feet and pulled my knife. The figure pulled its knife and advanced. I charged, using my left arm to block the figure's counter attack, so I could stab it in the heart. The figure was quick enough to redirect the attack into its side. I quickly adjusted and ripped the knife out. The figure didn't make a noise as I twisted its arm behind its back and stabbed it in the throat. Even though I was certain I had severed its spinal cord, I ripped the knife out through the front, severing all veins and the windpipe. The figure dropped without the slightest sound. It was the worst thing I had ever seen and yet, it didn't seem to be dead yet. I watched as the figure tried to get back to its feet. After almost ten minutes of struggling, the figure fell motionless. I cleaned my knife on its cloak and walked back to my hotel, leaving the body to be discovered. This body would lead me to the other seven, but only if I left it for the cops.

The next morning I got up expecting to see a big ruckus in the streets, but it was surprisingly quiet. The body I had left laying in the street was gone before anyone could find it. The first chance I got, I went to examine the spot where I killed the figure. There was no blood, but a strong smell of bleach hung in the air. I looked for signs of a body being pulled away, but I found nothing. I walked into the woods while no one was looking to see if I could pick up a trail. It took me several hours, but I was able to find a trace of the figures passing through the woods. I followed it to the edge of a field. There was a barn about a football field's distance from me, but other than that there was no signs or roads for that matter. This place was completely concealed from the rest of the town unless you hiked. The day was half gone so it was time to leave, but not before I spotted something truly interesting. The barn door opened. A young woman walked out of it and looked up toward the sun. She had to shield her eyes, but she never dropped her gaze. The door cracked behind her. She lowered her gaze in a sulking manner and went back in. It was a cult, but to what end was beyond me.

It took me half the time to get back to the hotel room, but I had unexpected company. The Sherriff was there. He looked grave, but stead-fast. I approached him as if he was a welcome guest, but he didn't regard me in the same manner. I stopped about a foot short of him and waited for an explanation that didn't come.

"Can I help you officer?" I finally asked.

"You're going to have to come with me," Sherriff Hamilton stated.

"Alright," I replied calmly.

The Sherriff sat me down in what had to be an interrogation room. It was my first time in one which was kind of surprising, but I wasn't bothered by it. The Sherriff stepped out for a minute, probably to make me sweat or something like that. Since I had the free time I started trying to figure out what was going on and how to resolve it. These people were extraordinary, but very dangerous. I had to take care of them, because I severely doubted that the police could handle it. Even though my objective was clear, I couldn't help but to be curious as to what these people were and why they did what they did. Before I could find out, I had to get out of here.

When the Sherriff came back in, he was accompanied by my boss. They looked as though they had been arguing and judging by the fact that my boss was in the interrogation room, he won the argument. I stood up and nodded to both of them to know what was going on. Neither answered me, but both sat down opposite me. I decided to retake my seat and let them tell me what was going on.

"I know you didn't do anything wrong by your standards, but you broke curfew. We can't have you here doing that, because you could get hurt. Worse than that, no one could find you all day," Sherriff Hamilton informed me.

"That would be because I left town yesterday," I lied.

"Without a car?" Mr. Dufton questioned.

"Walking is good for you. I hiked through the woods and camped. I was about fifteen miles out of town. That's why it took me so long to get back today," I continued the lie.

"Well, I can't have you doing that again. You have two choices. Stay in town and follow the curfew or leave town until this is all settled," Sherriff Hamilton offered.

"With your permission Mr. Dufton, I think I will stay in a neighboring town. I doubt we will be able to get any work done so long as these disappearances continue," I requested.

"He's right. I can't let you start building until we have this under control," Sherriff Hamilton informed my employer.

"Very well, but I will not be paying any of your expenses until it is time to start work," Mr. Dufton agreed.

"That's quite fair," I agreed hoping that this would give me the time and room to get this job done quickly.

They let me leave without any trouble. I went and packed my stuff and Mr. Dufton gave me a lift to the next town. Once there I bought a bike and rode back toward the town. I stopped about five miles outside of the city limits to keep out of sight. I pulled the bike into the woods and started figuring out where I was. It took a few minutes, but once I got my location figured out, I started heading for my destination. It took me a few hours to get close to where the barn was. The sun had set just over an hour ago and the woods seemed to become deadly, but I didn't stop. I pushed forward hiding when I heard something move, but I never came across the people from the barn.

It had been dark for several hours before I came to the clearing. I was closer to the barn than I was earlier, but it was still quite a run to avoid being spotted. I followed along the trees trying to get closer, but it seemed as though whoever built the barn had no intention of anyone sneaking in. I got to a point where the fence cut across the field. I decided to follow it and see if I could get into the barn without being seen. I stayed low and kept my eyes on the barn doors, but there was no movement. I knelt down on the other side of the fence and examined the door. It didn't look like it was wired or anything of that nature, but I couldn't be careless. I ran across to the barn and took a knee by the crack in the door. I looked through and saw a light in the back of the barn. I looked the door over and decided it was safe to open. I pulled it open just a little further and slipped in.

The barn was almost completely dark. The light in the

back casted a small amount of light over the whole barn, but the source was behind a wall. I looked around and spotted ten pallets, five on each side of the barn. I walked toward the back looking at everything trying to figure out what was going on in this place. The barn itself showed me nothing of any worth, but I still hadn't seen behind the wall that blocked the light.

I heard a man swear from behind the wall. He was ranting about his big plans and the perfect race needing more soldiers. I pulled one of my daggers and took a knee by the door to watch the man through the crack. He was looking over several notes he had scattered on a desk. What truly bothered me was the equipment he had against the wall. Most of it was surgical tools, but some of it looked like things you would find in a kitchen. What was this guy up to? I decided I was alone enough to find out. I opened the door, but a wire pulled a bell off of the desk, alerting the man to my presence. I charged in and put my dagger to his throat before he could so much as try grabbing a weapon.

"Terrible alarm system for such small quarters," I commented as I made him face me. He looked to be in his mid-fifties. His clothes were tattered and torn, but over all he looked to be quite healthy.

"Well, I haven't ever needed it before. Usually, no one gets to the barn before my children kill them," the man retorted.

"So what has the mad scientist been up to out here in the barn?" I asked hoping that he would tell me so I didn't have to go through all of his notes.

"The perfect human race. What every human on this planet is always working on whether they know it or not," he informed me.

"But what you're doing isn't making humans, but something else entirely," I pointed out.

"But they are humans who have absorbed the strength of those they consume. It's something you couldn't understand," he mocked me.

"They are monsters in the eyes of all others," I spat.

"But they are my children and to me they are the next step in human evolution. No one else matters. Too bad Abel was killed. Now I'm short a son and a mate. I guess Joan is of no further use to me," he said blankly.

"So the one I killed last night was called Abel," I thought out loud.

"That you killed?" he asked shocked at the idea that I was the one who killed Abel.

"Yes, I am a monster who hunts other monsters. I am an avenger who is quite able to kill all of your children," I stated as I pulled out a knife and drove it through his hand and the desk. The man yelled in pain.

A noise from above caught my attention. I looked up just in time to see one of the hooded figures leap off of the rafter. I stepped out of the door just in time to avoid the figure's attack, but it bounced at me, catching me in the chest. I watched the lantern that was giving off the light, fall as I fell. The lantern shattered and fire took hold of the man's notes. The fire spread as I rolled the figure off of me. I got to my feet as quickly as I could, but the figure was just a little faster than I was. It backhanded me, knocking me off balance. The figure took a step forward to hit me again, but rammed my dagger into its gut. The figure grabbed me and launched me across the barn. The figure put its hand on one of the beds as it made its way toward me. I reacted to the best of my abilities and launched a knife at the figure's hand, nailing it to the bed. The figure kept walking expecting to rip the blade out of the frame, but it didn't. I ran up to the figure and grabbed my dagger, ripping it out the figure's side. Of course, the figure punched me in retaliation. I hit the bed next to me and bounced into the floor. I kicked the figure's leg, dropping it to its knees. It grabbed my leg and started pulling me toward it, so I kicked it with my other leg. It jerked hard sliding my throat right into its hand. It tightened its grip around my throat, trying to suffocate me. I pulled out another knife and put it through the figure's forearm. The figure released me, so I used this opportunity to make a run for it, because while we were fighting the fire had spread to the beds and was soon to be on us.

I turned when I got to the door and watched as the figure was engulfed in flames. I ran out the door and stopped to see if the fire would consume the whole barn. The fire reached the doors and I knew that it would burn to the ground. I turned and hooped the fence to try getting back to the road and my bike, but I stopped when I noticed the two figures standing about thirty yards in front of me. I drew a knife in each hand and turned to take one last look at the burning barn. To my dismay, the one from inside the barn was walking out the door still covered in fire. It was on of the females, probably Joan that the man had mentioned. The fire didn't seem to be slowing her down, so my odds were slim. I turned to face the other two, who to me were the bigger threat, but they were running past me. One grabbed Joan's arms while the other grabbed her head and twisted until it broke, then ripped it clean off. I was startled, but still ready to fight if they tried to take me next, not that I thought I had much of a chance.

"You should relax. We aren't going to kill you," a male's voice came from the taller of the two figures.

"My name is Mary and this is John. We only kill to survive and you don't seem to be trying to kill us so we won't attack you," Mary explained as she pulled her hood back. John followed Mary's example and pulled his hood down.

"We have to move. The others will be on their way and the three of us can't take on all six and expect to win," John insisted.

"Alright, lead the way," I insisted.

John nodded and started in the direction I had come from. Mary smiled and fell in line behind him. I followed, but only just. We ran for several miles before John and Mary slowed down. They kept walking as though they were still being pursued. I did as they did, which basically had us blending in with our surroundings as we went. Finally, we reached the highway and my bike. I turned around to see if the smoke was still rising, but it was too dark to tell. John and Mary didn't look back as they started down the road heading toward the town I was suppose to be staying in. We walked for over three hours before we started to see signs of the town. It took us another hour to get to my hotel. We went into my hotel room and secured the door. John looked out the window to ensure we weren't followed. He seemed to be satisfied so he moved to the bed to sit next to Mary.

"Now a story if you would," I said as I began to get comfortable with their presence.

"Father took us at birth. He got a hold of our DNA and decided it was as close to the perfect strains he needed for his project as he could get. He fed us other people to boost us. We trained every day. After we turned five, Father paired us off and gave us names based on the Bible and our behavior. Mary and I are paired together. You killed Abel the night before last. We killed his mate earlier tonight. That still leaves; Adam and his mate Eve, Cain and his mate, as well as two others. Adam, Cain, and Eve are the ones to worry about. Adam and Eve know how to create more of us. Cain is as lethal as they come. To be honest, we just want to live in peace, but Father's plans won't allow such a life. So when we came across you at the barn, we decided to get out while we could," John explained.

"But you're not out," I stated calmly.

"What?" Mary demanded.

"Until things are set right, the two of you are a part of this. There is no way out, unless you help me stop the threat," I answered with a shrug.

"He's right, Mary. We are part of this, and we more than most have the skills that could put an end to the threat our brothers and sisters pose upon the world," John agreed.

"Then I guess we need to become friends," Mary said turning her gaze from John to me.

"To start with, we need to get the two of you identities and help you blend in," I stated.

"We have all of our birth records. We know who we are and have documents to prove it," Mary piped up.

"We have been prepared for this day for a long time. Father wanted us to be put back in the world, and you forced his plan into reality a little early," John explained.

"Well that makes me feel better," I said sounding annoyed.

"We will go and start our work. May I have a way to reach you?" John asked.

I handed a piece of paper with my number on it and nodded toward the door. John nodded as Mary stood up to follow him. They walked out the door and disappeared into the night. I stared after them for a minute wondering what they were going to do. I shut the door and went to bed, deciding it was best not to think about it too much. It took them about two weeks to decide that it was safe to let us work. I went back to the other hotel and rushed to get done with my work on schedule, even though we had been delayed. I was about a week away from completion when I got a strange text message from a computer. It read:

> Very impressive. I think you are just what I'm looking for. I will be giving you information on potential targets in the areas you are in. Don't try to trace this number or track me down. I don't know if I can trust you yet, but I do know you have killed over twenty people over the last two years and that you seem to be very gifted at it. I am offering you a partnership. Hope to work with you soon.

I closed out the message and looked around. I sent Judy a message letting her know that someone had found me and wanted to help, but I didn't know if I could trust them so she was needed on standby. What was the world becoming?

11

My next job took me back toward California. I decided to go visit Jessy when I was done. I remembered her saying that she didn't need my help, but I wasn't going to leave her to do it on her own. My new informant found out where I was heading and tipped me off on a target that needed to be eliminated. The man's name was Tommy Staton. He was a serial killer, but no one could catch him, let alone convict him. He was too good at cleaning up his mess, but that didn't stop my new informant from adding him to my list. I decided to take care of him and my job before going to see Jessy, allowing me more time to spend with her.

I tracked Tommy down, which wasn't easy. He made himself extremely hard to find and never went the same place twice. I got lucky and found him at a club, unfortunately, he wasn't alone. He had three guys with him, all of which were carrying guns. I watched them from the bar for over an hour, just waiting for one of them to go to the bathroom. Either this guy taught them well or he hired some of the best, because they all went together, never straying more than a foot or two away from each other. I watched them make their way to the back, but they didn't stop at the men's room. I got up and followed them.

I stopped when I saw the four of them standing around a girl who was leaning against the wall like she was puking, in the alley. I watched, waiting for them to make a move, giving me some time to take at least one of them out. I pulled out a knife as they started walking toward the girl. I opened the door which creaked, alerting them to my presence. I hide the knife as the guards turned to face me, leaving Tommy to his next victim.

"Guys, what is this. Don't you know running a train on a girl who is too drunk to say no, is just wrong," I tried to play it off.

"You need to leave," the one in the center stated in a menacing tone.

"I don't think I do," I laughed, but that was when it got interesting.

Tommy stopped his advances on the girl and darted away. The guards as well as myself all looked after him, dumbstruck by his sudden flight. I decided there was no better chance than this and pulled my knife back out. I drew the blade across the one in the center's throat, slicing it open. He grabbed his throat and dropped to his knees, gargling blood. When he fell, I glanced at the girl to see if she was ok. She had drawn two guns and aimed them at the other two guards who were none the wiser. She pulled the trigger and dropped both of them, putting a smile on my face. Then, she redirected the guns at me. I dropped and rolled into her. She tried to readjust, but I was faster than she was. I rolled back to my feet, shouldering her back against the wall. She put both guns to the same shoulder. I shifted as she pulled the trigger, moving my shoulder out of the line of fire. I tried stabbing her with the knife in the same motion, but shifted her abdomen out of the way and elbowed me in the side of my head. I swung my arm up and over hers, grabbing her throat and putting my knife to her back. She raised her arms and put both of her guns to my head, waiting for a reason to pull the trigger.

"I thought they said no one else was going to take this job," the girl stated.

"Wait are you a hit man or rather hit woman in your case?" I asked like an idiot.

"I use the term assassin. What are you? A vigilante?" she mocked.

"I use the term avenger. Besides, I've killed more than Tommy has or ever could," I corrected.

"Really now, I wonder if anyone has a price on your head," she wondered out loud.

"I think I made a big enough impression for any hit man to come after me," I stated thinking back to Thomas and the others.

"Well, we assassins have a code of honor that hit men can't follow. Now are we going to kill each other or just stand her getting to know each other better until the cops get here?" she retorted.

"I don't kill anyone who doesn't deserve to die," I stated as I let her go and stepped back, pulling my head out of harms way.

"Then why are you after Tommy?" the assassin questioned turning to face me.

"A guy tracked me down and now he wants to give me information on people that need to die. According to the intel, Tommy is a serial killer that can't be caught," I explained.

"The parents of one of his victims hired me to kill the bastard since the cops can't seem to get him," the assassin volunteered her reason.

"Good reason," I agreed.

"So you're going to just leave him to me?" the assassin implied.

"Nope, killing these people is just way too much fun," I declared.

The assassin turned as though she was about to walk away, but just like that, she kicked me, bring me to my knees. She smiled as she walked away, figuring she got her point across. I took a deep breathe and stood back up. I launched my knife toward her. It hit the wall right where her face was about to be. She stopped, but that was the last I saw, before I turned and disappeared into the night.

I spent the next couple of days working and tracking down leads on Tommy. He wasn't easy to find, not that my work schedule gave me much time to look for him. It was a week after I had encountered him and the assassin, when my informant sent me a message. It told me where Tommy had hired the thugs from and that; he was bound to go back since it was the only place to hire thugs on the west coast. I took his advice and checked them out. Sure enough, they were the ones that Tommy had hired his thugs from.

"I need to find Tommy," I informed the boss.

"I'm sorry; we don't give out information on our clients. It's bad for business," the boss retorted looking over at a small group of his men, who started walking toward me.

"No bad for business would be pissing me off, cause then I would take your product off the shelves, permanently," I warned him, but neither he nor his men listened as they gathered around me.

"I don't take kindly to threats," the boss said as he nodded to the men behind me.

One of them put his hand on my shoulder. I swatted it away and planted my elbow right between his eyes, breaking his nose and dropping him to his knees. I blocked the punch coming from the other one that was behind me and kicked the one standing on the boss's right. He fell back, as the boss started to back away, figuring that I was able to do more damage than he anticipated. I pulled the one who swung at me, toward me and broke his arm. I turned to look at the rest, who all had their hands up, with their guns in the floor. I looked behind me to see what they were staring at, and ended up looking at the assassin with her guns drawn.

"You didn't take the hint at all did you?" the assassin asked sarcastically.

"The knife didn't tip you off to that fact?" I retorted with a shrug.

"You almost hit me with it," she snapped.

"No I didn't," I informed her.

"No one is that accurate with a knife," she claimed.

"Stick around, I'll show you exactly what I can do with any sharp object," I said with a smile as I turned to the boss. "Now I would like an answer to my question."

"He hired four more guys, didn't say what happened to the other three. He doesn't know it, but I have a tracker on all my guys, just incase they need backup," the boss informed us.

"Then I recommend that you give us the tracker for at least one of the four guys you assigned to him," the assassin insisted.

"I agree with her," I added when he looked at me.

"Very well," the boss said as he pulled a device out of his pocket.

I claimed it from him and started out the door without a word. The assassin looked at me like I was stupid. She shot the boss in his arm to make a point and turned to follow me out the door. I could tell by her reflection in the glass that she hadn't put her guns, up but that was only part of what I was looking at. She was drop dead gorgeous. A perfectly portioned body with a beautiful face, it was a wonder she even became an assassin instead of a model or something. I walked out the door so I would stop looking at the glass like an idiot and continued toward my car.

"And where do you think you're going with that?" the assassin demanded.

"Home for a bit, then I'm going to kill Tommy," I answered without stopping.

"The hell you are. He is my target, and unlike you I'm getting paid to kill him," the assassin yelled.

"Who cares who kills him," I said while shaking my head. A bullet breezed by my head causing me to stop and turn around.

"I will not take money I haven't earned. Now give me the tracker," the assassin demanded.

"Why don't you just work with me?" I suggested.

"For all I know, you'll be my next target. I refuse to get close to anyone anymore," she explained.

"Then don't get close. Just tag along," I said as I opened my car door and got in.

I sat there waiting for her to make up her mind which didn't take as long as I thought. She climbed in my passenger seat and buckled up. She looked straight ahead and sat there without a word. I started the car and went back home not caring if she was planning on shooting me or working with me. It didn't matter to me, so long as Tommy was dead.

We got back to my place within a few minutes. I got out and went straight to the hotel room without bothering to look and see if the assassin was following me. I got to my room and unlocked the door. I left it open so she could just walk in behind me. The only sign that she was there was that she shut the door behind her. I set the tracker on my nightstand and knelt over to open my suitcase. I undid the extra slot that hide my knives and started pulling out the ones I wanted to use. For all I knew the assassin had a gun to my head, but I kind of doubted it for some reason, and I was right. She was just sitting on my bed, most likely waiting for me to get done.

"You haven't told me your name," I said in an attempt to start a conversation.

"Is my name important?" she asked in retaliation.

"Depends on if you think it is," I returned.

"It's Sarah. What's yours?" she answered.

"Charles. It was my great grandfather's name," I answered her question.

"What made you a killer?" Sarah asked, seeming to become interested in me.

"A rough life that took a turn for the worse about two and a half years ago," I stated blankly.

"That's what happens to us all," Sarah said as she lay back on my bed.

"So what's your story?" I decided to ask.

"I was sixteen when a group of men attacked me and my girlfriend. They didn't like the fact that we were together so they planned on killing us. She was first since she was older, but when they went to kill me, the cops showed up and scared them off. Six months of training and then I went after them all. Because of that I swore off men and love. I became an assassin to pass the time," Sarah confessed.

"Love escaped me every chance it got. Funny because I couldn't love at first. Then after I was pushed to the edge, a guy with a grudge decided to mess with my head. He hooked me up with a friend of his so he could fuck her and prove he was more of a man than I was. They were my first kills. I carved her up. I burned his dick off and destroyed his car, his pride and joy," I confided.

"They deserved to die," Sarah stated as she stared at the ceiling.

I stood up and looked at her. "So many do," I stated.

Sarah sat up and looked me in the eyes. I met her gaze with my own, starting to see that she was just like me, one of the few. She stood up, but never took her eyes away from mine. We kissed, who started it, I don't know, but we kissed. I put my hand up to her face and took a step in. We both fell on the bed, but all she did was wrap her arms and legs around me. My hand went to her back as we continued kissing. She started pulling at my shirt so I stopped and removed it as she undid my pants. I bent over and started kissing her again. She kicked her shoes off and undid her pants as my hand slide down her side. I slipped my hand up her shirt as I kicked off my own shoes. She pushed me up and pulled off her shirt. I stood up and pulled off my pants. She slipped hers off as I climbed back on the bed and back on top of her. It was dark before we stopped, which was only because we had a job to do.

We followed the tracker to another club. This was closed down for reconstruction. It was the building I was here to redesign. I looked annoyed as we walked around to the back. I let her take point since she had the guns. We slipped in the back down without a noise. We split up and moved toward the stairs, checking every corner for his guards. There was no one downstairs so we started upstairs. We poked our heads up first to make sure the coast was clear. Sure enough all four guards were standing outside of a door down the hall. Sarah got ready to stand up, but I caught her and put up one finger, telling her to hold on. I pulled out four knives and stood up, releasing all of them at once. All four guards fell with a thud. We quickly made our way to the door, before Tommy could open it and see that we had caught back up with him, but the door didn't open. A muffled screamed reached our ears, telling us why Tommy didn't hear the thud of his guards. He was in the middle of torturing and killing another teenage girl.

I kicked the door open, and Sarah breezed by me, shooting Tommy in the leg to keep him from running. Sarah walked over to the girl, who was pretty beat up and cut up. I walked over to Tommy and grabbed him. I pulled him out of the room so Sarah could take care of the girl. I pulled Tommy all the way downstairs and made him sit down on the grill, which I then turned on. I hit him in his jaw to disorient him. Sarah came down with the girl and let her out the back door, giving her instructions for the cops. As soon as the girl was out the door, Sarah turned and raised her gun to finish her job, but I was right there to stop her.

"What are you doing?" Sarah demanded.

"What I do to those who deserve it," I responded as I approached Tommy who started screaming as smoke began to rise from his ass.

"Please don't kill me!" Tommy screamed.

"I will no matter what you say," Sarah declared raising her gun again.

"But not until I make you suffer like you made all those girls suffer, like the one we just saved," I interrupted as I pressed Tommy's hand to the grill.

He cried out in pain, so I hit him. I glance back at Sarah who had a smile on her face, but still hadn't lowered her gun. I pressed Tommy's other hand to the grill and yet again he screamed in pain, but this time before I could hit him, Sarah shot him in the shoulder. I looked back at her with a curious grin. She seemed to be very amused. I pulled out a knife and jabbed it into Tommy's leg. He cried out for help and Sarah shot him in his other leg. I pulled out my knife and stabbed him in his side. This time, before he could even let out a sound, Sarah shot him in the head, ending our little game of torture.

When we left the club, Sarah went her way and I went mine. I have no idea who hired her, but I had high hopes that I hadn't seen the last of her. I went back to my hotel and found a card with her number on it, informing me to call if I ever needed her help. I put the card in my wallet with a smile on my face. I took a quick shower and went to bed. The next morning my hotel phone went off.

"Hello?" I answered.

("Well it looks like someone with similar tastes beat you to your target,") a voice spoke over the phone.

"You must be the texting informant. I was there, but someone else had a bone to pick with him, so I let the other take the kill shot," I corrected.

("Then congratulations. I'll be in touch,") the voice informed me.

12

I made to Jessy's place when she was about six months into her pregnancy. Her sister was there taking care of her cause she remembered how hard it was and that Jessy was there for her. I volunteered to relieve her so she could go spend time with her husband while he was off. She was more than happy to leave me and Jessy alone, and spend so quality time with her husband. I sat down next to Jessy and just started watching TV with her. She slide over and curled up next to me. I put my arm around her, letting her know that I was there. It wasn't long before she was asleep. Remembering what happened last time I carried her to her bed I decided it was best to stay still and let her sleep. The next morning I woke up to find that Jessy was already up and that Beth was back. Beth looked annoyed, but wasn't saying why. Jessy was beaming, most likely because she woke up next to me.

I was in the shower when a text came to my phone. I checked it, unsure of whom sent it to me, but it was very clear once I read the message.

> I know you are trying to get some down time with an old friend, but there is a matter that needs your

> attention before it gets any worse. There have been a series of killings in Washington State. That isn't a very long drive from where you are at, so I figured you wouldn't mind. All of the victims are young females. They were all raped, but there was no evidence left behind. The cops can't handle this job so YOU have to. Go online for more information and the location.

I did as he said and tracked down the information. I spent the rest of the day with Jessy and Beth, because I didn't know when I would be able to come see them again. Beth still looked mad, but wasn't telling me anything. Jessy followed me out to my truck when it was time for me to leave. Beth shut the door behind us without a word. I hugged Jessy and got into the truck. I looked back at the house and decided to ask.

"Why is Beth mad at me?" I finally asked.

"Cause she knows how I feel about you. And its not you she's mad at. It's me," Jessy confessed.

"Why would she be mad at you?" I asked.

"Cause I haven't done something she insists I should," Jessy murmured.

"What is that?" I inquired.

"Nothing to worry you with. Go take care of business and come see me when you can," Jessy insisted.

I smiled and nodded before starting the truck. Jessy stepped back, a tear running down her face, as I started to pull out of the driveway. It took me all of twenty minutes to realize what I saw, but the moment I did, I called Jessy to check on her. She swore she was fine even though she was locked in the bathroom to avoid her sister's lecture. I cheered her up enough to get her laughing before I had to let her go. It was a long few hours of driving alone after that.

I pulled off the road for the night deciding that I would better off starting in the morning after a decent nights sleep. In some aspect I was right, but then again so very wrong. I woke as the sun started to rise the next day. I made my way toward the city with all the trouble, but what I found when I got there made me feel guilty. I drove by a scene where they were removing a body out of the woods. It was a young girl who looked to have been killed a few hours before now. I could have saved her if I had of just left when I got the information. She was on my head and that made me want revenge for what had happened.

I got in touch with the local forest ranger. He let me know where I could go to set up a camp site. He helped me get everything I needed to avoid any legal trouble and then gave me directions to my camp site. I got there with about four hours of sunlight left. I used a map the ranger had given me to determine that I was about eight miles from the dump site. I used the map to determine where the other dump sites were to give me an area to search. The problem was that there was seven dump sites scattered across a twenty mile radius. That covered most of the woods between this city and its neighboring town fifty miles away. I had reserved the camp site for a week, but it could take longer to find the killers when they seemed to only be active at night. I looked over the map one more time and decided to start heading away from the most recent dump site. I was about seven miles in when the trees covered the sun. It got dark very shortly after. The moon was almost full, giving me more than enough light to keep my flashlights put up. It was another hour of walking before I finally decided to take a break. I leaned against a tree and started munching on my snack. It seemed like my choice of direction was getting me nowhere until laughter drifted to my ears.

I did my best to avoid making any noise as I crept toward the laughter hoping it wasn't a bunch of kids goofing off. I saw a campfire about thirty yards ahead of me. I could make out a few people up dancing around it like they had no sense. I figured it was just a couple of kids partying it up, but decided to get just a little closer to be on the safe side. There were four guys and two young girls none of which could have been more than twenty-two years old. One of the girls was up dancing around the fire with three of the guys. The other was sitting against a tree. She looked as though she was having trouble staying awake. I was about to turn and walk away when one of the guys pushed the dancing girl through the fire. One of the other guys caught her and pushed her toward the other girl. The fourth guy walked over and made her take a drink. She coughed some of it up, but he managed to make her swallow enough of it to take affect. She started looking like the other girl, which let me know that I had found the right place. I tied a bandanna around my face to keep the girls from seeing me. Then I pulled up my hood and got ready to kill the guys before they could kill the girls.

I pulled out two of my throwing knives and stepped out of the shadows. I launched them at the closest, but he had already spotted me and started diving out of the way. Only one of my knives hit its mark, in his shoulder. The other three turned hearing the commotion. Two of them grabbed the girls while the other pulled out a hunting knife. I pulled out my bowie knife and stepped into full view. The other three took off into the woods leaving the last one to fend of himself. I turned toward him, eager to start avenging the girls. He had already pulled my knife out of his shoulder and was back on his feet.

I turned to show him my full body. He sized me up before making a move. He lunged forward with a downward slash, which I stopped. I twisted his arm, forcing him to release the knife. He used his other arm to hit me as hard as he could. I retaliated by slashing him. He dropped as his intestines tried pouring out. He kept his insides maintained as best he could, but it left him completely helpless against me. I pulled the bandana down and smiled down on him as he looked up at me, waiting for his death. I picked up the knife I made him drop and jabbed it into his uninjured shoulder. He let out a cry of pain and lost his grip on his stomached, letting his intestines fall out onto the ground. He whimpered as he started to fall over. I watched him for a minute to make sure he would die before help would come, then I turned to pursue the others.

They probably had about a five minute head start on me, but they were carrying or dragging an unwilling extra. This gave me the advantage I needed to catch up, just as long as I could track them, which was hard since I was in the dark. I ran after them for just over an hour without any trace of them, but I wasn't about to give up, not with the girls were still alive. I finally caught a break and found evidence that I was on their trail. It was a sleeve from one of the girls' shirts. I would have missed it if it wasn't a bright color against the dark ground. I stopped for a minute and listened to see if I could hear them in the distance. I heard a few twigs break under their feet. They were only a few yards ahead of me. I picked up speed, hurrying to save the girls and punish the boys who deserved to die.

From out of nowhere a tree branch hit me in the chest, knocking me off of my feet. I rolled to get back to my feet, but one of them was there with the branch and hit me again, knocking me into a tree. I pulled out my hatchet and my bowie knife and deflected his next swing. I used the hatchet to clamp down on the stick and jerked it away from him. He got pulled toward me trying to keep a hold of his stick, so I shifted the knife and planted it in his chest. It was a heart shot so I just pulled my knife out and started trying to pick up the trail again.

It took some time, but I was finally able to get back on their trail. I wasn't sure how far ahead they were, but I was bound and determined to catch them before they could harm the girls. I moved as quickly as I could, keeping my eyes pealed for any sign that I was close or one of the other two stayed behind to ambush me. The night was half gone and my job was only half done, but I seemed to be getting closer. The trail split into two. I could only guess that they split up to throw me off. I knelt down and examined each trail trying to decide which one was the one I had to follow. Both of the had two sets of footprints, one male and one female, which made me believe that they each took a girl. It didn't matter which trail I took, because I had to find them both.

I took the one on the left deciding that it would be easiest to follow and quickest to take care of. I followed it for twenty minutes before I found them both in a small clearing. The guy had the girl pinned against a tree with his hand up her shirt. She looked terrified as he started to unzip his pants. I quickly and quietly walked up behind him, avoiding letting the girl notice me and give me away. I grabbed the arm he had up her shirt and his throat and launched him across the clearing, into a tree. He turned to face me as I moved in front of the girl to defend her. The guy took a step forward and put his foot right into a bear trap. I pulled out a knife and took a step forward, but the girl caught my arm.

"I owe him," she stated as she reached for the knife.

I opened my hand and let her take the knife. I walked her over to the whimpering figure so she could exact her revenge. The guy lashed out, but I caught him with a backhand, silencing his rage. The girl put the knife to his throat and jerked hard, cutting deep. He started choking on his own blood and fell back, drifting into Death's arms. I helped the girl over to a fallen tree and sat her down. I took my knife back and cleaned it on the guy's shirt, before putting it up.

"Have you saved Lily yet?" the girl asked.

"That's where I'm headed now. I need you to stay here until help comes, because I don't exist, ok?" I requested.

The girl nodded her head so I turned and went back down the trail to finish what I started. I ran as fast as I could without tripping over my own feet. It was over an hour before I started to slow down, believing that I was getting close and I was right. There was a fire in a clearing up ahead. I could see Lily hanging by her arms from a tree. The last man was nowhere to be seen. I approached the clearing as slowly as I could trying not to catch his attention, figuring he was hiding somewhere waiting to ambush me. As I went to step into the clearing, I felt something tighten around my ankle. I was swept into the air, left dangling from a tree. The last man walked from behind the tree Lily was hanging from to see what he had caught. He looked rather happy to see that it was me. He put his hand on Lily as he walked past her and gave her a nudge to make her spin. As her back came into view, I could see that she had been stabbed once in her lower spinal cord. He paralyzed her. Anger welled up inside me.

"So you're the mystery man that came in here and started killing my merry little bunch," the man guessed.

"You're next," I stated while keeping a straight face.

"My name is Fred. You already killed George, Mike, and Itch. Odd name I know, but his parents were hippies to the very end. He of course, is the one who killed them," Fred introduced.

"Which was he?" I asked trying to keep him distracted while I found the rope.

"You're first kill. Mike was the guy who left the other trail for you to follow. He was rejected by women a lot so I knew he'd stop and have his way with the other one, most likely getting killed in the process. It drove him nuts getting rejected by every girl he ever talked to. They wanted nothing to do with him to be honest. And poor Itch was treated like he was a girl. That's why he came to hate them so," Fred explained.

"That just leaves pawn number two, George you said his name was?" I inquired finally seeing the rope I had to cut.

"The most devoted lover I've ever met. He loved every woman without thought or hesitation. They simply used him to get what they wanted. It was usually money. He even tried men, but it was no different. Then they all met me. I gave them an outlet for their pain and rage. We were like brothers, but I can't truly care for anyone," Fred explained.

"Sounds like me," I stated blankly as I tried to get one of my knives.

"You've been hurt too much to care, haven't you?" Fred guessed.

"Why do you think I started killing?" I retorted.

"So you and I are just alike. You were brought here to complete me. The others were just a means to an end, but you're the real deal. You're my match," Fred tried to piece together.

"That's where you're wrong," I stated bluntly, finally freeing my knife.

"What do you mean?" Fred demanded.

"I kill those who wrong others," I stated.

"As do I. Those girls were just teasing us. They had no right to show us attention that they didn't mean! They are the exact type of people that made us the way we are!" Fred declared.

I launched my knife, cutting the rope. I pulled the rope off of my feet as I flipped onto the ground. Fred took a step back. I stood up and faced him, determined to make him understand where he went wrong and how I was right.

"I kill those who destroy good people. The ones who push them over the edge, to the point of no return. I kill those who rape women, who kill for pleasure, who exploit others for their own gain. And I kill those who decided that the world is beyond saving, those who seek to destroy it. You just want to make yourself feel better," I informed him as I drew my bowie knife intent on finishing the conversation.

Fred took another step back and tripped over a stick. He tumbled into a tree and tried to push himself up so he could make a run for it, but I was quicker. I pushed him against the tree and stabbed him in his leg. I pulled the knife out and took a step back. Just as I expected, Fred tried running and fell over. I followed him away from Lily and the fire. He crawled trying to stand whenever he could find something to brace himself on, but he wasn't strong enough to hold himself up and fell every time. I waited until we were about twenty yards away from Lily before I slashed his arm, leaving him helpless and hardly able to move. He rolled over and looked at me, finally accepting his defeat. I knelt down and slow dug my knife into his shoulder. He stifled his cry of pain and looked me right in the eye. He wouldn't break like so many of the others. Just like me, he longed for death and when he said I was his match, he meant I was the one who had the right to kill him for becoming something he wasn't. I wasn't sure when, but this was going to be my fate. I could only hope that Judy or Sarah was the one to pull the trigger.

I walked back to the fire, to Lily. Her blood was no longer flowing from the wound and her body had already lost its color. I had failed to save her. She was one of the few and it was my fault. If I had not of gone the easy route, both girls would have survived. Mike didn't have the guts to kill the other girl, but she would have been scared for life. I bet if I were to ask her, she would willingly take that fate so that Lily could have survived. Her life was in my hands, just like Kelly's. That was the third person I let die. This one held just as much importance because I could have saved them both were last time............ I would have died too.

I walked back to my camp site, arriving just before dawn. The forest ranger showed up an hour later asking if I saw anyone go by around dawn. She didn't realize that she was describing me before I changed into some clean clothes. I told that I didn't notice anything out of the ordinary and that I would keep an eye out for her. I stayed that night and got a good nights sleep under the stars, trying to clear my head. It wasn't easy, but after a few hours I was finally able to let go and fall asleep. The next day I was more resolved than before. I knew what my mission was and how it would all end. I was more than happy to die if I made the world change for the best first. I packed up and headed to my next job, one more failure, but a better man.

13

A call from Judy woke me up at six in the morning. I realized that I was in Nevada and that I was an hour behind her, but I'm a night owl. She called to get me to come for a visit. She had a problem that she needed my help to resolve. I told her I would be done by the end of the week and would catch the first plane out and leave my truck with Jessy.

It had been just over a month since Lily died on my watch. I accepted that I couldn't change the past and pressed on, but nightmares plagued my sleep. I saw Kelly, Lily, and my unborn child every night. I begged for forgiveness, but they never answered. I didn't have any idea why I had this nightmare, nor did I know why they wouldn't answer me, especially Kelly, but the fact was that I had failed them and didn't deserve their forgiveness. I finished my job just as I had been the entire time, lifeless.

The first good feeling I had since Lily died was when Jessy opened the door to let me in. I hugged her and kissed her as soon as I got my foot in the door. She seemed to be glowing even if she was moody. It was the fact that she was only weeks away from having that wonderful baby boy that she had been carrying around for months. She was more beautiful than ever.

"This is unexpected," Jessy commented after I took a step back.

"Judy needs my help with something. I decided flying would be faster and decided to leave my truck here, where you could use it," I explained.

"Will she need you for very long?" Jessy asked as she touched her belly. I knew she wanted me there with her when she had the baby. I wanted to be there so no matter Judy's request, it wouldn't take long.

"I promise that I will be there right next to you when you give birth to little...... You never told me his name," I realized.

"Samuel," Jessy answered my implied question.

"I like it. I promise to be there for you when Samuel is born," I confirmed.

Jessy smiled at the thought. I couldn't help but to smile back at her. I kissed her forehead and slipped her the keys. I turned just in time to see the taxi pull up. Jessy grabbed my arm and pulled me back so she could kiss me on the lips. I smiled as I looked at her glowing face, but I had to turn around and go take care of Judy's problem. I wouldn't be gone long. I couldn't be gone long even if I wanted to.

I made it to Alabama a few hours later. Just like the first time, Judy was waiting for me at the airport. She was alone, but worry covered her face. I gave her a hug as I got to her. She smiled and opened her trunk for me to put my bag in. It was a quiet ride to her house, but she broke the silence when we pulled onto her street.

"I have a stalker. He keeps breaking into my house. I asked what I could do and they started sending patrols, but I was told that if I killed him or hurt him in any way, I would be arrested for manslaughter. That's why I need your help," Judy explained.

"Drop me off here. Take everyone to your parents. I'll take care of him and you will have an alibi," I explained.

"I should be the one to kill him," Judy stated.

"Not when the risk is so high," I informed her.

"But he is my problem. Besides, you took care of that kid the day you started killing. That was your problem and a high risk situation," Judy tried.

"But I'm better at getting myself out of any situation than anyone else. That includes you," I pointed out.

"I can't change your mind, can I?" Judy asked.

"No. Just make sure he doesn't know you are gone. Leave your car and take Jason's," I insisted.

"Make him suffer," Judy requested as she came to a slow stop a few houses down from her own.

I got out and walked into the woods deciding to hide until Judy and the family was gone. Once I watched them pull off of their road I slipped in through the window Judy had left open for me. I locked it behind me and looked over the house, trying to figure out how he was going to get into the house and where to wait for him. It took me an hour cause there was about three easy ways for him to get in which made it very difficult to find a good spot that would keep him from seeing me no matter where he came in. Finally after the sun had started to set behind the trees, I found a spot next to the entertainment center. The light was blocked from all sides making it easy for me to blend into the shadows almost as if I wasn't there at all. I downed a bottle of water before taking a seat to start my wait.

It was after midnight before the police drove by flashing their light around, looking for someone suspicious. I figured he'd wait until they passed to make his move because they weren't likely to return for at least an hour after they were gone, if at all. I continued my wait and was rewarded for not twenty minutes after the police passed; I heard a creak followed by a window opening. It was one of two windows that with the right tools could be unlocked from outside. The noise was coming from behind me, Alyssa's room. I took a slow breathe listening to what he was doing. His foot steps drew closer and closer until he was walked right past me. I slowly stood up and followed him across the house into Judy's room. He turned on the light to her room before going in. I stopped because there was a mirror on her wall that would show me to him the minute I walked in the room. I stood next to the door and waited for him to come out. He knew she wasn't here and was probably looking for a souvenir. It was almost an hour before he turned the light out and walked back by me. This time I swung, catching his head and slamming it into the wall. He twisted and tried throwing a quick punch to my gut, but I caught his wrist and twisted it, dropping him to his knees. I kept twisting until I heard a cruel snap and then I released his arm and kneed him in the face. He fell back and tried rolling away, but I stepped on his foot, breaking it in the process of stopping his fleeting attempt. He cried out in pain as I twisted my foot on his now broken ankle. I kicked him in the side to roll him over. I knelt next to him, allowing the light to show my face. Surprise covered his face as he seemed to realize who I was.

"You're the one who taught her," he said in complete amazement.

"What do you mean?" I demanded.

"She is so graceful when she throws knives. If she wanted to kill me, she only had to grab one. I would have let her kill me if only she used a knife," he whispered.

"You saw us practicing?" I inquired.

"You are lethal, but she was just so graceful. You scare me, but she fascinates me. I want her to kill me," he insisted.

"Not your call and far too late to get things changed. I'm your executioner now," I said as I slid a knife into his chest, piercing his heart.

He took two more short breathes before he stopped altogether. I slid my knife back out and cleaned it on his clothes. I went out of the house the same way he got in to avoid suspicion. I hiked two miles before setting up a tent in the middle of the woods. I made sure to stay out of sight until the next night when I went to get some real food at McDonalds. Judy met me there and took me back to the airport so I could go back to Jessy. Judy stopped me before I got out of the car.

"Guess what I found out?" Judy asked.

"No idea," I answered honestly.

"I'm pregnant," Judy stated with a huge smile on her face.

"Congratulations," I said.

My phone started going off. It was my mom wanting me to come home and visit. I called a taxi to come get me so Judy could go home. Then I called Jessy to let her know that I had to go visit my mother and that I would be back by the end of the week. She sounded relieved to know I would be there soon. She was seven and a half months pregnant and to the point that I wanted to be there for her.

I made it to my mom's just after midnight. The door was locked so I used my knowledge of the open windows to get in since Jessy had my house key on my car keys. Mom was a little surprised to find me on the couch the next morning. She woke me up demanding to know why I didn't let her know I was already there. My answer was simple, "You were in bed."

I spent the next two days visiting all of my old friends who were still around. Mom insisted on me being home for dinner every night so she could find out what was new. It was while I was out that I found a target without even trying. There was a guy that I knew who had a bad habit of trying to get with every girl he could, then cheat on them with any guy that wanted him. What made it worse was that he had five kids, none of which he took care of. Well it was five when I left years ago. Now he had seven with another on the way. He was cheating on the woman that was supposed to be his third or fourth wife with another girl and two guys. She was upset and crying when I came across her in town. I sat there for over an hour trying to comfort her, but it wasn't easy and she needed someone to replace him and I wasn't that man. It did make me realize that she needed a reason to leave him and it was someone to treat her right. I couldn't do that, but I could kill the man who was causing her all this pain.

I gave the girl the great idea of going to the club with some friends and letting her parents watch her two kids, only one of which was his. I convinced her not to tell him as a punishment for what he was doing. What she didn't know was that I needed her to have no idea what he was doing and the same of him so when he got home I could take care of the situation. She did exactly as I had hoped. He arrived at home just after ten. It was obvious that he was pissed to find no one waiting there for him, but I planned on clearing that up after I let him try calling her. She had apparently turned her phone off, something I hadn't thought of, but it worked to my advantage. I walked up to the door and knocked.

"Charles what brings you here?" he said as he opened the door.

"Just thought I'd see how you two are doing," I lied.

"Well, I'm a little pissed because she left with the kids and I can't get in touch with her. Maybe she's leaving me. That bitch better not!" he answered.

"Now now, maybe she has a reason. Have you been cheating on her with any guys and/or girls?" I asked hinting that I knew.

"Go the fuck away," he demanded.

I stopped him from slamming the door in my face. "I'm here to open your eyes to the truth of your pathetic life," I stated.

I kicked him in the stomach and walked in. He straightened up and tried to yell, but I hit him in his throat, shutting him up. He fell back on his couch, choking. I sat next to him and threw my arm around him, pulling him close so I could whisper into his ear.

"No one can save you. You had plenty of time to save yourself. I mean how old are you? Twenty-eight? Thirty? In the last twelve years of being a man, you never figured out how to be a man. That's kinda pathetic," I mocked him.

"You don't have the right to judge me," he coughed.

"Very true, but I'm not judging you. I'm solving you. This is a judgment call. It's an awakening. The only one you seem to get. I open your eyes to the fact, and fact being the key word, that you have failed to be anything less than a fiend. My job is to kill you. I'm sure I'll be in your shoes as far as the whole being killed for who I am, but that doesn't change the fact that you are about to die," I explained.

"For what? Being a good father? Taking in that ungrateful bitch? Loving everyone? What did I do so wrong?" he demanded.

"You aren't a good father. The fact is that only one of your kids sees you more than once a month. You have seven. As for that ungrateful bitch as you called her, she was getting along just fine without you. You needed her. And loving everyone doesn't mean you fuck everyone. You are a cheater, the worst father I have ever met. You use women. Why shouldn't I kill you?" I pointed out.

"Cause I'm a good person," he claimed.

"That's between you and God," I stated as I stabbed him in his throat with a pen shaft. "You'll bleed out in a couple minutes, but it will be unbearable."

With that I got up and walked to the door I checked to make sure no one was looking before opening the door and leaving. I knew that she would stay gone until one or two in the morning so no one would catch me if I walked back to my car which was parked a little over a mile down the road. I enjoyed the walk in the cold air. It made me sleepy. Christmas was a few days away and I decided to spend it with Jessy. I had already saved up some money to get her some presents and had already left the ones I got for my family under my mother's care. I didn't need to be here for the holiday when Jessy needed me more. That was my last night in Alabama. I was on one of the earliest flights out the next day.

I was overflowing with excitement when I spotted my truck waiting for me. I was expecting to see Jessy get out of the driver's side, but Beth's husband was the one that greeted me. He handed me my keys and climbed in the passenger's side. I looked at him with some confusion because he didn't tell me where Jessy was. He looked at me, puzzled by my lack of motion, but then he got the "I figured it out" face.

"Beth has Jessy on bed rest for the moment. There were complications while you were gone," he finally explained.

We drove in utter silence. Beth's husband wasn't a very big talker, but he loved her and that's what counts the most. It took us about twenty minutes of driving to get to Jessy's, but the silence made it seem so much longer. Jessy's parents were there, so whatever was going on was more serious than I thought. I parked and got inside as quickly as I could. I said hi to everyone as I waited for someone to tell me what was going on. Then Jessy walked out. She was pale, but otherwise as beautiful as ever. She walked over to me very slowly so I met her halfway. She hugged me so softly it was as though she was hardly trying. I looked at Beth for an explanation and she nodded toward the kitchen. I followed her in there to find out what was happening.

"Jessy's stress levels are through the roof. She hasn't eaten anything in the last couple days," Beth explained.

"What's stressing her out so much that she won't eat?" I asked.

"You are," Beth spat, irritation starting to set in.

"What do you mean?" I demanded.

"She is constantly worried about you. When you said you were going to be a few days longer, she stopped eating. You being so close and yet so far away are hurting her," Beth explained.

"I can't be here all the time. She knows that," I tried, but Beth cut me off with a "shut the fuck up" look.

"It doesn't change the fact that she cares about you way too much. I don't know why she bothers. What did you ever really do for her?" Beth asked herself.

"Something that only three people alive know," I stated blankly.

"And what is that?" Beth snapped.

"I killed Derek for what he did to her," I confessed.

Beth's face was a mixture of horror and shock at my confession. It seemed as though she couldn't believe that I had done that for Jessy. The fact was that I was a killer and Beth had no idea that Derek was just one of the first. She didn't realize that Jessy always seemed to know, even though I never said a word. Beth was clueless as to everything that happened and everything that was there between me and her little sister.

"Does Jessy?" Beth asked.

"She knew without me ever saying a word. She sees something inside me that no one else sees. It's crazy, but true," I explained.

Beth walked up to me and gave me a hug as tears

started rolling down her eyes. She was happy to know the truth, even if she didn't approve. I spent the rest of that week with Jessy, Beth, and their family. Jessy's color and health returned with my hand pushing her to take care of herself. I even got her to promise that she would keep taking care of herself, even if I wasn't there. She promised because she realized that she was about to be a mother and that her son would need her, even if I wasn't there.

I bought a lot of baby clothes for the little guy. Most were big enough for him to grow into just incase he wasn't as big as he needed to be. Jessy seemed to be overjoyed by the active interest I was taking in Samuel. It confused me that she would be so thrilled by the idea, but then again, she did have high hopes that she could change my mind about everything. The holiday came to an end and work called, just as I expected. I told Jessy that I would be back in time to spend a few weeks with her before and after the baby was born. This seemed to calm her and make her glow even brighter. I didn't have to worry about her doing anything crazy this time.

14

My next job took me to Virginia. I had some family not too far from where I was working so I went down to visit them. They seemed overjoyed to see me, especially my grandparents. Neither was in any kind of condition to travel and my life kept me busy. If I remembered correctly, I hadn't seen them since I was fourteen. Hard to believe I went ten years without seeing my own grandparents.

While I was there I caught one of my cousins shooting up. I quickly pulled the plug on that. He wasn't old enough to even buy tobacco, so he had no right doing drugs. I destroyed his supply, all the while he was cussing me out. I turned to him and pinned him against the wall. His mother came out to see what all the commotion was. At first she went to cussing me out, but then she saw what was on the ground and changed her target. It was apparent that this wasn't the first time my cousin had been caught, but it was going to be the last time he got out of legal punishment. His mother took him inside and made arrangements for him to be sent to boot camp. That night I pulled him off to the side to find out who his supplier was.

"I'm not telling you," he snapped.

"Do you want to die, because that's what will happen?" I stated.

"My supplier's been on the stuff for years and he's still in good health," he boosted.

"Dealers never use, because it's addictive enough to cost them money. He lied to you. Now I want a name, because no one messes with my family," I demanded with a look that would make the average man piss his pants. As a matter of fact, my cousin pissed his.

"Don. He hangs around the park," my cousin said before he slipped into his room, undoubtedly embarrassed that I made him piss himself.

The next day, I went straight to the park when I finished my work. Don was no where to be found. I did come across several kids who were using in the park bathrooms and anywhere they thought they could be left alone. I decided it would be best not to mess with any of them. The risk that Don would hear about it and escape me was too high. I figured out that Don showed up right after the kids got out of school and was gone within an hour, leaving anyone who might be looking for him a very small window of opportunity.

I got done with my work just after two the next day. I made it to the park just after school let out. I glanced around and spotted Don on the other side of the park. He had a crowd of about twenty kids around him. That was too many witnesses and potential distractions to try catching him. I waited until his crowd was gone to make a move. I followed him back across the park, most likely to his car. He turned a corner. I moved to follow him, but he had slipped in behind me. I heard the cock of a gun, and reacted before he could pull the trigger. I spun around grabbing the gun and sliding it right out of his hand. I put the safety on and threw the gun as I continued to spin behind him. He twisted, throwing an elbow in an attempt to hit me. I shifted my elbow under his, forcing him to miss. I finished spinning when I grabbed him by the throat and slammed him into the bathroom wall.

"Damn, who the hell are you with all those fancy ass moves?" Don demanded.

"You've been selling to minors. They aren't old enough to decide what to do with their lives let alone how to end it," I snapped.

"Hey man, I'm just following the boss's orders and he says that kids are his biggest customers. You don't upset my boss unless you want to die," Don stated with a shiver that ran up his spine.

"And you don't mess with people's kids unless you want to be strung up and stoned, but lucky for you, I don't do public executions. Now I want a name and an address," I demanded.

"He will kill me and my girl," Don said before spitting in my face.

"I'll kill you a lot slower. That gives you two options. Tell me and I will kill you quick, then I will kill him and save your girl. If you don't like that one, I can torture you until you tell me. That way you suffer for a few hours while he goes and gets you girl because you didn't show up with his money," I offered.

"The only house on the hill. Other side of town. Don't know the address. His name is Theo. You won't be able to kill him. You won't make it past his bodyguards," Don informed me.

"None of them will live very much longer," I said as I slipped a knife into Don's throat.

I put the knife through to the wall, and then with a quick shove, into the wall to hold him there. He looked natural after I put something over his neck to cover the blood. I knew that he would eventually bleed out enough for it to seep through his shirt and show everyone that he was dead, but it bought me enough time to take care of his boss.

I decided to wait until I had the cover of darkness to make a move. Don was right about the bodyguard, but he was underestimating me. There were two guards at the front door, two more at the front gate, and six walking in a circle around the property with dogs. I still had no idea how many had to be inside the house, but I did notice that there was no back door. That had to be a sign that there was a tunnel under the house as an escape route. I would have to cut the drug boss off before he could get to it, otherwise things would get messy. I noticed a garden shed at the very back of the property, right next to the road. It seemed to be the most likely exit to me, so that became my target.

I made my way around the back to see if there were any guards stationed near the garden house, and sure enough, there was a car parked across the street. One of the two men inside got out and walked over to the stream a few feet away. I grabbed my bow and took aim, striking him down. He fell into the stream, keeping his partner from knowing that he was shot. The partner got out of the car and started calling to him. He walked around the car and was only a few feet away from the stream when I shot him too. He fell to the ground, without alerting anyone. I walked over to the body and moved it into the stream to remove it from sight. I inspected the car and found that it was bulletproof. Nothing I had would penetrate it, therefore if the drug boss made it to this car, he would be safe. I checked the tires and found that they were just regular old tires, so I sliced them. I opened the car door and looked for the keys. One of the two men must have had them, but that was fine by me. I pulled the door panel off and cut the wire that locks the door. Then I removed the locking mechanism altogether. I did the same to the other front door, so he had no way of locking me out, just in case. As an extra precaution, I punch a hole in the gas tank with one of my knives.

I made my way back to the front and covered my face, so the cameras couldn't pick me up. I loaded two arrows and took out both guards at the front gate. I climbed over and launched a knife at the dog and guard that were coming through on their patrol. I started walking their patrol in reverse so I could run into the other five units and take them out, before they could become a problem. Once they were all dead, I preceded to the front door. I came from the side, letting me slip in behind the guards. I launched a knife at the one farthest from me, and grabbed the other one, snapping his neck. I walked right in the front door and had two guys waiting for me. They both drew their guns, but I was just too quick. I threw a knife at each, dropping both of them. An alarm went off, lighting the house up with red and white. Why the guy added white is beyond me, but he did. I grabbed the guns from the fallen guards, deciding no to chance it and went to work. I put a bullet in all four of the guards I saw, as I climbed the stairs. I kicked in the first door I came to when I got up there, just to find two little girls hiding on the other side of their beds. I paused, but the guy that charged out of the next room still took a bullet.

"Please don't hurt us," the older of the two girls begged.

"I would never hurt someone who looked as innocent as the two of you," I assured them.

"Then why have you come?" A woman's voice called from just down the hall.

"To kill a man who believes he has the right to sell drugs to kids," I answered her without moving, knowing she had a gun trained on my head.

"There was a time where my husband would have killed a man for refusing to sell to a kid, but not since those two little girls were born," she stated.

"Then how do you explain Don being forced to?" I asked, slowly turning to face the woman who was threatening my life.

"Don doesn't sell to kids. He sells to their teacher, but not the kids," she denied.

"Don's dead, but he was more afraid of what your husband would do to his girl if he didn't sell to kids than telling me where to find the man who as good as had a gun to his head. Your husband keeps you in the dark to protect you. He either loves you or deems that you would be a liability if you knew. You know him better than anyone, don't you? Which do you think is the case?" I said placing doubt in her conviction.

"Are you going to kill me too?" she asked, tears starting to roll down her face.

"Get as far away from drugs as you can. Take care of your daughters, cause if you see me again, I will," I answered.

"The tunnel leads to the garden shed. There is a car

parked across the road to pick him up. He should be halfway through the tunnel now. You'll have to run to catch him before the car leaves. If you let him escape, he'll hunt you down and kill you," she informed me.

"I took care of those guards and the car. I won't let him come back and kill you for making the right choice," I assured her.

She nodded. I ran back down the stairs and shot out one of the back windows. I jumped through it and made my way across the back yard. The drug boss ran out of the shed. He saw me running toward him and started shooting. I dropped to avoid getting hit. He turned and ran for the car. I got back up and started after him again. I stopped when I got to the road. He turned and unloaded the rest of his gun, trying to hit me, but couldn't aim well enough to even graze me. He threw his gun and turned around looking for his two guards. When he realized that they were no where to be found, he jumped in the car. He pulled keys out and tried to start the car, but nothing happened. I slowly walked across the road, in no rush to end his misery. The drug boss realized that the gas hand was on empty and went to get out and run, but then he saw me and how close I was. He hit the spot the door lock use to be, but when he felt nothing, he looked to realized that the door could no longer be locked. I opened the door and pulled him out of the car while shock had hold of him. I pushed him to the ground and stared down on him, waiting for his wits to return so he would know why I killed him.

"Are you aware yet?" I asked.

"Why are you……" he began, a sign that he would at least understand me.

"You made your men sell drugs to kids. One of them is someone I know. I will not allow that to happen. This is what happens to people who I catch doing the world wrong. I kill everyone who wrongs another, because I was wronged, but from my pain came rage and perfect skill. I am a killer, but I channel my skills toward those who need to be removed from the equation. I can't be your judge, but I am the one who sends you to face him," I informed him as I pulled out a knife.

"I'll be better," he promised, with no intention of committing to it.

"Too late," I stated as I sliced his gut open. His insides started to fall out. There was trace of disease or drug use. He wanted the world to use something that he himself did not. Too bad the drugs still killed him. I slit both of his wrists and walked away, knowing that he would be dead within a matter of minutes.

I finished my job and went back to Jessy right in the middle of the first week of February. Jessy was in a lot of pain, so just like last time, Beth had her in bed a lot, even though walking around would help her along. I was in often to see Jessy, but I slept on the couch, against Jessy's wishes. We took her in Friday night, after her water broke in the kitchen. Jessy's mother and Beth were the ones that went in with her, even though she wanted me there. I was perfectly fine in the waiting room after hearing how my brother's first kid went. It wasn't until early the next morning that Jessy's son, Samuel Christopher, was born. It was February eighth, at three in the morning. Jessy's mother, Beth, and I were the only ones awake when it happened. I was the first one in to see her after they gave her Samuel back. He was so much smaller than either of my brother's kids. He had bleach-blonde hair, and when he cried, he could clear a room.

I stayed at the hospital for the most part, until they sent Jessy home. My boss called me for a job, but I convinced him to give me another week before we got started. I spent that week helping Jessy around the house. Beth and her family stayed to help Jessy learn to take care of the baby and to show that they would be there whenever she needed them. As much as I hated it, I learned how to change diapers so I could be more helpful to Jessy when I was in town. It was an eventful week for everyone. Judy got some time off and flew down with her family, to finally meet Jessy and Samuel. Judy kept giving me odd glances after she first laid eyes on Samuel, but she wouldn't tell me why. "You'll figure it out someday," she would say whenever I asked.

Judy and her bunch went back that Sunday. I had to be in Colorado by Tuesday. It was about a six hour drive depending on traffic and stops. I stayed until the following morning so Jessy could get one more good night of sleep before I left her to handle it. She wanted me to stay in bed with her that night, but I argued stated that it would defeat the purpose if I woke her up every time I had to roll out of bed to take care of the baby. She laughed and let me have my way. Unfortunately, it was the last night I stayed with Jessy for quite some time.

15

I was finishing up a job when I received a mysterious phone call. The caller never told me who they were, just that I had to go home or people would die. I got in touch with my informant to find out what he knew of the situation. After several hours of waiting, I got an answer, Mike and Kay went missing while they were out on a date. No one had heard from them and their son was with Mike's parents. I asked my informant to try helping me find out who was behind this. While he was working on that, I made my way toward my hometown. I did my best to make sure no one knew I was in town. I stayed hiding in a hotel room for the better part of a day before my informant called me back.

"What do you have?" I asked the moment I answered the phone.

("Not as much useful intel, that's for sure,") the informant stated.

"Well, why don't you fill me in on what you did find out?" I requested.

(There was a contract taken out on you a while back. No one acted on it until the bounty was raised,) the informant informed me.

"Who put out the hit?" I demanded.

("No contact information is available. I can't even backtrack the cyber intel to find the guy. All I can tell you is that he will post the pick up point and time after your death is recorded in the newspaper,") the informant filled me in.

"Thanks. Let me know if you find out anything else," I requested.

("Hold up. There is a group who showed an interest in your bounty. They arrived in Alabama on a private plane two days ago. That's right before Mike and Kay went missing,") the informant added.

"Thanks," I said right before hanging up the phone.

I couldn't be sure, but I thought I knew who put out the bounty, but considering they made damn sure they couldn't be tracked, they wouldn't have the slightest idea where these bounty hunters were. I went to the last place that Mike and Kay were seen and started there, looking for anything that would lead me to where they went next. There was a parting in the bushes at the edge of the parking lot that seemed out of place. I walked over and looked through them. Sure enough, Mike and Kay's car was at the bottom of the ditch. I slid down to get a closer look. The driver's side and passenger's side windows were shattered. The attackers waited for them to get in their car. There was blood on the steering wheel, most likely Mike's. It was while examining the passenger side that I found a clue. It was part of a shirt, most likely cut off when the guy broke the window. It had an odd design that would help me figure out where it came from.

I examined the design and then put it back where I found it, just incase the police actually managed to find the car. I crept up the hill and looked around to make sure I wasn't going to be spotted before I could get out of the ditch. It was while I was looking around that I spotted a man wearing a shirt with a torn sleeve. The design was the same as the torn piece I found on the car. He was waiting for me to come investigate. They were trying to trap me. I memorized the man's face before sliding back down into the ditch so I could get away without being spotted. I climbed out by the parking lot entrance and made my way to where I saw the man. He was moving away on foot. I followed as he slowly walked down the street. I followed for over an hour before he stopped to grab a bit to eat.

He sat there eating his burger for over ten minutes. I started getting uneasy, because no man should take that long to eat. He was too relaxed to be looking for me. A shadow on the ground caught my attention. I spun around and put a knife to the source's throat. I stared him down as he dropped his gun. Another guns barrel buried itself into my back. I tilted my head slightly so I could see who was behind me out of the corner of my eye. It was the guy I had been following. He used a napkin to wipe his face as his friend reached for my knife. It was too crowded to actually shoot a gun without alerting a lot of people, so I went for it. I threw my elbow back, catching the one still holding the gun in his jaw. I jerked the hand I was holding the knife with, slitting the other guys throat. I shifted one more time and sliced the last one's arm open, forcing him to drop his gun. I kicked him square in the chest, knocking him against a wall so I could drill him for information. I saw him clench his jaw and thought nothing of it, until foam started pouring out of his mouth. He had a cyanide capsule hidden in his mouth, just incase he was captured. I searched them both for clues, but all I found was a message written in a code that I would not have been able to crack, but I was betting that my informant would have it taken care of within the hour.

Well, I was almost right. My informant took about an hour and a half to break the code. The message was simple instructions on what to do if they successfully killed me. They were to go to the hideout decided on before their arrival until the payment was received. It made no mention of Kay and Mike, or and clue to the whereabouts of their hideout. With no other clues, I had no other choice but to be patient, which was far from my strongest virtue.

It was the next day that my mother called to inform me that a man came to the house and dropped off a letter for me. I asked her what he looked like, but her only reply was that he was a tall, white man with dark hair. He made himself so boring, that there was nothing to say about him. It meant that the letter was the only clue I would have access to. I slipped into the house that night and got the letter while my mother was at work. It read:

> I know you killed the other two. They were meant simply to let us know you showed up. You're even better at this game that we would have predicted, but that makes this game even more exciting. There are a total of ten of us. If you want to keep

> your old flame and her current one alive, you simply have to play. If you get through rounds two and three, we will spare the husband. If you get through round four and five fast enough, we will spare her, because you will have killed us all anyway. Now if you are wondering what round one was, well it was the two who tried to ambush you. Round two, however, will take place at five the morning after I deliver this letter. If you don't show, they both die. Here's your clue: The Lord's word RINGS throughout the land. Good luck.

I knew what the clue was without thinking. There was a church with a bell tower by the dentist's office. Putting rings in all capital letters just made it too easy. I had three hours before I had to be there. I knew that the ones I would be facing would most likely be there getting ready, so I decided to drop in early. I wondered the grounds until five on the dot, without any sign of them, but as soon as five hit, the bell rang and two men walked into view. One of them was holding duel daggers. The other looked to be holding a crossbow. A light breeze brushed against their backs, pushing their odor into my face.

"So you two are round two?" I guessed.

"If you want to view it that way, be my guest," the one with the crossbow stated.

"We look at this as your final round," the other stated.

"And why would you count me out on such an early round?" I inquired.

"No one ever makes it past us," the one with the daggers stated.

"Well, I'm going to have to disappoint you," I called

as I pulled my jacket off, revealing an array of knives and throwing stars, not to mention a machete strapped to my side. The two men exchanged glances after seeing my armory.

"That's a first," the one with the daggers said with thrill in his voice.

"Most people bring guns to fight us. At least we won't have to kill you quickly to avoid getting shot," the one with the crossbow added to clarify.

"Very true, but you still have to watch my blades," I stated as the first ray of light hit the sky and my first two knives left my hands. The one with daggers blocked my knife, while the other rolled to the side, trying to shoot me with his crossbow. I caught the bolt and slapped it and he immediately began reloading. I moved to grab two more knives, but the other one charged, forcing my attention toward him. I ducked beneath his first strike, launched two throwing stars at his partner and spun around, drawing my machete with my left hand to block his second strike using his left. He tried to cross over with his right to finish me, but I caught his wrist with my free hand. I shifted sliding my elbow into his face, forcing him back. I turned just enough to see his partner shoot at me again. I pushed him back and used the machete to deflect the bolt. This time, the one with the crossbow didn't immediately try reloading, refusing to chance another barrage of knives.

"Impressive," he stated as he slowly reached for another bolt.

"I think we were wise to come after this guy," the other decided as he stepped forward and charged again.

I launched a knife catching the one with the daggers by the foot. He tripped as I jumped to avoid the bolt whistling toward me. I launched three knives at the one with the crossbow. He had to use the crossbow to try blocking the knives. He dodged one and blocked another. The third not only hit him, it cut the crossbow's string, disabling the weapon. The one with the daggers pulled the knife out of his foot and slowly stood up. This time I charged him. With his foot injured, he was far to slow to stop me from hitting him. Both of his daggers flew into the air as I disarmed him and slit his throat. His partner pulled out a knife and prepared to continue fighting. I lunged forward and launched a knife. I stopped just short of him to watch him fall, my knife in his throat.

I checked both of them and found another note. I collected all of my knives and erased any sign that I was there. I went back to my hotel room and washed up before reading the next note. This one read:

> Very impressive. I watched you fight and if you are reading this, you won. Even better, you're the first to ever make it to round three. Now for the sake of being fair, I will give you all day to rest before round three begins. This next one is at sundown. Now as for your clue: I'll simply say that this one won't be a WALK in the PARK. See you soon.

I spent most of the day resting. The next round was at the park in one of two parts. The most likely was the natural trail. The most apparent was the walking track by the entrance. Considering the natural trail was out of sight, they would almost certainly be there. I arrived at the park to find that there were baseball games going on. I made my way to the trail and found that there were three people walking around it. I let them get in front of me; no longer sure I was in the right place. That changed when the three in front of me stopped at the very back of the trail and turned to face me. They all took off their jackets to show armor chest plating. They each wore gloves with metal plating on them. They could only be fist fighters, which under normal circumstances would have given me an advantage, even against three opponents. This situation, on the other hand, was far from in my favor.

The first one lunged at me. I blocked his punch and almost took a blow from one of his teammates. I took a step back to figure out what I was going to do. Before my mind got very far with that, they attacked again, this time as a united front. I blocked most of their attacks, but two of them got through. I stumbled back and one of them tried to take advantage of it. I triggered a hidden blade and met him, planting the blade firmly in his waist. He hit me in response, but the damage was already done. The other two moved to either side of him, to cover him if needed. I stood up and waited for their next attack. It didn't come. They were waiting for me, and I aimed to oblige. I launched six knives and ran forward. I caught the already injured one in the throat and the one to his left in the arm. The one in the middle dropped. The one to his right shifted away from the group in agony. The other met me head on. I caught his first strike and stabbed his bicep while he connected with a second. I elbowed him in the face and wrapped my arm around his head, snapping it with a violent pull. The last man standing shifted his stance to protect his injured arm. I launched a knife at his foot which he shifted his stance to dodge, but opened his injured arm for my real attack. I grabbed his arm and wrapped it around mine, breaking it in several places. I grabbed him by the throat and triggered the hidden blade, releasing it into his neck. He died before I let him go. Just as I did before, I collected all of my knives and checked the bodies. Just as before, one of them had a note on him. I left the park the same way I went in, unnoticed.

I went back to the hotel and opened the note. It read:

> You continue to impress. You will be going on the round four. That would be me, the leader of this merry band. The other four will be round five, which is a very special round, but enough about that. We have round four to attend to. You must come to the tallest abandoned warehouse tomorrow by noon. We will duel as if we were cowboys, but better. See you soon.

I decided it was best to get some sleep before the big fight. I knew that the leader had to be a great fighter, but what truly bothered me was what round five was going to be. I knew there would be four men left, but it didn't make sense for the leader to be the second to last round in a series of fights. There was a trick that I would have to figure out in order to survive the final round, if I survived the forth. My dreams plagued me, but they were nothing compared to what my life had brought me. I woke the next day covered in sweat, but ready to kill any who stood in my way.

I spent the next couple of hours getting something that could help me in any situation. When the time was growing near, I made my way to the checkout desk so that I could leave when this was all done. The drive was a bit longer than I figured, but it came to an end and I came to the next round. The double doors were open, inviting me into what was intended to be my place of rest. I sighed and began walking. It was a dark place, but the path to round four was easy to find. The group had drawn arrows on the walls, leading me to them. I entered a room with several levels all open to the main hall. It was a great spot for ambushing someone, which was the likely scenario considering Mike and Kay were tied to chairs in the middle of the room. A figure entered the room from an entrance across from the one I entered.

"Welcome to round four. You can call me Hood. I will be your next opponent, and may I say that it will be an honor facing and hopefully killing you in combat. Your goal is to defeat me, but keep in mind; I intend to kill all three of you. If you fail to kill me before I kill you or either of them, you will all die," Hood introduced.

"So you go back on your word?" I questioned.

"I'm sorry. I don't know what you mean," Hood said puzzled.

"You said that Mike could go if I made it through rounds two and three," I stated.

"Oh that, well that was the promise of one of the guys you already killed, so I'm not obligated to honor that arrangement. Makes it much more interesting this way," Hood claimed.

With that said, Hood charged toward Mike and Kay, drawing his sword as he drew closer. I launched six throwing stars to divert him. It worked just enough for me to draw my katana and meet his sword. Hood pushed me back and lashed out at me. I blocked his strike and tried to counter, but he was much quicker than I expected. He stopped my counter and threw me back a few feet. He charged after me, trying to follow up. I rolled to the side and launched three more knives at him. He deflected these as well, but was less prepared for me to be behind them. I slashed upward in an attempt to take out at least one of his legs, but narrowly missed his legs, still catching his left arm. He launched another attack. I jumped over it and rolled away. I launched three more knives and this time came at him from his left, hoping to use his injury against him. He used his left arm to swat my katana away as he slashed downward. I stepped back, just missing his blade, and jabbed my katana at him. He tried to side step, but wasn't quick enough. My katana went straight through his right shoulder. He grabbed my katana and tried to lift his arm in an attempt to cut me down, but my katana had done too much damage for his arm to work at all. I shifted my grip on my katana and swung my left arm down. My katana sliced down to his stomach, cutting off his thumb in the process. I slide my blade out and took his head to finish the fight.

I heard a noise from the level above and rolled, barely avoiding a bullet. I launched two knives, freeing Mike's feet. I charged across the room and stopped at a very good guess, that save me from another bullet. I sliced through the rope holding Mike and Kay and started running without a pattern across the floor. Mike turned and started untying Kay as I tried to draw the snipers' fire. One stood up to get a better shot, so I launched a barrage of knives that made him tumble down to the room, weapon still in hand. I started to relax until I heard another gun fire from right above me. Mike went ghostly white as Kay dropped to her knees. I took a step forward causing a bullet to miss my head by just over an inch. It made me jump back into reality, and I ran through one of the double doors and up the stairs to kill the last three. I heard Mike cry out in pain, and just as I made it to the top of the stairs, another gun went off. Fear gripped me; fore I was afraid that I had failed to save not one, not two, but three people. I was afraid that I had just allowed Mike and Kay's son to become an orphan. Another shot sounded and shock passed through me. I finished my run up the stairs and spotted one of the snipers. I walked right up to him and planted a knife in his stomach and slowly twisted it. I pulled it out and replanted it into his lung. I looked down to see Mike holding a sniper rifle, tears pouring down his rage-filled face. I pulled my knife out and pushed the sniper over the railing. Mike watched him tumble to the ground and stared for a few seconds before returning his gaze to me. I leapt over the railing and landed just in front of the dead sniper. Mike stared at me. I didn't know what he was thinking, but I would accept whatever he did next.

"This is what you became?" Mike asked as he looked over the remains.

"This is what I was meant to be. Killing came too easy to me. It was a natural development. I don't regret what I've done," I answered honestly.

"Would she have died if you hadn't of become this monster?" Mike demanded.

"I can't answer that. No one knows how different life would have been if I had never killed. Perhaps, she died in your stead," I tried.

"What's that suppose to mean!" Mike yelled.

"I wouldn't have given you the money to treat your cancer if I hadn't travelled the path I'm on. You would likely be dead now instead of her. Maybe even all three of you, due to the guy you owed money. I can't foresee what would be, but I do know what is. You have to try picking up the pieces for your son's sake. He needs you," I stated.

"And what about you? What about the cops? What do I tell them?" Mike asked.

"Do you want me to go to jail?" I asked without any sign of emotion.

"We need you to keep killing those who must die," Mike decided.

"I'm glad you believe in my cause," I stated.

"I will figure out what to say. Then, I will join your endeavor. The wicked must be stopped so that the world can become a good place," Mike declared.

"Make your son your priority above all else. I have a handful of people that keep me human. Never forget what keeps you going," I informed him as I turned and walked away.

My informant let me know that I was in the clear as I made my way back to my job. He kept me posted on what the cops were doing as far as the murder of Kay and their kidnapping. Mike did as he said and covered so he could join me in my quest and let me do what I do best.

16

New York beckoned me back. My boss had found me work, but more importantly, the gang violence was getting to far out of hand. I decided that while I was in town, I could help the police out and drop some of the gang members off a roof or something along those lines. It took me a few days to get my baring as far as where the gangs were and weren't. Most fights, robberies, or murders happened in alleys. As far as turf went, it was disputable. There were two gangs fighting over the same area. It was their turf war that was causing most of the violence that was plaguing the streets. I decided to just wipe them both out and get it over with.

The first few days on patrol didn't go so well. I missed four gang fights because I was on the other side of the turf. Oddly, the scenes looked as though there were no survivors from either side. This didn't seem to make sense, but I had no way of checking to scenes due to the overly effective police work. My informant was being quiet. I could only guess that he or she was being careful for one reason or another.

It was the end of the first week before I found any action. There was a six-man brawl in an alley just down the street from my hotel room. I ran into the alley and the brawl stopped. They all looked at me with puzzled looks on their faces. I looked the scene over, but hardly any blood had been spilled. As a matter of fact, it didn't look anything like the other four scenes. That's about as far as my thoughts got because all six of them charged at me. I decided that since these weren't the ones shedding all of the blood, that I wouldn't kill them. I side-stepped the first one and elbowed the second one in the temple, dropping him where he stood. I Spartan kicked the third one, stopping him cold. The fourth one swung a pipe at me. I dropped to my knee and punched the top of his, breaking his leg. The fifth came at me from my left. I shifted to my left knee and planted my right knee into his chest, dropping him flat on his back. The first one tried to kick me in the gut. I caught his foot and spun, throwing him to the ground. I turned, anticipating the sixth one to make a move, but he was running down the alley, trying to escape. I backhanded the one I just put on the ground, bouncing his head off of the cement. The third one started sliding away, deciding that he wasn't about to win the fight. Two of them were moaning in pain, one was screaming due to his broken leg, while the other one wasn't able to make a noise.

I stood up and walked up to the only one who wasn't making any noises, the one I Spartan kicked. He kept trying to slide away from me, like I would let him go, but I had questions that he might have answers to. The others started trying to move away from the scene since my focus was on the other guy. He finally gave up on sliding away and started to stand. When he was on his feet, he tried staring me down. I grabbed him by his throat and directed him toward a wall. I slammed him into the wall to make a point of how serious I was.

"A lot of fighting going on between your gang and another," I pointed out.

"So, what's it to you?" the gang member spat.

"Innocent people get hurt over stupid reasons. The whole lot of you should be ashamed. I want to know who is the one shedding the blood," I explained.

"They started this," he spat.

"The gang member who is killing everyone. Someone is a loose cannon, and guess what; he isn't just killing their guys. He's taking your gang out too. I want a name," I demanded.

"I don't have that information," he stated, starting to relax.

"Then connect me to the man who does," I declared.

"If, and only if, he agrees to meet you, you'll get the answers you want. Be at the third bench in the park from the east side in two hours," he said.

"I will, but you better be there, with or without your boss," I warned.

I let him go and he ran down the alley and disappeared around the corner. I went back to my hotel room and prepared a few precautions, just incase the deal went south. I went to the park an hour early. I found the bench and scoped it out. My precautions were unnecessary, because the bench was in the middle of a large clearing. It was perfect for avoiding ambushes, which I was sure, was the plan. At five minutes to the deadline, I walked over to the bench and took a seat. A group of six men walked toward me. The guy that told me to be here was among them. He and one other guy walked all the way to the bench, while the others spread out as if keeping watch.

"This is my boss," the gang member introduced.

"I'm here to stop the killing of my men," the boss stated.

"I can help you with that, but I do want the violence to stop altogether. But, at the very least, I want to take the only killer out of the mix," I explained.

"He isn't one of mine, but once I realized what was going on, I started collecting information on him. It wasn't easy, but I managed to get his name, but that was it," the boss explained.

"So his name?" I inquired.

"Thomas. He denounced his last name years ago when he took to the streets. He sticks to the area about three blocks south of where you met my boys. Good luck killing the son of a bitch. By the way, don't let me catch you out after you finish him off. I will kill you," the boss finished with a warning.

"I've probably killed more people than you have, so avoid threatening me, unless you want to get added to the count," I said with a smile as I stood up and walked away.

I scoured the area that I was directed to. It was good to know that I could still find my mark, even without my informant. I came to the last building in the area, without any sign of the man I was looking for. But that last building was the one I needed to find. There was blood on the door to warn anyone and everyone to stay away. Funny thing was, the blood seemed more like an invite to me.

I kicked the door in and made my way into the building. The first few floors were empty, but when I got to the fifth, life came out of nowhere. Empty wrappers and soda cans were thrown all over the place. I made my way further down the hall to an open room that seemed cleaner than the rest. I poked my head inside to find a pile of books next to a bed. There was a large pile of wax on one side of the bed and a box of matches next to the pillow. This was someone's haven, their Fortress of Solitude so to speak, and I was intruding.

I took a step back, deciding to find him and talk to him if I could. I looked away from his paradise just in time to see him swing at me. I managed to dodge his attack and take a few steps back, but he was quicker than I would have guessed. He followed me down the hall, swinging at me every chance he got. I ducked and side-stepped every shot he took trying to talk to him, but it did no good. He wouldn't stop unless I made him, and I was running out of room to back away.

I took the offensive and deflected one of his attacks, following up with an elbow to his face. He swung his arm around catching me and launching me down the hallway. I rolled back to my feet and turned to face him. He tried to kick me, but I caught his leg. He slammed his fist down onto my back, dropping me to the floor. He grabbed me by my neck and threw me back into the corner. I pulled a knife out of my pocket as he came barreling back at me. I deflected his swing and tried to plant the knife in his throat, but he stuck his hand in the way. My blade went straight through, but all it did was piss him off. He grabbed my head and tried to bounce it off the wall. I spun around, dropping to one knee and kicking the side of his with all the force I could muster. He dropped to his knee, so I took this chance to get out of the corner. I leapt over him, kicking him in the head as I cleared him. He rolled onto the floor and pulled the knife out of his hand. He lobbed the knife at me, but it just flew over my head and out the window. Thomas charged toward me. I stepped forward, spun around, and kicked him square in the chest. He stopped, but just for a moment. He swung for a face shot, so I ducked and went up for a jab to his face, but he elbowed me through the wall. I stumbled around, trying to get my footing while Thomas came in the opening he had just made with my body. I finally got my footing as he got through the hole, so I did the first thing that came to mind. I jumped up and planted both feet into his chest. I flew back, going through what was left of a kitchen table, while Thomas went back through the hole.

I ran toward the door to try changing the setting of our fight, but Thomas met me at the door. He took a step forward and started to swing. I slammed the door, in hopes to hit him in the face, but he just put his fist through the door. I grabbed his fist and pulled, dragging him through the door. H tripped over the bottom and fell face first. I jumped up and landed on his back. I ran out the door and toward the stairs. I heard Thomas yell from the room. I turned at the stairs and waited for him to watch me run down them. It was a good plan, until he hit me from the side. We slammed through the wall and into the bathroom sink. I grabbed the largest chunk of the broken sink and smashed it into the side of his head. Thomas stumbled, tripping over the tub and wrapping himself in the shower curtain. I took the advantage and dropped my elbow on the back of his head. While he seemed to be somewhat subdued, I decided to try talking to him.

"Thomas, I can help you. I came here to kill you, but after seeing the books, you're just like me. I can help you channel your rage and use it for something good. Let me help you," I tried.

"You came here to kill me," Thomas repeated.

"You're killing innocent people. You have to stop. Let me help you. I can show you how to know when to kill and when to walk away," I explained.

"I won't let you kill me. I will kill you first!" Thomas yelled.

He ripped through the shower curtain, as if he were emerging from a cocoon. I kicked him in his leg to throw him off balance, but all it did was tick him off. He punched me dead in the cheek, knocking me off of my feet. I hit the floor and rolled to my feet and prepared for next attack. Thomas came barreling out of the bathroom. I jumped out of the way, and he put his head through the wall. He pulled his head out of the wall and I decked him. He swung his monstrous arm at me, but I jumped back to avoid it. He spotted me and did what must have been the first thing that popped into his mind. He charged me. This time I couldn't avoid it and was caught in his overpowering grip. He barreled through the room and straight out the window. When he realized we were falling he threw me in an upward motion. I looked up at the sky as I fell to what ever fate was to have me. My body met something solid and everything went black.

17

Mary was there, holding an infant child in her arms. She smiled at me and looked down at the baby. She beckoned me to come look at the child. My heart raced as the thought that I would finally meet my only child sank in. I started forward, not moving fast enough. Then, as if it was all a dream, they were gone. An emptiness filled me, and then, the world went dark.

I expected to be in the hospital when I woke up, unable to move. I was wrong about one thing. I did wake up in a hospital, but not only was I alright, I felt better than ever. I sat up and looked around. It was the hospital from my home town, or that's what it looked like. I slide out of bed and went to the door. There was no one around. I crept down the hallway, determined to leave unnoticed. From out of nowhere, a man swung at me with a sword. I ducked, narrowly avoiding the blade. Two more men started toward me from the other end of the hall. I turned to face the guy that already engaged me. He put both of his hands on the hilt and swung again in a downward motion. I side-stepped, using my forearm to knock the sword out of his hands. I elbowed him in the face and followed up with a knee to his chest. He fell back, but the other two were already too close for me to avoid. One had an ax, while the other had duel daggers. Deciding that being unarmed was a bad idea, I turned to pick up the sword I had knocked out of the other guy's hands, but it was gone. I turned just in time to avoid the first strike from the guy with the ax. The other guy tried to anticipate my moves and strike, but instead I palmed him in the chest and followed up with a palm to his face. The guy with the ax elbowed me in the back and tried pinning me down, but I spun sending him into the wall. I used the momentum from the spin to give a little extra power to my knee as I planted it in his back. I took off down the hall while they were all down. A guy with a katana stepped into my way. He slashed with his sword, so I dropped to my knees, sliding into him. I went for a gut shot and put my hand completely through his chest. His katana fell from his hands as he dropped to his knees. I pulled my hand out of his body and pushed him out of the way. I looked down at him as I stood up. I looked back to see his friends walking down the hall. I decided not to wait for them and ran.

I made it out of the hospital and sure enough, it was my home town. I didn't understand what was going on. I was starting to believe I had been out for a lot longer than I realized, but I had to find someone to get some answers. I went across the street to my former place of employment, but didn't recognize anyone that was working. I walked outside to check the date on the newspaper. It was dated almost two years after I went to New York. I was out for a very long time, but I wasn't sure why I had a group of assassins after me. I decided to go to my mother's house to see if you knew anything.

I ran all the way there, not having a phone or any other way of getting in touch with anybody. A car, the only car

I saw the whole time I was running, stopped in front of me. A man got out and nodded to the driver who sped off. The man left pulled a gun and pointed it at my head. He smiled, but didn't pull the trigger. I tensed up, unsure of what was about to happen or why.

"Impressive," he spoke. "Your training takes you to a level we never expected out of any of our prey. I hope you can endure the suffering; fore everyone you love will die before your very eyes. There's nothing you can do to change that."

"What do you want?" I demanded.

"To torment you until you willingly die. That's how my team works. I am just here to postpone you until my man is done preparing your family for their execution," the man informed me.

"I will kill you all," I warned as I started toward him.

"They aren't the first team and they won't be the last. Just like you aren't the first target, nor will you be the last," he said as he put the gun to his head and pulled the trigger.

Shock filled me as I watched him fall. I didn't understand what had just happened, but I knew it was part of the enemy's plan. I pulled myself together and started running as fast as I could manage. I got my mother's house to find the man with the ax hovering over my brother and father's dead bodies. He had beheaded them. My nephews were hanging from the roof. My sisters were cut open. My mother was tied to one of the columns on the porch. The ax wielder turned to me. He nodded at me right before he turned and took her head off.

Rage poured out of me as I charged toward the axman. I grabbed a stick as I passed it. The axman swung as I made it to him, but I rolled. I got to my feet behind him and clubbed him in the back of him head, shattering the stick. The axman fell forward but caught himself before he hit the ground. I threw the stick down and decked him before he could stand up. He elbowed me in my stomach before I could straighten back up. I dropped to my knees as he started to stand. He started to swing his ax toward me, but I pushed off of my knees, slamming into him before he could hit me. We both stumbled, but neither of us fell. I straightened up and faced him. His hood made him looked like an executioner, but I planned to be the one doing the executing today. He came at me, swing his ax around his head, trying to keep me at a distance or cut me in half, I was unsure which was his goal. I kept taking steps back, waiting for my chance to strike, but he just kept swinging.

I got tired of waiting for him to make a move, so I made my chance. Right after the ax passed, I dove at his feet, taking them out form underneath him. I rolled away from him to get on my feet. I was up first, but not by much. He swung his ax in a wide arc, to keep me away, but I was in his circle as soon as the ax passed. I started with an elbow to his face. I wrapped my arm around his head and started kneeing him repeatedly in his chest. Unexpectedly, he picked me up, launching me over his shoulder. I landed flat on my back and rolled as he tried to drop his ax on my chest. I rolled until I was able to get to my feet. Axman was right behind me, still trying to cut me in half. He swung at me again, this time I caught his attack. I pulled him toward me and elbowed him in the face. I kneed his hands, forcing him to let go of the ax. As soon as I planted my foot back on the ground, I put the other knee into his chest. We both went down, but I rolled, returning to my feet. The axman sat straight up and looked around, his gaze stopping on his ax. I ran up and dropped to my knees behind him. I wrapped my arms around his head and snapped his neck. I laid him back down and went to grab his ax, but it was gone. I looked back at him before going to my brother's car and driving away.

I made it to Judi's just over an hour later. Horror struck me as I witnessed the next to impossible. I watched as the one who had two daggers cut Judi down. He was completely unharmed, but Judi was covered in blood, too much to be her own. It was then that I realized that there was a trail of blood leading out of her house. It dawned on me that the man with daggers didn't just kill her, but her whole family. I jumped out of the car as it barreled toward the man with daggers. He rolled out of the way, giving me enough time to get to Judi's body. She was already dead. I picked up her katana so I could avenge her death.

The man with the daggers wore a cloth that covered his mouth and nose, but his eyes bore into me. We walked toward each other, not seeming to be in a rush to kill each other, but I could feel the blood rising as each step brought me closer to this man. Finally, we were within striking distance. He attacked first, slashing at me with his right weapon. I blocked his attack and shifted the katana to block his second slash with his right weapon. He repeated this pattern three more times, before spinning around in an attempt to catch me off guard. His spin slash came from above. I shifted my sword to slide his dagger off of it and blocked his second swing. I shouldered him, forcing him back a few feet. I swung my sword in an attempt to take his head off, but he leaned back, narrowly avoiding my slash. He made a stabbing jester that I swatted away. He spun and swiped his other dagger toward the ground to attack me in an upward motion. I jumped back to avoid getting hit. He followed up by thrusting his sword at me, my heart as his target. I grabbed the dagger with my bare hand and pushed it away. In one swift motion, I planted Judi's katana in his back. Blood started dripping off of the cloth that covered his face, as he started to sink toward the ground. I twisted the blade before pulling it out. I kicked him, forcing him face-first into the ground. I looked over at Judi, regretting that I put her in the middle of this mess.

Since my brother's car was parked in Judi's house, I stole her neighbor's car. I had to go find Jessy. I knew that if they had found Judi as quickly as they did, that Jessy wasn't safe. Her neighbor's car was definitely the fastest car I had ever driven, but it was a convertible, which was a major problem for me. I sped down the interstate with the car topped out the whole way. I stopped only for gas, but I had an ever growing uneasiness stirring inside me. I could shake, but at the same time, I couldn't figure out what was causing it. I got back in the car and sped off, only a few hours away from Jessy.

About a hundred miles away from Jessy's, a car got on my ass and stayed there. I was going at least a hundred and twenty miles and this guy was staying with me like it was nothing. At first I thought it was a cop, but then I saw the driver. He had a hood that threw a shadow over his eyes. I floored it, trying to put as much distance between the two of us as I could, but he just stayed on my ass. Finally, I ripped the e-brake, pulling a full three-sixty. Now I was behind him, but he didn't seem to like that too much. He slammed on his brakes, causing me to slam into the back of his car. It all happened at once. His car went flying ahead, while mine began to flip. Without a seatbelt, I was launched out of the car. I hit the side of a van that got caught up in the collision, falling to the street, hurt but very much alive. I looked up to see the car I was driving falling toward me. I rolled under the van and made it to the other side as my car landed on the van. All four tires and every window exploded under the pressure. I looked ahead to see that several cars were involved and that most had been launched into the air. A very sad looking car hit the ground and bounced up about three feet, revealing the man who caused the whole thing. He ducked beneath the car as if it were just a low bridge, as he proceeded toward me. I looked at the ground right next to me to find Judi's katana laying there. I could only assume it fell out of the trunk when the car hit the van. I picked up the weapon and stood to greet my new foe.

He stopped about ten yards away form me. We stood there staring at each other for what seemed like an hour or more. The breeze was swirling around us as if it was an arena for us to fight in, one that was well on its way to becoming a tornado the minute our swords clashed. As if we heard someone yell "FIGHT," we both charged each other. Our swords met and the wind seemed to pick up. I moved to step into him, but he simply threw me back. He slashed his sword down and brought it over his head as he charged me. I side stepped his attack, but he followed up with a backslash. I blocked it with my katana, forcing his sword to go over my head. I countered with a jab to his chest, but he shifted his sword, swinging it to intercept mine. I took a step back, pulling the katana level with my face as if I were notching an arrow. My opponent held his level to the ground, waiting for me to attack. I stepped forward and swung in a downward motion. He, of course, blocked my attack and countered with the same attack. I blocked and so went our battle for the next couple of minutes. Neither of us made a decisive blow that even drew blood. Then, without warning, he stepped in trying to take charge. I blocked his attack and slipped into his defenses. I elbowed him in the face and spun behind him. I slashed at his head, hoping to take it off, but he was able to block my attack. My katana slide over his, allowing him to swing his sword down toward my feet. I reacted before I could even realize what was going on. I did a backflip to avoid his attack, landing on one knee. Surprise filled me as I realized what had just happened. My opponent seemed unsurprised and continued his attack. He grabbed his sword with both hands and did a downward slash. I deflected his attack and pushed myself forward, slicing through him in the process. We both stood perfectly still for a very long time, but eventually, he fell. Blood covered the road, but I stood up and started walking, determined to get to Jessy.

It was over an hour before I found a car I could steal. I was surprised that the cops still hadn't found me yet, but there was still something unsettling about what was going on. I had never been able to complete a backflip before, and after being hospitalized for so long, my physical body should be worthless. Even stranger, I don't remember the sun going down and I knew I was driving for well over twenty-four hours. It then dawned on me that I hadn't eaten or used the bathroom the whole time I was awake. I concentrated hard on being in Jessy's living room, and suddenly, I was standing in her living room. Her scream floated in from outside the door. I ran outside to see the last first man that attacked me at the hospital torturing her. He looked at me as I walked out the door. He pushed the knife he was using through her chest and left it there. He stood up and walked between Jessy and I.

"You figured it out," he stated as he looked back at the road.

"I'm still hospitalized," I confirmed.

"That's right. This isn't real, but if you die in here, you're really dead. That's why we want to kill you here and now. It would seem that very few can match you in the real world so, we were sent to kill you in the dream world. Are you ready to accept your death?" he asked as he raised his blade toward my face.

"I'll die when I'm good and ready. Before then, I get to send you to Hell," I informed him.

"Think what you want, but I've never lost," he stated.

"You're in my head. I can't die," I stated as we charged each other.

Our swords shot sparks as they clashed. No one could see the blows we were delivering to each other. After a few minutes passed, we managed to push each other back. When we looked each other over, we were both covered in cuts. Our clothes were virtually destroyed, but we were both standing tall. He was the first guy to use the dream factor to his advantage in his fight against me. It was odd that no matter how much faster and stronger I became, he was able to keep up with me every step of the way.

"You caught on very well. I commend your talents, but you will never be a match for me," he allowed.

He pointed his sword to the ground and smiled. He slashed his sword in my direction. A wave of wind swords sped toward me. Without thinking about it, I stomped the ground, causing a sound wave that destroyed the wind swords. A hint of shock covered his face for but a second. He composed himself and launched another wave of wind swords. He followed them after me, hoping to catch me off guard. I exhaled and all of the swords vanished, I blocked his attack and countered. He managed to block my counter and took a step back. I stepped forward and pressed my attack. He blocked my next two strikes as I pressed on forcing him back. He stood his ground and tried to take the offensive, but I was too fast. I leaned to the side, avoiding his attack. I swung Judi's katana over my head, and took his off.

I looked over at Jessy's bloody corpse. A mixture of emotions filled me as I realized that this could really happen. I had a job to do, and I was willing to pay whatever price was asked of me. The one thing I couldn't allow was someone else dying because of my actions. I wouldn't stand by and let anyone suffer for what I was. Maybe I needed to stay asleep. Maybe the world would be okay without me. I didn't really know, but I could hope.

A figure appeared behind me. I turned to him, expecting more fighting, but he didn't show any signs of aggression. He stood there for long while, just staring at me. I was compelled to stare back. Finally, the figure pulled his hood back to reveal the first man I killed. He looked at me as if he was admiring me.

"I am sorry for the form I came as, but my job is to simply remind you what you are. This man would never have changed. He would have ruined lives, and you saved them. God didn't make everyone to go to Heaven. I regret to say that some of you have to be Hell bound warriors, so that the other sheep can stay with the Lord. You have done much more than expected of you, and you have started a growing change that will continue to reshape the world you were born in. I cannot guarantee where you will go, but I do know how you will continue to live. You will save people in your own way, but never forget that you are saving people. Good luck," the figure explained before vanishing into my dreams.

I decided to take one last look at Jessy, but her body was gone. I spun around and watched Jessy's house disappear. The world began to fade and once the ground was gone, I began to fall. It seemed like I was falling forever, but sooner than I realized, I landed on something and blacked out.

18

My eyes shot open. The light was blinding. I tried to move, but my body was too heavy. I was gasping for air, struggling to move. Hands grabbed me, holding me in place. I struggled harder, refusing to be taken. Finally, my eyes came into focus and I realized that I was trying to fight a group of nurses. I stopped struggling and took a deep breathe. The nurses started running tests on me to see if there was any permanent damage. They seemed satisfied with the results and left me to myself.

I spent the next couple of days moving any part of my body the doctors would allow, trying to get myself fully functional. After the third day, they were comfortable letting me get out of bed. They wanted a nurse to help me until I got my muscles back to full strength, but I wouldn't have it. By the end of the week, I was back on my feet at almost one hundred percent. I signed the papers to get myself out, but a few men were in the lobby waiting for me.

"I'm glad to see that you're finally awake," the leading officer stated as I moved toward the exit.

"Three years is a very big chunk of one's life to lose. I had just turned twenty-five when I got taken out of the equation for awhile. Now I'm half way through being twenty-eight. I'm a lot closer to death than I use to be," I said to the officer.

"We need you to come to the station with us. We found you under some very interesting circumstances. We need you to help us figure out what happened," the officer stated as he started to lead me out the door.

"I'll be honest with you Officer?" I started waiting for a name to finish.

"Stein," he filled in.

"Officer Stein, the last thing I remember was being told that I had a job in New York. I don't even remember packing for the trip. Worse than that, I have no idea if I drove up here or flew," I stated honestly since most everything after the phone call that sent me to New York really was a blur.

"None the less, we have questions we need to ask. Who knows, maybe we will jog your memory," Officer Stein insisted as he lead me to the police car.

Thanks to the traffic, the ride to the station was a very long one. I followed Officer Stein into the interrogation room so he could ask whatever he thought he needed to. I sat down and waited for him to begin. Another officer walked into the room with a large box and set it down on the table opposite of me. The officer just smiled and left the room. I looked at the box a little confused about what was going on, but I was getting a bad feeling. Another man walked into the room. He was FBI. Officer Stein shook his hand and left me to the FBI agent.

"My name is Agent Marks. I have to say that you are a remarkable man to have pulled off everything you've done," he introduced as he sat down.

"I'm sorry, but I don't know what you're talking about. I thought I was brought here because I was mugged or something like that," I lied.

"You were found in a dumpster five feet from a man who had fallen from the fifth story of a rundown building. On top of that, for three years, people died everywhere you went. Know anything about that?" Agent Marks pointed out.

"I remember Derek dying. The rapist. Um, I remember that everyone, but Kelly died tragically from that New York office. Then Kelly died while pregnant with my child. There was that series of murders in that small town I went to. It delayed work for a little over a week. I can't think of anything else," I recalled minus most everybody I killed.

"Did you know the guy that was hired to kill Kelly in the first place and soon after succeeded, was found dead? He was tortured before the murderer finally killed him," Agent Marks tried.

"If you ask me he deserved it," I spat.

"Do you not recall taking a woman out to dinner the night before her car ran off a cliff?" Agent Marks demanded.

"Heather. I didn't have much time to get attached to her," I stated as if barely remembering.

"What about your Texas field trip? Five bodies, one of which was your step mother's father," Agent Marks persisted.

"He's dead?" I asked honestly forgetting that I killed him.

"Alright, how about the fact that more people have

been murdered in your home town after you decided to leave than ever before?" Agent Marks challenged.

"I'm from Syracuse, New York, dude," I stated blankly.

"Not that home town," Agent Marks spat.

"Oh, that one. How does my career choice have anything to do with people dying?" I inquired.

"I'm not sure yet, but I will find out the truth and then you will go to prison, and you will never get out," Agent Marks threatened.

"Good thing I have nothing to hide. Otherwise, I might have to be scared of your threat. But since I'm clean, I guess you are the one who has to be careful. If you take it too far and come up empty handed, it could cost you your job. I really don't want to see that happen, so please be careful. Good cops are hard to come by," I said figuring that he didn't have enough to do anything more than blow steam out of his ass.

"You aren't leaving here until we can account for a few of those murders," Agent Marks stated as he got up and opened the box.

"Alright start at the beginning," I said very unenthusiastically.

"How did you meet Heather?" Agent Marks asked.

"I bumped into her by accident. I offered to buy her a new meal since I knocked hers out of her hands. I asked for her number and took her out the next night," I stated.

"Did you have sex with her?" Agent Marks asked.

"I assume you're looking at the police report which states that I stayed the night with her. Yes, we had sex," I stated with an attitude.

"Alright, did you know prior to Derek's death, that he rapped Jessy?" Agent Marks asked.

"I was the only person she ever told. I was trying to convince her to step forward," I stated, suddenly missing Jessy.

"Did you take matters into your own hands?" Agent Marks pressed.

"I was three hours away, on another job. I stayed in for the most part of that job, making adjustments to my design for the house," I defended.

"Tell me about the night you left everything behind to start your new career," Agent Marks demanded.

"I called my friend Judy. She was off for the next two days, so I asked her if she wanted to hang out before I left. We went out clubbing. I was mad at my family so I didn't want to stay in town and deal with them. Why is that night important anyway?" I asked already knowing the answer.

"A young couple was killed a couple miles out of town. A few people that were interviewed about it said that you and the young man in question had issues about the girl. They were both tortured, which means it was personal. Most times a woman is tortured, the man will rape them, but not in this cause. She had crosses carved into her breasts. Her face was carved up, so badly that no one could ever love her. A love crime if you ask me. As for the guy, he was tortured in a way that would make the crime a revenge trip. The murderer burned his balls and his dick until there was nothing left. I think you killed them. I know it in my gut, but the thing is I need evidence. The only clue we have, are knives used to kill the pair. This killer developed a MO that is being repeated. The man who killed this pair never stopped killing. If I can get evidence that puts you at any of these crimes, holding the knife no less, I can convict you for all them," Agent Marks explained as he threw pictures down in front of me.

"I'll admit that they were part of the reason I left. They and a lot of other people used me until there was little to nothing left. Don't you think that if I was the one who killed them, that everyone else that used me would be dead too. My own family used me. Almost everyone I knew in that God forsaken town used me to get what they wanted. If I decided to get revenge on those people, I'd simply drop a bomb on the place," I snapped, unable to maintain full control of my anger.

"You could just be working your way around until you can have your revenge on everyone. You're not dead yet, which gives you plenty of time to finish unsettled business," Agent Marks countered.

"Anyone could die at any given time. That much is guaranteed. Besides, life is a much better way to have revenge. Karma is a bitch," I spat, still mad at his accusation, true or not.

"You're going to stay here until I find out the truth. Do you understand?" Agent Marks stated.

"Unless things have changed since I was put under, you can't hold me for more than forty-eight hours I believe," I said forcing Agent Marks to understand that he couldn't hold me regardless of his feeble attempts.

"They haven't changed, but I will have everything I need by the end of the day," Agent Marks threatened.

"You can't find anything to convict an innocent man, without tampering with evidence. Besides, how long does a statue of limitation last?" I asked.

"Excuse me?" Agent Marks asked as if he didn't hear me.

"Don't crimes stop getting investigated after awhile? Or does it still count as long as someone wants it solved?" I asked, trying to get him off my back.

"I'm still on the case. That's all that matters," Agent Marks stated as he leaned across the table.

"Something tells me that you aren't as in the right as you're saying," I guessed.

A man dressed just like Agent Marks walked in the door. Agent Marks looked frustrated at this man's appearance. The man gave him a "you should know better" look as he approached the table. Agent Marks took a deep breath and looked away, trying to avoid eye contact. I turned to the new man to find out what was going on.

"I'm sorry Mr. Beast. Agent Marks was in the wrong for bothering you. There has been a continuing increase in kills by the suspect, even though you were still in a comma. I'm sorry for any inconvenience you have endured. You're free to go. I believe that there is a woman in the lobby that is here to pick you up," the man said.

"No, Steve. He did it. I know he is the guy we are looking for," Agent Marks started to argue.

"That's enough. You are out of line and looking at suspension. Don't push your luck," Steve spat before Agent Marks could finish what he was going to say.

"Thank you for letting me know that I won't have to be sitting here for the next two days, Mr.?" I inquired.

"Special Agent Smothers," he introduced.

"It's a pleasure to meet you. Agent Marks take care," I stated as I stood up and started for the door.

"Oh and Mr. Beast, you are on our suspect list, but at this time we can't try to detain you. Keep your nose clean or I will bring you in personally," Special Agent Smothers informed me.

I nodded to let him know that I understood and walked out the door. I looked around to see who it was that came to pick me up. It wasn't until I got to the front of the station that I discovered Judy waiting somewhat impatiently for them to release me. She stood up when she realized that I was walking toward her. She hugged me when I was within range. I was glad to feel the touch of someone I knew. I followed her out to her rental car so we could go back to the airport and get back to our home state. It was a long plane ride, but we managed to make it bearable. My mother agreed to pick me up from Judy's house the next day. It gave the two of us time to catch up. Judy had come a long way since the last time I had seen her.

"So how are things?" I asked as we started walking the track at her local park.

"Busy. I tried taking up where you left off, but I had to be fairly localized. It didn't make it easy. I met two friends of yours. They helped me keep your ghost legend going. John and Mary can do things that I doubt even you can pull off. It hasn't been easy on any of us, even Mike and Josh," Judy explained.

"Josh?" I asked unsure of who she meant.

"That's right; he never revealed his identity to you, now did he? He was your texting informant. After you went down, he found me and started working with me. He's the one who brought all of us together. Well only after you connected us, but he played connect the dots none the less," Judy continued to fill in the blanks.

"I guess a lot has changed since I landed in that dumpster. Have you talked to Jessy?" I asked, hope filling my heart.

"She can't wait for you to visit her. Samuel is going to be three in about four months, and you haven't spent any time with him. He won't recognize you," Judy answered.

"Well that was a bit out of my hands. I'll be with her before Halloween. Thank you," I told her.

"For what?" Judy asked.

"For keeping me alive. A legacy only lasts as long as someone keeps it going or remembers it. You kept it going. All of you did. For that I thank you," I explained.

"It's who we are. I may not be as much of a killer as you are, but I do my part," Judy said with a nod.

"I know, but you did well. If you hadn't of continued my work, the police would believe it was me without a doubt," I stated knowing she would appreciate that she kept me safe.

"We need to get back. My kid should wake up anytime now, and you need to get some sleep because your mother plans on picking you up way too early for either of us," Judy informed me.

"Alright, let's go," I agreed.

We went back to her house. Everyone was still in bed, but before the hour was up, her youngest kid was up crying. I laid there thinking about how much probably changed in my absence and what I knew had changed. The world wasn't that different, but the people around me weren't the same. The ones like me were out there doing what I had been doing all along. It was a great feeling, knowing that I was changing the world by finding others who wanted what

I wanted. They were helping me solve some of the world's problems. At the rate things were going, we would create a life changing movement that would make the world a far better place. I didn't expect to see the changes myself, but I knew that within the next couple of generations, the world would be free of fear for the innocents. I couldn't sleep that night, because I felt as though I hadn't reached my potential. I felt as though I wasn't reaching everyone who needed my help. I was only able to help those in the United States. That was only a fraction of the world, and everyone needed help. I knew I couldn't do it alone, but now I had a team that help me make a difference. We wouldn't be able to save the world, not yet at least, but soon enough the world would be able to start changing for the better. It was time to get back in the game.

The next day came before sleep did. My mother's voice rang through the house as Jason let her in the door. She came into the room I was in and hugged me before I could even get my pants on. It was a bit embarrassing considering Judy was standing outside the door laughing at me. I got dressed and made mom wait until I was completely ready to go before she got to hug me again. The car ride home was dull, as she explained that each of my sisters had a little girl. One was name Courtney and the other was Stephanie. David was finally on his feet, trying to fill my shoes as the family backup. Mom was remarried to the guy that was her boyfriend, even though they both agreed to never marry again. My dad was now in a wheelchair thanks to his accident a few years back. I let all the information soak in as we got closer to the place I once called home. I didn't plan on staying long because Halloween was only two weeks away, and I was going to be with Jessy that day.

After mom went to work, I started practicing to get my skills back to where they needed to be. When I was satisfied that they were where I had them, I continued to practice, determined to advance as far as I could. That night I sat down with the whole family and had dinner. I finally got to meet my nieces. My nephews had grown a great deal, but neither recognized me, couldn't blame them since they were so young when I was hospitalized. It was a nice dinner none the less. I went to bed that night ready to get back to practicing the next day. I practiced for two more days before I decided it was time to go to Jessy. I called her the last night I was going to be at my mother's. She was so glad that I was going to be there the following night and couldn't wait to see me. She admitted that she was scared that she had changed too much for me to want to spend time with her, but I promised that I would never feel that way. I spent most of the night on the phone with her, just talking about anything and everything. It was the most peace I had ever felt.

19

The next day didn't seem to be short enough. The plane ride was unbearable. My mother was nice enough to let Jessy use my truck while I was in a comma, so I didn't have any other means of getting to her. Thankfully, she was the one waiting at the airport for me. Her smile took my breath away as I approached her. She took a step forward and I embraced her in my arms, unable to contain my joy at the sight of her. I loaded my things into the back of the truck, thankful that it was a sunny day. I opened to door to get in and found a very curious looking little boy in the back seat. He looked me over before sticking his tongue out at me and giggling. Jessy scolded him, but I assured her it was quite alright and stuck my tongue out at him. She, of course, scolded me too, which made him laugh again. Samuel was growing up quickly, and I missed it.

It was a quick ride back to Jessy's house. She insisted on driving because the streets had changed and there was a much faster way than there use to be. She helped me put all of my stuff in the guest room. She promised that we would have plenty of time to get reacquainted after Samuel went to bed, but for now we were to behave as if he were in the room at all times. I laughed, but nodded in agreement. That night we had dinner as if we were one big family. Samuel was warming up to me, but that's just the way kids were. I helped Jessy with the dishes while Samuel watched his favorite show before he was off to bed. I watched as Jessy tucked her little boy in for the night. He stared up at me, still trying to figure me out. I smiled as Jessy and I walked out of the room, leaving the door cracked to let in some light.

"You're doing a great job with him," I assured her as we walked down the hallway.

"I do my best, but I think if you came around to give him a male role model he would be better off," Jessy confessed.

"I'm here now, and I would have been here to help you every step of the way if I hadn't of been in that accident. You know that don't you?" I promised.

"I know. He's more like his father than I would have thought, even though he hasn't been here to raise him," Jessy said blankly.

"Why don't you ever talk about his father?" I asked, suddenly curious.

"Because he has things that keep him from us, that's all," Jessy said as if she was holding back the full version.

"All you have to do is call and I will be here, for both of you," I promised.

"Don't say things you can't stick to," Jessy begged.

"Have I not always been there for you? I realize that I haven't been everything you've asked me to be, and that I am something terrible, but I have done more for you than anyone else," I guaranteed her.

"Yes, but you haven't been the one thing I really need you to be," Jessy stated, starting to walk away from me.

I grabbed her hand and told her the undeniable truth, "I know I'm a monster among men. I know that I can't stop killing, at least not yet. There is one more thing that I can't deny. I love you. I always have. I'm here to be with you. I can't stop being what I am, but if you want me, you have to ask. I hate to say that I will still have to leave from time to time for purposes I don't want you involved in, but I'll always come home to you. If you want me, I'm yours."

"Are you serious?" Jessy asked, unable to believe me.

"I've lost time that should have been spent with you. In that time, I could have finished the work I've been doing, but I won't let this set back stop me from being with you any longer. I hope that one day very soon, I can stop and stand by you until we die old, together," I confessed.

Jessy put her hand on my chest as if she couldn't believe that I was real. She took a step closer when her hand didn't go through me. I wrapped my arms around her and held her tightly. She started crying in my shirt. I set my chin on the top of her head to let her know that I was there for her. She buried her face into my chest and let it all out. I picked her up and carried her to her bed. I set her down and laid next to her, holding her tightly. She cried herself to sleep that night. I fell asleep shortly after she did, still holding her in my arms. I was afraid that my dreams would be filled with her death, but my dreams were just that, dreams.

The next morning, I was up before Jessy. I decided it was my turn to surprise her with breakfast this time. I made my way toward the kitchen, but a sudden thud caught my attention. I grabbed a pen out of my bag and made my way into the kitchen. Nothing prepared me for what I found when I got stepped into view. Samuel was just standing there with a big grin on his face, the one kids always have when they were doing something bad and hoped you didn't see. He kept smiling as he walked by me. I watched him pass with curious eyes, but could not see any sign of what he had done wrong. I decided to pretend I hadn't seen a thing and went to where he was standing to start on breakfast. It was when I turned around that I discovered what Samuel had been up to. There were three knives in a triangle pattern on one of the cabinet doors. There were several other notches where the process had been done before. I walked over to the cabinet to examine the knives and discovered that they had all been thrown. Samuel had more accuracy with a knife than most four year olds had with any projectile. It dawned on me at the moment that the reason Jessy never talked about Samuel's father around me was because I was his father.

It hurt realizing that I had the family I always wanted and had missed it. I knew that my work wasn't over yet, but at the same time, I knew that I had to make up for lost time here with my family. I went ahead and fixed breakfast. Samuel went into the living room and turned on the TV. I wasn't positive, but I thought I heard Bugs Bunny. I finished cooking breakfast and set a plate on the table so Samuel could go ahead and eat while I went to wake Jessy up. Samuel was at the table as if he knew what I was thinking. I walked into Jessy's room and sat down on the bed. She groaned and looked up at me as if I was a dream. I smiled down at her and waited for the smell of breakfast to hit her. It did, but instead of saying anything, she kissed me. My stomach was in my chest before I knew what to think. She let me go and leapt out of bed, heading straight for the kitchen. She stopped when she saw the knives. She looked at Samuel and then at me. I walked into the kitchen and stopped to let her say what she felt she had to.

"I guess you figured out who Samuel's father is," Jessy stated.

"Yes, and I wish would have told me. I always wanted this. After Kelly, I thought it was impossible, but here it is right in front of me, right when I decided it was time to be with you," I said honestly.

"So last night wasn't a dream?" Jessy asked, tears running down her face.

"It was as real as those knives are," I promised.

Jessy took another look at the knives. She then turned her attention toward our son. He just kept eating away as if we weren't even in the room. I put my hand on her shoulder as she continued to stare at our son. She finally stopped crying and looked at me. I met her gaze, waiting to hear her voice. She took a deep breath, but just sighed. I tilted my head toward the table and she nodded in return. I pulled her chair out before taking mine. She stared at her food for a minute without so much as touching her fork.

"So what happens now?" Jessy asked.

"I have a few more things to take care of, but I was hoping it wasn't too late to start a family with you," I informed her of my desire.

"You mean?" Jessy started but was unable to finish.

"If everything goes as my plans are beginning to, I can stop killing within the next couple of years. By then, I was hoping we would be ready for a wedding. When I thought of it, I was hoping that we could have a couple of kids together, but now I know we already have one. I want to be with you. I want to live instead of doing," I explained.

"Are you proposing to me?" Jessy asked suddenly filled with a mixture of excitement and delight.

"I believe I am. What do you say?" I confirmed.

"Yes, Oh God yes. I've wanted you to ask me that question since I first met you," Jessy confessed as she gave me the answer I hoped for.

"I love you, Jessy. If you can wait just two years, everything will be perfect," I said as a smile slide across my face.

"If you haven't figured it out, I'd wait until the end of time for you," Jessy said as she began to cry.

"Foolish as I am, I don't think I can wait that long," I assured her.

I looked over at Samuel to see what he thought, but he just kept playing with his food. I held Jessy tightly as I began planning my next move. I had two years to get everything out of my system. I intended on starting with a man who came to power in Central America. He went by Crow, but nobody knew his real name. It would take a few weeks to plan the attack and almost as long to prepare. After that was taken care of I didn't figure it would take much more than a week to complete the task.

The next day I started making phone calls. I needed a team if I was going to take Crow down. Judy was my first recruit. She was more than happy to have a chance to show me her finely tuned skills. My second phone call was to Josh. I asked him to track down John and Mary for me, and then I needed him to track Crow's movements so I could figure out the best way to kill him. The last guy I called was Mike. He agreed to meet me, but I got the impression that he was less than willing. Jessy was disappointed that I had to leave out to meet with Mike, but she decided to let it slide for his kid's sake. I kissed her on the forehead before heading to the airport.

Mike looked like hell when I found him at the restaurant that we agreed to meet at. He was poorly saved, and his shirt was filthy. I sat down in front of him and waited for him to focus. He looked me over and then finished his beer. I put a twenty on the table and signaled for the waitress to bring us another. Mike just stared at me until the beer was set in front of him. It was like a wake up call for him, but he took a drink anyways.

"You look like shit," I finally stated.

"I could say the same about you, but for a guy that was just in a comma, you look fit," Mike spat.

"I need a sniper and I hear you're a lot better than any civilian I could find," I decided to get straight down to business.

"You're a lot more straight forward than I recall. What's the job?" Mike asked.

"Crow," I stated.

"The guy whose soul gets linked to a bird?" Mike mocked.

"The Crime Lord in Central America," I stated.

"Wait, I saw him on the news. You're fucking crazy," Mike spat.

"Yes him, and no I'm not crazy, at least not legally. Look, you will be far from harm's way. I promise. I've already looked into a means for paying everyone for their time, that way nothing is really problematic. It's up to you, but I figure we can each go home with over a hundred thousand," I explained.

"Won't that be suspicious?" Mike asked.

"Depends, Josh has the means to make it slowly appear in a taxable manner that keeps the Federal government out of our hair. So what do you say?" I asked one last time.

"How can pass that up? I need the money to take care of my son. Let me know when to make my travel arrangements," Mike agreed.

"Meet me and the rest of the team in Andrews, Texas in a week," I informed him.

"The team?" Mike inquired.

"Judy, Josh, you, John, Mary, and myself," I listed.

"Interesting team," Mike commented as he lifted his glass and finished it.

We both left the restaurant and went our separate ways. Josh confirmed John and Mary's involvement later that day. I went back to Jessy's to spend time with my family before I was off to risk my life for a better tomorrow. The week went by faster than I wanted it too, but none the less, I had a job to do. Josh called to let me know that John and Mary were off to secure the route we were going to use to get across the border. I left Jessy the way I wanted to, with a kiss and a promise to return.

We all met up at the hotel in Andrews. We each had a different room, but were using mine as the center of operations. Mike stayed in a corner with a beer in hand, while Judy helped me go over the basics. Josh sent us information from his room since he was grounded for getting into a fight in school two days before. We waited for John and Mary to return so we could explain the plan to them. Once all the details were set in motion, we made our way south toward the boarder. About two miles shy of the boarder we ditched our car in a parking lot that would allow us to pick it back up on our way out, and made our way to the crossing. John moved ahead of us to scout, while Mary stayed behind to guide us through. It seemed to be a lot easier to cross than anyone would have predicted, but we did have an elite team of killers who specialized in not getting caught. Once across and out of harms way, we hoped a train and made our way further south. The train got us within twenty miles of Crow's headquarters. We went into the nearest town and checked into a hotel under John's name. It was a small room, but we didn't need much since only three of us needed to sleep for more than two hours. I contacted Josh the minute we set up shop.

"We're in," I said when he answered.

("Alright. He's out right now, but according to his PTA he should arrive at ten tomorrow morning. He has a meeting with the president at one. I recommend making your move at eleven and being out no later than twelve-thirty. How's Mexico treating you guys?") Josh informed me.

"It could be nicer. Josh I need you to track this cell phone. When I'm within a football field's length of Crow's facility, I need you to shut down his surveillance system. Can you do it?" I requested.

("I'm way ahead of you. I've been recording all of his recent activities. He has a group of hostages in his basement that could use our help. Other than that, I'll cut the cameras and send the footage to some government official who will turn it in and never be able to trace it to me,") Josh informed me.

"Excellent. Talk to you when I get around to it," I said as I hung up the phone.

"So Josh is covering the surveillance system, I've got the wall, Judy has the entrance, and John and Mary have your back?" Mike asked to confirm.

"In light of recent information, I think we need to make a few adjustments," I said in reply to his question.

"Such as?" Judy asked.

"John do you think Mary could handle a rescue op while the two of us take care of the big guns?" I asked.

"I don't doubt that she can, but the decision is not mine to make," John said from the door.

"I will save the hostages. I will need help covering them all for an escape though," Mary answered as I turned toward her.

"Alright, I got an idea. John, help me clear the halls all the way to his floor. Then, I will need to start clearing a path for the hostages. Will that work?" I suggested.

"For the hostages, yes. I don't think it is wise for you to finish Crow alone. Too many chances for a complication," Mary stated.

"I'm with Mary on this one. At least let me start clearing the path so John can stay with you," Judy piped up.

"I'll be fine. I'm in better shape than I ever was and I will kill Crow," I assured them.

"I may be able to clear most of the path and let Judy and Mary finish the rest," John offered.

"No. Judy must stay at the entrance to cover our escape. This is the best plan," I stated firmly.

"As you wish," John decided.

"Alright, now we need to have a quick weapons check," I said to change the subject. "Mike, how much ammo did you bring?"

"I have two straps each with twenty sniper rounds. I have two back up clips for my handgun," Mike listed.

"Judy?" I went to the next.

"Twenty throwing knives and a dagger. I can hold the entrance," Judy assured me.

"We can hold our own," John assured me when I turned toward him and Mary.

"Very good. We're set," I stated and stood up.

"How about you?" Mike asked from his corner.

"Thirty throwing knives, twenty throwing stars, two daggers, and a katana. Satisfied?" I retorted.

"Impressed to be honest," Mike stated. The others nodded in agreement at the number of weapons I intended on taking with me.

"Good, now let's get some sleep. John, can you take first watch?" I asked.

"Of course. If Mary and I get four hours of sleep, we will be at our very best," John answered.

"Alright. Mary, you get second watch. Lights out in an hour," I said as I made my way toward the kitchen for a snack.

The next hour went by quicker than I expected, but that night went by faster than it should have. We all had a rough time sleeping. It wasn't the fact that we were about to kill a lot of people, because we had all killed. No, this was the first time any of us had ever made a play this big, including me. I did a tally that night and realized that I had killed seventy-six people in my life. That was more than anyone in this room, including John and Mary. I was about to put myself into triple digits and that scared me more than anything. The thing that comforted me that night was the thought of ending this so I could go spend my life with Jessy. My family was all that mattered.

20

Mike

I don't know why, but I fell asleep in the corner I stuck to. Charles and the others were up before I was, but I had my suspicions that Charles didn't get much sleep. Judy was putting on her sexiest outfit that didn't slow her down on the draw. John and Mary were always ready, so all they did was stand by the door. I just got up and grabbed my bag. I had a sniper suit in my bag that would help me blend in. I would change when I got to my position, might be too risky to change before leaving town.

We moved out around ten-thirty. Everyone was on edge, but that was to be expected. Out of the five of us here, Charles was the only one who had never worked with the rest of us. I'll admit that we had all seen him in action and we all agreed that he was without a doubt the best at what he did. I didn't know how well he would work with others. None of us had ever really worked with him on any of his marks. I was told that he worked with an assassin at one point, but no one knew for sure. We followed him to a truck that seemed to just be waiting for us. We all hopped in and let Charles drive us to our next destination. We stopped about half a mile from the compound. There was a cliff to our right that gave me the best vantage point to snipe from. I nodded to the others, knowing that this was my stop, and made my way through the trail that took me to the cliff. It only took me fifteen minutes to get to the top. There didn't seem to be anyone watching this spot, even though it was indeed a perfect sniper's nest. I set up shop and waited for the others to let me know that we were green.

At eleven on the dot, I got the green light. I had already done a head count. There were twenty men on the wall. Some of them walked out of sight for a minute or so, but I could hit them all. I decided to start at the back to throw them off. It worked. One, two, three, four, ten, fifteen, all twenty were down, now I just watch and wait.

Judy

Charles dropped Mike off at the trail entrance. Once Mike eliminated the wall guards, it was going to be my turn. We walked the rest of the way to the compound to make ourselves harder to spot. John and Mary moved ahead of Charles and me due to their natural speed. Once we were all in position Charles gave the green light to Mike. We watched the guards, waiting for them to fall, but nothing seemed to happen. Charles glanced back, but seemed satisfied and returned his gaze to the wall. Sure enough, the guards started falling. Once the last guard was down, Charles turned to me and nodded.

I smiled and climbed out of the ditch. I brushed the dust off of my skirt as I walked to the front gate. The guard didn't seem to notice me approach so I knocked on the window, cause he had to open the gate from the inside otherwise the plan would never work. The guard jumped at the sudden noise, his hand going for his gun until he saw me. Confusion covered his face as he looked around me to see if I was alone. I slowly walked over to the window to see what I wanted.

"Um….. I'm lost, do you speak English?" I said acting dumb.

"Yes, I speak English. What do you want and how did you get here?" the guard asked.

"I'm not really sure. I was driving and I must have taken a wrong turn. My car broke down about two miles down the road. Do you think I can borrow your phone?" I explained as I played with my spaghetti strapped shirt.

The guard held up one finger and walked back to his desk. I didn't understand what he said over his radio, but a minute later two more guys came into the room. They all stood there looking me over and talking in Spanish. They all smiled from time to time whether they were looking at me or not. I was starting to think that they were coming up with other plans for me. Finally, the guard turned toward his desk and hit a button. The door in front of me opened. I walked inside and one of the other two guards closed the door behind me. I smiled as I started toward the phone, but the second new guard stepped in my way. I gave them a startled look, but then the main guard started to undo his pants.

"How about you help us before we help you," he said as he started toward me.

"Only if it's to hell," I answered as I pulled my first knife and buried it into the one by the door.

Shock covered their faces as I ripped the guard's guts out. I launched the knife at the one by the phone to stop him from picking up the radio. The main guard turned to run, but his pants fell to his knees, tripping him. I walked over to him and planted my knee in his back. I put my second knife to his throat and held it there.

"That's not how you treat a damsel in distress," I whispered in his ear right before I slid the knife across his throat.

I walked over to the desk and hit the button to release the door. I walked over and opened it, letting the others know that the coast was clear. The others started this way, but the twist of a doorknob caught my attention. I turned around just in time to see another guard enter the room. He was looking over paperwork and did not immediately notice his dead comrades. I launched my knife across the room, catching him in his throat. He gargled on his own blood as he fell to the floor. The others were in the room now. Charles nodded to me as he made his way across the room. Mary smiled as she parted from the group and went to rescue the hostages. I took out a knife and sat down to await their return as planned.

Mary

We left Judy to hold down the exit as we made our way to our different goals. Mine seemed simple enough. I had to save the hostages while everyone else got to kill the bad guys. I knew I'd get some action, but not as much as Charles or John. Heck, I figured that even Mike would end up killing more than me this day. I followed the hall that Josh had directed us to go down to find to hostages. There were two guards at the other end, but I wasn't afraid of two men. I ran up to them, before they even knew I was there. They both shifted to shoot me down, but I had already put my hands through their chests. I pulled my hands out of their chests and looked to either side of me. They were alone, but I wanted to make sure. I turned to the right and continued to head toward the hostages.

There were two more corners between me and the hostages. Each corner had two guards that I was more than happy to take care of. I finally made it to the hostage room. It was more like a dungeon. They were either chained to the wall or locked in the underground cage just below my feet. None of them looked at me, undoubtedly thinking I was one of the guards. I walked over to the nearest and broke his chains. Shock filled his face, and then the room. All eyes were on me as I continued to break them free. One of them shouted. I turned to see why. Three guards had just walked in with a strangely dressed man. They drew their guns and started barking orders at the freed hostages. I was over there before they even knew I was in the room. I ripped the center one's throat out. I dropped to my knee in the same motion and planted the same hand in the one on my left's knee, snapping it. I stood up and elbowed the last guard in the face. His head popped off and flew across the room. I turned back to the one on my left and planted my palm against the side of his head, bouncing it off of the doorway. I grabbed the oddly dressed man and pushed him into a freed group of the hostages.

"Hold onto him while I free the rest of you," I ordered.

Immediately, several sets of hands clamped down on the man's arms. I finished freeing the others and looked around. They were all gathered around me, waiting for directions, orders? I took a breath and walked over to the entrance. I picked up the three guns and walked back to the center of the room. Everyone's eyes followed me where ever I went. I stopped and turned toward them all.

"Who wants to be brave enough to help defend this group from any more guards that decide to get in our way?" I asked calmly.

It was a very quiet few minutes as they all left me standing in the cold. It seemed as though this man had made them scared, too scared to fight. After what seemed to be a very long time, a boy no older than sixteen stepped forward and held out his hand. I gave him the smallest gun. He turned and raised it above his head. Two more boys about his age nodded to each other and walked forward to claim the other two guns. I took a breath and smiled.

"Now, we wait for backup," I said proudly.

John

We left Judy in the guard shack and I watched as Mary ran off in the other direction. I wasn't worried about either of them. Mary could handle herself and Judy was in a safe spot with her own skills to back her up. Mike was so far out of sight, that they would never even catch him. I wasn't worried about myself, because like Mary, I could handle getting shot a few times. It was Charles that I worried about. The role that he and I played was dangerous enough, but now he intended to face the last of them alone. He was good, better than any human I had ever known, but those were impossible odds.

We pushed on. I moved ahead to clear the way, but Charles was no slouch. He pegged three people that I didn't even see coming. True, I killed five guards while he was trying to catch up, but to notice things that eluded me was a far greater feat. We made it to the main building as planned. There was a great deal of guards by the door. I ran toward them in order to wipe them out. Four knives whizzed by my head. Only two guards were left standing as I reached them. Horror filled their souls as I leapt into the air and caught the closest by his head. I landed behind him and grabbed the other's throat, ripping it out as I pulled his head off. Charles ran past me and cracked the door. He closed the door and took a step back, holding up three fingers. I nodded and went to the window on our left. Charles kept watch while I pulled the window out and climbed in. The three guards were all standing by the door. They didn't notice me walk right up to them. I snapped the first guy's neck. In the same motion put my finger in the guard to my left's throat. With the other arm, I grabbed the last guard's head and smashed it into the wall. Blood ran down the wall until I let him go. Charles walked through the door and motioned toward the stairwell.

We made our way up the stairs. There didn't seem to be anyone watching them, but once we got to the floor we needed, things got interesting. There were close to twenty guards patrolling the hallway. Charles had predicted this much. We stood on either side of the door waiting for an opening to strike. The two closest guards turned their backs to us. Charles nodded to me and I returned the jester. We charged through the door. Charles started launching knives while I took down the closest two. Charles ducked into a side room as they took aim. I spun around and jumped through the window. I grabbed the edge and pulled myself up. I started making my way to the other end of the hall, deciding it was best to attack from behind. I caught a glimpse of Charles engaging two of the guards just outside of the room he was hiding in. I got to the last window and went straight in. I pulled out my two hatchets and went to work. I took one's head off and planted one of my hatchets in another's chest before anyone even knew I was there. Based on the amount of bodies on the floor, Charles's knife barrage had claimed five of them. I moved out of the line of fire and launched both of my hatchets, taking out two at Charles's end of the hall. I straightened up, forcing the guard in front of me to miss. I wrapped my arm around his head and snapped his neck. I grabbed his knife and used my elbow to divert the next one's gun away from me. I recoiled and planted the knife in his chest. Grabbing his gun, I moved to the next and pegged him in the face with the butt of the gun. I pulled the gun across and smacked the guy next to him in the side of his head. I spun around and planted the end of the barrel in the first guy's skull. I stopped my spin and jabbed my hand into the second guy, severing his spin. I stood up and ran to the last two men. They turned to run, but Charles was in their way with one of their friends still on his blade. I was on them before they had time to consider any other options. I grabbed their heads and smashed them together, crushing both of their skulls.

"Twelve in the hall. I think you're losing your touch," I said to mock Charles.

"I'm only human. Can't kill everyone for you, besides, bullet hurt like hell when they hit me," Charles retorted.

"What's that mean?" I asked unsure of why he would say that.

"You're bleeding," he said as he pointed at my leg and my gut.

Sure enough I was bleeding in both locations. I pulled up my shirt and removed the bullet that was in my kidney.

I used the knife Charles offered to cut my pants open enough to remove the other bullet from my leg. We looked at the carnage as Charles started toward the elevator. I stood up in front of him to stop him.

"John?" he asked, a little confused.

"I'm up by seven. You don't need to do this last bit alone," I offered.

"I'm not alone. Mike's got the room in his sights. Plus, when I'm done in there we may be tied. Mike's got twenty kills right now anyway," Charles pointed out.

"I have twenty-two," I stated.

"And I'm up to fifteen and no wounds. Beat that," Charles challenged.

"Alright, let's see what fate deals me next," I accepted.

"Then go help Mary and leave these guys to me," Charles said as he turned and walked into the elevator.

I tapped the headset and let Mary know that I was on my way to aid her.

Mary

John let me know he was headed my way. Judy chimed in to let us know she was ready and waiting. I stood up and the hostages did the same. I smiled and lead them out the door. Two of them were holding on to the oddly dressed man who informed me that he was a professor. I decided to take him with us to find out what he knew so for now, the hostages were taking care of him. We made our way back the way I had come. There were a few guards who had come and found the ones I had already killed. They had already radioed it in, so this place was about to become a mad house. I ran up to the first set of guards and put them both down with my daggers in their backs. The next two guards were shot down before I even got to them. I turned and nodded to the three who had taken up arms to help me.

We came to the exit. I got ready to start fighting my way through guards, but was surprised. Two bodies came flying through the door. John stood up and pulled his hatchet out of the other body. He was wounded, three shots from the looks of it. He had already removed two of them so the third must have happened in the yard. He smiled when he saw me and nodded back at the door. We ran out into the yard. There weren't as many guards as I expected, but there were already four men down so I could only assume that John had started without me, that was until I spotted the knives. Four men came out of the main building. I was over there before they even took aim. I slit the first two's necks and planted my daggers in the second set all in one motion. The hostages started running across the yard, wildly trying to escape. The three that had accepted the guns spread out and started exchanging fire with the guards. The gates opened and they started to flood out. Guards started to pool into the yard. I looked over as John came up behind a group of them and put them all down. The door behind me opened. I instinctively turned with my daggers ready. Two men ran out the door, looking at the escaping hostages. They didn't even notice me until my blades pierced their chests. I stood up and turned to see two men running for the gate house. I took a step toward them, but then I spotted Judy and stopped.

Judy

I stepped into the yard and planted my knife in the guard that was making his way toward me. In one swift motion, I pulled it out and shifted it in my hand. I launched it at his partner who was ten feet behind him. I pulled out two more knives and launched them at the two guards that were trying to sneak up on Mary. She turned and watched them fall. We both looked at each other and nodded. I turned and started helping to hostages through the gate. Two men came running at the hostages from the other side. I pulled two knives, but a young man shot them down before they could open fire. The boy stopped and helped one of the hostages who had tripped over their own feet. Another guard came out of the same door as the hostages. He opened fire. John was there in an instant, putting him down hard. I turned to look at the boy, but he was on the ground. Mary was there before I could take the first step. He was alive, but badly injured. Mary picked him up and started out the gate. John dropped another guard that came out of that door. I looked up just in time to see two guards poke their heads out the windows from the second floor. I caught both of them in the throat before they could open fire. Charles came over the headsets.

Mike

("Alright everyone, it's time for you to retreat to Mike's position. I'll catch up when I'm finished here. Take care of the hostages. John, seal the gate behind you, permanently, I've got a back door,") Charles said over the headsets. I looked at the gate to see a flood of people. Judy and Mary came out with them. Mary was carrying a young man who looked to be injured. John was nowhere to be seen.

Suddenly, the gate dropped. John came barreling out a window as the gate house blew up. I watched as the group of people moved away from the compound.

I looked at my watch. It was almost noon. Charles had just over thirty minutes to get out. What was worse was the fact that he asked me to back him up in the room. He said he'd let me know when he needed my help with a code phrase. It was simple really; he just had to say my name. I found the room that Crow was in. Charles was tied to a chair. The man in front of him punched him. The man doing all the talking handed Charles's headset to one of the other men, who smashed it. He was my first target. There were twelve people in the room. I took a breath and opened fire. I dropped three of them. I pulled the trigger a fourth time, but I forgot to reload after clearing the last of the wall. I panicked as I tried to reload fast enough to save Charles's life.

Charles

I finished telling the others my final orders, even though I was told to lead them into a trap. Crow grabbed my headset and gave it to one of his guards as another hit me for my uncooperative behavior. They pulled most of my weapons, but they didn't find my newest toys. I decided to wait until Mike made his move to make mine. The window cracked and three men went down. I triggered all of my hidden blades. There was one on each arm and a razor on the front and back of each shoe. Triggering the ones on my arms freed me from my bonds. I pulled my feet up and kicked the two guards in front of me, pushing the chair backwards. I rolled out of the chair and onto my feet. Two guards moved toward me. I turned toward one, planting my right hand against his face and my hidden blade in his throat. I took a step away from him and swatted away the other guy's punch. I opened my hand and smashed my palm into his face, planting my other hidden blade in his mouth. I pulled my hands away from the two guards, letting them drop to the floor. I spun around avoiding a bullet and kicked the guy in the gut. He bowed over and I caught him with a pen I took off of the desk. He fell over as the next two stepped between me and the door. Crow must have run out of the room during all the commotion. I took a step forward and the pair tried to meet me. I did a spin kick, catching both of their throats with my razor heel.

I grabbed my weapons as I ran out of the room. There were four guys waiting for me at the other end of the hall. I was ready and launched a barrage of knives to meet them. All four of them went down as I started running down the hall to catch up to Crow. I rounded the corner as Crow and his remaining guards were entering the elevator. Two of them walked out to meet me, but there was still several in there with him. I pulled out six throwing stars and launched them, hoping to catch the elevator before it closed. My plan worked as only one throwing star didn't go in. I ran up to the guards and pulled my katana. They both went for their guns, realizing that this wasn't going to be a fist fight, but it was too late. As I drew my katana from my shoulder harness, I swept it down and up killing the guard on my right. As soon as the deed was done, I shifted and brought the katana over my head and took the other guard's head off. As the two bodies fell to the ground, I turned to my right and walked to the window.

I broke the window and climbed out. I turned around to see the window John had used to get behind the guards earlier. I threw myself toward it. I landed on the outside and rolled into the hall to avoid hurting myself. The elevator dinged alerting me to Crow and his men arriving. I stood up as the door slid open. The color drained from Crow's face as he saw me standing there. Two of the guards were on the floor dead. The other six ran out to kill me. I held my katana as they approached. I slashed the one on my left and pulled back across, stabbing the one to my right. I released my katana and continued the attack. I blocked the swing sent my way from the one behind the guy I just killed. I met his attack by planting my hidden blade in his throat. I pulled the blade and drew one of my daggers, spinning to the left side of the hall. I stabbed the guy that was standing there. Releasing the dagger, I spun around while removing my other dagger from its sheath. I stopped and lifted one of the two remaining guards over my right shoulder. As he fell, I planted my dagger in his chest and let it slit him open as he fell. I grabbed a knife from my pack and pegged the last guy in the chest with it, dropping to a knee as I forced him to the ground. I stood up, covered in blood, but alive and unharmed.

"Holy shit," Crow said as I stood in front of him.

"I've come to kill you. God will decide your fate, but I am the executioner who will rid the world of your crimes, crimes of which have helped destroy this world," I announced.

"And what of the crimes you committed today?" Crow challenged.

"God will do with me what he deems is right. As for killing your men, you pulled them into this, not me," I pointed out.

"You set my slaves free. You stole from me. Where is the justice in that?" Crow spat.

"How are they your slaves?" I asked.

"They owed me, and so I am letting them work off what they owe. They are my property until their debt is paid," Crow boasted.

"No human belongs to another. There are only two bonds that allow that kind of talk. One of them is the bond between husband and wife. The other is the bond between parents and their kids. You have neither bond with anyone we set free this day. You're done. Accept it because there is no going back now," I informed him.

"Do what you think you must, but others will take my spot. Corruption is human nature," Crow stated.

"That may be true, but there are those who can have great lives. And now that I've been born, there will always be those who will kill anyone like you," I countered as I started toward him.

Crow pulled a gun, but I was too quick. I launched the knife I had in my right hand, catching his hand before he could pull the trigger. The gun fell to the floor. I walked up to him and grabbed him by his throat. I pulled him to the broken window and pushed him to the floor to cower while I pulled a rope out of my bag. I was ready for this moment, but it was obvious when I pulled the noose out of the bag, that Crow was not expecting to hang. I put the noose over his head and tied his hands to the rope to where there was a little bit of slack. I tied the rope to the most secure object I could find. Crow stood up and took a breath. He opened his mouth to speak, but I hit him, sending him out the window. Just as I had planned, his hands were torn off by the force of his body falling with slack in the rope. He jerked violently until he spit blood out. He went limp so I walked away, leaving his hanging body as a warning against the corrupt.

I met up with the others at the truck. Mary had taken a hostage of her own. We moved quickly catching the first train and getting on it. It didn't take long before the train was stopped. I knew this was coming so I had the others follow me to an open coal container. We climbed in and waited for the search to stop. Once the train was moving again, it was a straight shot back to the boarder. We did just as we had on the way down to get back to the United States. We all parted ways and went back to our lives, each of us taking something back with us.

21

I made it back to Jessy's but all was not well. Tears were on her face as I walked in the door. Worry over took me. My phone began to ring. It was a number I was unfamiliar with. I answered, unsure of the caller.

"Hello?" I answered.

(Mr. Charles Beast?") The voice asked.

"Yes, this is he," I answered.

("This is Detective Wallace from your home town. I'm afraid I have some bad news,") Detective Wallace introduced.

"David?" I asked certain he was dead.

("Your brother is fine. Your sisters and mother are dead,") Detective Wallace corrected me.

"How?" I demanded.

("I can't tell you that because we have yet to make any arrests. Your brother needs you though. I'd like you to come down and help him with the arrangements,") Detective Wallace requested.

"I'll be on the next flight out," I assured him.

I hung up the phone. I turned as Jessy walked into my arms, wrapping hers' around me. Samuel was standing in the hallway. He knew something was wrong, but was unsure of how to react. I remembered when I was like that. Now I knew how to act. I had to take care of the problem since the cops weren't able to. I turned to grab my bag, but Jessy grabbed my arm to stop me.

"I've already made arrangements for us to go with you," Jessy said as she made me look at her.

"Jessy, I can't...," I began.

"You need more than blood for this, Charles. You need love," Jessy stated, cutting me off.

"I know that no matter where you're at, you love me without fault," I said pulling her into a kiss.

I let her go get her bags and the bags she got ready for Samuel. I went ahead and got Samuel set up in my truck. I helped Jessy put the bags in the back and then we were off. It was strange having her with me for this. She wouldn't let go of my hand. It was comforting, but more than that, I didn't think about the blood I was soon to spill. I thought about the family that was with me, the family I longed for. It was peaceful for me.

The plane took far too long to board. I would have been out of my mind with frustration if Jessy had not been there. We loaded the plane and finally got off the ground. Judy was at the airport waiting for us. She hugged us both, offering her condolences and her help. I assured her that I could handle it and thanked her anyways. She took us to meet my brother in Fayette. He looked like hell, but I could tell that he was trying to keep up appearances. We moved everything into his car and made the rest of the trip with him. We ended up in a hotel room because Mom and the others were killed at her house. David lent me his spare car to use while we were down. Something about the way he was behaving was suspicious. I decided to corner him later that night.

"David," I said when I caught him away from everyone else.

"Yea," he said without facing me.

"What are you hiding?" I asked.

"I don't know what you're talking about," he stated and started to walk away.

"I know better, baby brother. You know why this happened. Tell me so I can make it right," I demanded.

"They'd just kill you too," David spat.

"David, you have no idea what I've done in my life," I started.

"You can't kill. I never thought you could even fight. Yea, you proved me wrong, but you're no killer. You need to leave it alone," David warned.

"David, I've killed over a hundred men. I'm so lethal with a blade that I give a whole new meaning to bringing a knife to a gunfight. I can kill them all, without getting hurt or caught," I told him.

"How can you say that? I've known you my whole life. I know better. You aren't a killer," David argued.

With that said he turned to walk away. I pulled the pocket knife out of my pocket, opened it up, and launched it over his shoulder. He stopped as he watched the knife hit the dead center of his bird feeder. He slowly turned to look me in the face. Disbelief covered his face, as I knew it would. He realized that I wasn't lying. He pulled the knife out of his bird feeder and walked over to me, offering my knife back to me. I took it and put it up.

"What happened to you?" David asked.

"I broke and became who I was always meant to be," I answered as best I could.

"Mom, Angel, Rockie, and the others were killed over me owing someone money," David said and walked away.

I knew who he meant the minute he mentioned money. It was the man who put out the hit on me, the man that had his guys jump my brother, the man who had the guy in the blue neon hound Mike and Kay, the very man who ran everything illegal in the area. This time I intended to make him fully aware of what I could do. I went back inside to keep appearances, just as my brother was. Jessy could tell that I was planning something, but decided to wait before asking. Jessy cornered me after we got Samuel in bed that night.

"What did you find out?" Jessy demanded.

"Who and why," I said as I pulled a small bag out of my suitcase.

"Details," she demanded.

"There is a man in this area that runs all of the crime. David borrowed money from him awhile back. This man decided to collect and I got in the way. He took out a bounty on my head, but I killed the group that decided to collect. I can only assume that he got tired of waiting and had someone kill our family to get to us. Now, I plan on making it very clear who's got the means to kill and who should take a seat," I explained.

"How bad do you think it will get?" Jessy asked full of concern.

"I can handle anything he can throw at me," I promised.

"I'll hold you to that," Jessy said as I finished getting ready for my attack.

I went outside and walked to the nearest car dealership. I hotwired one of the cars and took it for a ride. It took me over an hour to find his house, but once I did, it was obvious why no one ever dared to do what I was about to attempt. I got out of the car and walked around to scope the place. A rustle in the woods behind me made me hide. A man came walking by. He was carrying a rifle and one handgun. I slipped behind him and went to strike when the moon showed me his face. It was Mike. I stopped and watched him for a minute to see if he would notice me. It took him awhile but he spotted me and walked toward me.

"I heard about your family. I didn't figure you'd need help, but I owe this man too. I'm not quiet enough to get in there without all of his men coming after me. I figure you can. I just want you to let me pull the trigger," Mike explained.

"I'll get you in and I'll watch your back," I promised.

Mike nodded and followed my led. I pulled out three arrows and notched them. I walked out of the woods and straight toward the front door. I let the arrows fly and both guards went down. The third arrow hit the camera just above their heads. I walked right up to the door with Mike right behind me. I opened the door and walked right in. Two guards rounded the corner. I put a knife in both of them and kept walking. I stopped just outside of the study and peaked inside. Our target was in there with three other men. Laughter flowed from the next room, alerting me to at least four more guards in the kitchen. I motioned for Mike to count to five after I went into the kitchen. He nodded and pulled out his handgun.

I walked over to the kitchen door. I looked at Mike and nodded. I took a breath and walked through the door. There was a man in front of me with his back to me. I pulled out one knife for my right hand and two for my left. I pulled the one in my right across his throat. There was one guy in the back sitting at the table. As I finished slitting the first man's throat, I let the knife fly, killing the man in the back. There were two more guys standing at the kitchen counter. They turned as the first man started to fall. I swung my left hand over the falling man and released the knives. Both men by the counter grabbed their throats as my blades went in. They both fell and I walked over to the door that led to the study to wait for Mike to make his move. I heard two gunshots and opened the door. Our target was cowering behind his desk. Mike was standing just inside the door with his gun trained on our target.

"Mike, what the hell! Charles isn't it?" our target said as he tried to get a grip.

"You killed her. It was your fault she died," Mike stated.

"And you just couldn't accept defeat, could you?" I demanded.

"So you're here to avenge your family. But Mike the only person I've been after is Charles. I don't know why you're here," the man claimed.

"The men that killed my wife, Kay, were mercenaries. I had a friend track them down. You were the one who hired them. You are to blame for her death," Mike explained.

"You don't get it do you? I hired them to kill Charles. She's dead because of him," the man stated.

"Charles is the best man I know. He does the things that everyone else is too afraid to do. Yes, he was the target, but he risked his life to save us. You put us in that position, not Charles," Mike said as he walked toward him.

"We are not judges. We are executioners who send you to be judged by the only one who has that right. You aren't the first, and I doubt that you will be the last. It's time for you to be judged," I said as I walked to the other side of the desk.

Mike looked at him one last time and pulled the trigger. Mike offered me a ride so we could eliminate the stolen vehicle from being evidence. He dropped me off about a mile from the hotel room. I used the walk to unwind. Jessy was still up when I got back. She was relieved to see me, and I to see her. I slept well that night, but only because I slept next to her.

The next day was the funeral. I was usually dressed in black, but never a suit. Everything was going as expected. David and I were given condolences from everyone, even some we didn't know. I kept my usual calm outlook. David was a complete wreck. As the funeral came to a close, Detective Wallace showed up. Unfortunately he was not alone. Agent Marks was right behind him with a large grin on his face. I looked at David and Jessy and shook my head to keep them from getting involved.

"Mr. Beast, we meet again," Agent Marks greeted as he pulled out a pair of handcuffs. "Told you that I'd get you."

"I'm sorry Mr. Beast, but you are under arrest for the

murder of Sam Night and eight other people," Detective Wallace said as Agent Marks put the handcuffs on.

Murmurs rippled through the crowd as the two officers escorted me to the back seat of their car. I didn't fight or argue because I had no intention of giving them a reason to use force, nor did I intend to cause a scene. The ride to the station was full of Agent Marks boosting about how right he was and how he would get a huge promotion for catching me at long last. It was nearly unbearable. I thanked Detective Wallace when he told Agent Marks to shut up because we were at the station. They put me in the interrogation room and walked out. I sat there waiting to see what they tried to claim would tie me to the murders. I always wore gloves, so finger prints were out of the question. The knives I used were untraceable. There was nothing that could tie me to the murders.

Detective Wallace was the first one back in. He set a Sunkist in front of me and took a seat. I took the can of soda and opened it. I drank half of it before setting it down and waited for Detective Wallace to explain. He just looked at me. I couldn't help but to find him familiar to me, but I couldn't put my finger on it. It was right after I picked up the Sunkist for another drink that I realized that I never said what I liked to drink. From there my mind went into overdrive until I remembered why he seemed familiar.

"James?" I asked.

"Took you long enough," James said as he started to relax a bit.

"Well it has been a very long time. Last time I saw you was when I was in fourth grade," I pointed out.

"True. Charles, I need to know if you had anything to do with Sam's murder," James tried.

"I came here to bury my family. I've only just been in town twenty-four hours. How could I know who killed them before you guys?" I contested.

"People have ways. Look, Agent Marks is hell bent on you being this big time murder. He wants to put you away and seems willing to do just about anything to make sure he does. I need to know everything you know," James stated.

"All I know about Sam is that my brother owed or owes him some money. He went after my brother a few years back and I got in the way. That's it," I said only what I knew would keep me off the chopping block.

"I'll do what I can. Just hang tight," James said just before Agent Marks entered the room.

"Agent Marks, I believe you have the wrong man," James said as he stepped between us.

"No I don't. The way he kills is unmistakable. He is the man I've been looking for. It's time I take him down," Agent Marks said as he pushed James out of the way.

"He's innocent!" James exclaimed.

"Confess!" Agent Marks demanded.

"To what? I didn't kill," I stated firmly.

"You know what," Agent Marks spat.

"You have nothing but hunches to lead you. Without evidence, you have nothing," James said.

Before any of us knew what was happening, Agent Marks pulled his gun and shot James. He moved to aim it at me, but I was quick enough to stop him. His free hand grabbed the table and pushed it into me. I used my left hand to keep myself from falling. Beating persisted on the door, but Marks had locked it on his way in. James was dying and I was running out of options.

"I know you killed them. I know that you killed Richard, Michael, Pedro, and Thomas. Thomas let me know before you got to him. You will die today," Marks stated, explaining everything.

"You're the fifth hit man. Thomas said he killed you," I said as I put everything together.

"You should have double checked. I may have to go down with you, but you die today," Marks stated as he took a step back to free his arm.

I kicked the table hard enough to throw it into the air. Marks hadn't noticed me grab the pen off of the table, but it was too late for it to do any good. Two rounds went through the table. Both would have hit me had I not moved to the side and taken a step forward. The door suddenly opened and I let the pen slip from my hand. The cops noticed what was going on and started ordering Marks to put his gun down. Instead of doing as he was told, he pointed the gun at me. Before he could pull the trigger, three shots rang in the air. Marks fell to the ground and all of the cops looked stunned. James was laying in a puddle of his own blood with his gun trained on where Marks was standing. Marks dropped his gun, then fell to his knees, then fell on his face. I watched until I heard something else hit the ground. I looked at James, but it was too late. James died because I hadn't finished a job I started. Rage filled me, but there was nowhere to send it, because Marks was dead.

I stayed in town three days longer than I had planned so I could attend James's funeral. I went to visit his family to find that his wife had died three years back and that his only living relative was his six year old son.

"What will happen to him?" I asked the child services representative.

"We will place him in a foster home until we can find a permanent home for him," she explained.

"Would it be possible for me to adopt him? It's the least I can do after his father saved me," I asked. Jessy looked at me with a mix of love and joy.

"It would take some time and we'd have to do a background check and inspect your house," she answered.

"Jessy?" I asked.

"I'd love to have him," Jessy agreed.

"But you don't have a permanent residence do you?" she asked.

"I do and Charles and I are engaged. He's moving in after we get everything sorted out here," Jessy piped in.

"Alright, if you would fill this out, please. As soon as we can, I'll set up an interview, but I'm afraid that he has to come with me until then," she informed us.

"That's alright. We'll see you soon, Anthony," I said as I patted him on his shoulder.

That night I did exactly what I should have the day Jessy turned eighteen. I dropped to one knee and used a ring to propose to her. She screamed yes, which would have set the mood, but it woke Samuel up. We sat there for an hour trying to convince him that everything was alright so he'd go back to sleep. Finally, we got him to sleep, but only after Jessy had fallen asleep. I laid there and watched them sleep. It was everything I wanted and soon enough I would have another boy to raise and protect.

22

It took me a little over a week to get everything set up in the house. Jessy helped me keep everything neat and the way she wanted it. I may be stubborn, but I couldn't win a single argument with her. Samuel was getting use to me being around the house. I found a local job that I enjoyed. We were just getting into a routine when Child Services showed up to start inspecting the house. A week after they finished, Anthony came to live with us. He was three years older than Samuel, but they seemed to enjoy having a brother to play with for a change.

Before long we were a happy family. Samuel's birthday was less than a week away and Anthony's was only four weeks after that. Jessy and I went shopping for the birthday gifts while Beth watched all of the kids. Beth was pregnant with her second kid which was due in six months. Jessy was going to start planning her baby shower after we made it through birthday season. Life seemed normal for change, more so than even my childhood. The day of Samuel's birthday party I received a phone call from John. I stepped outside to take it.

"Yea," I answered.

("It's John,") John informed me.

"John, I have caller id. I knew you were the one calling the minute the phone started ringing. What's up?" I pointed out.

("The man we brought back from Mexico gave us some information. He told us what the hostages were there for. They were being used in an experiment. It was a recreation of the experiment that created us,") John explained.

"How would they know about that?" I almost shouted.

("We asked the same question and got one name. Lilith,") John informed me.

"Who's Lilith?" I asked suddenly lost.

("Cain's mate. It would appear that Cain and Lilith are moving to expand our numbers. Mary and I aren't enough to kill both of them,") John stated, implying a request for help.

"Why can't you go toe to toe with your own?" I wondered aloud as one of the kids walked out the door to go to their waiting parent.

("Cain is the best fighter that was produced. Lilith is crafty and will no doubt kill us before he has to,") John explained the difference in abilities.

"So you need someone who is craftier and can keep pace with Cain? I can pull that, but I need two days," I said.

("Alright, but Charles, we only need you for one out of the two,") John corrected.

"What? Which one?" I asked.

("The crafty part. Cain would most certainly kill you in a fight. If you can get Lilith out of the way, Mary and I can handle Cain,") John explained.

"Well, alright. This is your target and I should let you have the lead," I said sounding a little disappointed.

("Meet us in New Mexico at noon in two days. We will find you where ever you land so just make sure you get to New Mexico,") John stated right before he hung up on me.

"You have business to attend to?" Jessy inquired as I walked back in the door.

"In two days. I'm not leaving on his birthday, no matter what," I promised.

"I know. You've started the path out of that life. You're almost there," Jessy said as she walked up to me and kissed me.

The party was great. I was proud that I was giving Samuel the childhood I never had. He was having a blast with all of the other kids, especially Anthony. There was a knock on the door halfway through the party. I told Jessy to let me answer it so she could handle the kids. I never expected to see the person that was standing at the door when I opened it.

"Hello Charles," Sarah said as she smiled at me from just outside my house.

"Sarah? What the," I began.

"This is our son, Patrick. Today's his fourth birthday and I promised him that he'd met his father today," Sarah cut me off to explain.

"This is awkward. You show up to one son's birthday

party with my other son that I never knew existed. Sarah, you have bad timing," I stated.

"So you have another son who is how old today?" Sarah asked.

"Today's his fourth birthday," I answered.

"How strange. Patrick, your father has a power number of eight, just like you and your half-brother," Sarah said as she walked her son in my front door.

"How about we not say anything about who his father is until, never," I recommended.

"I'll wait until everyone leaves. That's the best I can do," Sarah said.

"Fine," I agreed feeling that there was no other way.

The party went by much too slow after that. I kept waiting for Sarah to blow the top off of everything, but she stuck to her word and didn't say a word to Jessy. She helped Jessy herd the kids and their parents out the door while Anthony, Samuel, and Patrick ran around playing with the new toys. Then, came the moment of truth.

"Jessy, this is the assassin, Sarah, the one I told you about," I introduced.

"The one you slept with?" Jessy asked, suddenly not very friendly.

"You told her about us?" Sarah asked, surprised.

"I've told Jessy everything, but I don't think either of us expected this," I said pointing at her and Patrick.

"Wait, he's your son?" Jessy asked suddenly pissed off.

"It appears that way," I said trying not to piss her off anymore.

"Don't worry, if he wanted me, he would have come," Sarah assured her, which didn't help much.

"You're not helping," I pointed out.

"I only came because it seems that your blood is very powerful," Sarah stated.

"Come again?" Jessy demanded.

"His number is eight. You know, the number you get when you add your birthday until you get one digit. Since both of your kids have the same birthday, they both have the same number. They also have your gifts," Sarah explained.

"You mean the knife throwing?" Jessy asked.

"Guess you already caught him playing with knives. Has he killed anyone?" Sarah noticed.

"God no!" Jessy exclaimed, now really pissed.

"Has Patrick?" I asked.

"One of my marks had me cornered. Patrick saved my life. It was three weeks ago. He asked me to take him to his father as a birthday present right after that. They both have your instinct and skill. They will probably surpass you," Sarah explained.

"I'm going to raise Samuel away from that life," I stated.

"Charles, it's in his blood. He'll find his way to it. You did," Sarah pointed out.

"Life pushed me into this. I won't let it do the same to him. Sarah, you're welcome to bring Patrick here when you have a mark, but please do not bring him here if he will teach Samuel how to kill," I requested as I offered assistance.

"Alright, but how can you expect that to happen when you're just like me, in the fight?" Sarah challenged.

"I'm working my way out," I said to answer her question.

"For some of us, there is no way out," Sarah warned.

"There's no harm in trying for my family's sake," I stated.

"Well, maybe I'll see you on a mission soon, or maybe not at all. Take care," Sarah said as she headed for the door.

It was later that night that I left to meet up with John and Mary. It didn't take me but a few hours to get down there. I waited around for the better part of a day before it was time to meet up. They weren't hard for me to find once I got into town. I met up with them by a sewer entrance. I had no idea what was going on, but John and Mary were on their toes, so I decided it was best if I did the same. Instead of filling me in, they just went in. I followed, careful not to get ahead of them. This was their game and I was just a weapon to win it with.

We stopped at the first intersection. They took a knee, but I decided not to sink any further into the sewage we were wading through. John and Mary looked at me, waiting for me to follow their lead. I just shook my head and crossed my arms over my chest. Mary and John looked at each other and shrugged.

"They are hiding in this sewer somewhere. We need to find and eliminate their nest," John informed me.

"Wait! What do you mean nest? Their hiding spot?" I asked suddenly not too sure I liked this mission.

"The place they have been attempting to create more of us," Mary answered.

"Yup, this is going to be a very bad day," I decided the minute they told me what we were up against.

We worked our way through the sewer, making sure to watch every step. It was several hours after we went into the sewer that we found any sign of the nest. There was a middle aged man hunched over in one of the pipes. He didn't seem to notice us at first, but when he did, things got really messy. He turned toward us and glared for what seemed like a lifetime. I started to feel uneasy, but that was when he attacked. John intercepted him and cut him clean in half. He let out a hideous cry before his head went under the sewage.

Cries went off throughout the sewer. It seemed as though we had set off an alarm that could get us killed. There were three pipes leading away from us. We each took one and waited for the attackers. Mary was the first to see action. John was next. They each had three, but I was dry. Then, something stirred the water behind me. I drew my katana just in time to take one of their heads. That was when it got really interesting. There were two coming from behind us. I grabbed three throwing stars and prepared to launch them, but I heard a splash coming from the pipe I was watching. I turned and launched the throwing stars down the pipe, stopping the one that was making his way toward me. I spun, pulling a knife as I did. I was just in time to plant the knife in one of the others throat. I crossed my katana over and took his head off. I pulled the knife out and dropped to a knee. The other one missed her swing when I dropped. I jabbed the knife into her knee, forcing her to drop to my level. I pushed the katana into her neck, severing her spinal cord. I pulled the knife out and stood up, shifting the knife so I could throw it. I launched the knife, hitting my mark in his temple. He fell as Mary finished off her last opponent. John had the last one pinned against the wall.

"Did you just save my ass?" Mary asked as she saw the knife sticking out of the one behind her.

"Don't mention it. I don't want anyone knowing I was down here," I remarked.

"Where is the nest?" John asked.

"Mother won't let me," the last said.

From out of nowhere, a throwing star went clean through John's shoulder and into the last one's skull. Mary ran to John to check on him. I turned, launching three throwing stars in the direction the other came from. I heard two hit the wall of the pipe. I moved my katana just in time to deflect the other one. A woman came barreling in. She pressed down on me, but I was able to jump out of the way, or so I thought. She grabbed my foot and launched me at the wall. I dropped my katana as I hit, but still managed to land on my feet. I dropped to my knees, making it look as though I was hurt. I wrapped my hand around my katana and waited to see if she took the bait.

I looked up, expecting to see her face. She was going head to head with Mary. John was leaning against the sewer wall. I looked back toward the fight to see Mary get sent flying away from Lilith. I stood up and charged her. I almost caught her off guard, but when I got too close, the ripples in the sludge made her aware of me. She tried to swat me away, but I dropped beneath her swing. I started to drive my katana toward her for a kill shot, but she deflected it with her dagger. I spun around in one last attempt to take the advantage, and got lucky. I swept my leg behind her and took her to her knees. Mary and John were both there in time to save me from her dagger, and run her through. Mary then took Lilith's head off to ensure that she was dead.

We all stood up and turned to finish our search, but it was unnecessary. Cain was standing in our way. He had two swords, bastard swords if my eyes didn't deceive me. I couldn't see his face, but I could feel his rage as it built into an attack. John and Mary spread out. They motioned for me to back up. They wanted me to get out of this fight. I came this far. I intended to see it through. The stare down seemed to last forever as John and Mary got into comfortable positions to increase their odds. Unfortunately, they were both injured and couldn't guarantee victory.

"Why have you betrayed us?" Cain demanded.

"We aren't humans, Cain. The professor made us into something else. We have no right to do it to others," John answered.

"We have every right. We are the stronger race. We can do whatever we please. The professor gave us that right. You betrayed us. You betrayed him. And now, now you've killed one of your own, my mate. I will have revenge," Cain spat.

"We had to stop you. The humans are the ones that deserve Earth, not us," Mary tried.

"Survival of the Fittest is the principle that I believe. Human, do you think that your bread deserves this planet?" Cain asked me.

"We were put here to keep it. We've done a piss poor job of it, but God put us here. Who put you here? It wasn't anyone who had a right to say who could control the earth. It was a man who had a dream, a dream that could destroy the world, or improve it. You aren't following his dream. If you want to follow his dream, then merge with humanity, and make them better. Exterminating them isn't what he wanted of any of you. I know that I will die, but I'll have no regrets. I will have done what I could to make humanity better," I answered.

"You're the one who killed Abel. I must avenge all of my fallen brothers and sisters, and most importantly, my wife," Cain said as he started to lift his swords.

Cain charged me first. Mary and John both moved to intercept him. As I guessed, it was all part of his plan. He sent them flying into walls as they got too close. I dropped my katana the minute I saw him coming and grabbed my throwing knives. As soon as Mary and John were moved out of the way, I let them loose. I dropped to my knee and grabbed my katana just in time to use it to divert his attack over my head. I pulled the dagger I had strapped to my back, and tried to slice into Cain's throat. Cain took a step back and avoided the attack. Cain crossed his swords and took a step forward, slashing his swords like scissors in an attempt to take me. I used my katana to stop his swords and dropped to my knees. This gave me an opening to stab him in his gut. I took it, running my dagger into his stomach. Unfortunately, my katana was cut at the hilt by his scissor cut. As the shock set in, Cain's knee met my face and sent me flying. Cain caught my leg and threw me in the opposite direction. I expected to hit a wall, but someone caught me. I looked up to see Mary. Her eyes were on Cain, but when I looked back at him, John had one of his hatchets in Cain's side. Cain grabbed John and threw him at us.

Cain had us where he wanted us. We were all grouped

together, and his weapons were more than capable of slicing through all of us at once. Cain charged us. He moved his swords back into position to do his scissor cut, but this time I was ready with a counter. I pulled out two hunting knives and stepped onto a pipe behind me. I timed it to the best of my abilities. I jumped over his attack, landing inside his arms. I buried my knives into his neck and dropped. John had used his second hatchet to stop Cain's attack. Mary did a flip over them both and took off the top half of Cain's head.

Tired and beaten, we made our way back out of the sewer. It was a long drive home. I think it was only so long, because I smelled like sewage and I was black and blue from getting tossed around so much. When I got home I burned my clothes and got in the shower. Then I went out and cleaned the truck top to bottom. It took me all day to get rid of the smell, but I did it. Jessy came home with Samuel as I was finishing dinner. Jessy seemed surprised, but glad to see me. That night, I had the best night's sleep I could remember.

23

The next day seemed like it was going to be very uneventful. I got up and got Samuel ready for preschool while Jessy got ready for work. After they left, I got a shower and started cleaning. I even cleaned the dishes, which was the only bit of cleaning I hated.

It was just after noon when I finished cleaning. I sat down and turned on the TV. I was flipping through channels, looking for something worth watching. I passed a news report, but when I realized it was a live broadcast, I went back. There was a bank robbery just over two miles from where I was sitting. The robbers were armed and had at least twenty hostages. They were refusing to talk to the police and threatening to kill hostages if the police didn't stay back.

I stood up and looked and started toward the door. I stopped as I grabbed the doorknob. I couldn't go without covering my face. Worse than that, how would I get in the bank without the cops stopping me or the robbers seeing me? I went to the closet to look for something to cover my face. I searched and searched, but only found a clown mask. I picked it up and sighed. I didn't have a choice, so I went to put it on. I saw the rest of the costume laying there and decided to go all out. I grabbed one of my trench coats and put it on over the clown suit.

I got in my truck and drove as close as I could without alerting the cops or any civilians to my presence. I slipped into the building next to the bank and used it to scout the bank. I noticed a manhole that was uncovered and decided that it was the way the robbers got into the bank. I slipped into the sewer and made my way around looking for the way in. It didn't take me long, because they left a guy to guard it. I stepped into the open and started waving at the guy. He looked confused when he spotted me. I had a knife between my fingers, so when he started to point his gun at me, I launched it at him. He fired off a few rounds, but I had stepped behind a wall to be on the safe side. I waited for the splash and walked out. The guy was face down in the sewage. I walked by him and climbed the ladder they had made to get in.

Of course, the hole leads into the bathroom. I looked around before pulling myself up. I cracked the bathroom door. There were three hostages and one robber within my line of sight. I looked at my clown suit and shrugged my shoulders. I opened the door and stepped out, fixing my pants as a cover to pull a knife. The robber and the hostages all looked at me with wide eyes. I tilted my head from side to side as I walked toward the robber. He started the pull his gun toward me, but he was too late. I grabbed the gun, putting my finger behind the trigger to prevent him from firing it. I jabbed the knife into his throat. Instead of stopping like I usually would, I pulled it out and stabbed him a few more times. I dropped the robber and turned to the hostages. I put my finger to the lips on the mask and waved the knife in a no gesture to keep them quiet. I gave them the thumbs up and proceeded down the hall.

I ended up by the vault. There were two robbers in there with the manager. I stopped to think of a plan, but as I stood there, a shadow started moving at the other end of the hall. I prepared my knife and as soon as I saw the gun, I let it fly. The guy fell backwards without a sound as far as I could hear. I took a breath and tiptoed across the vault door and ran over to his body. I looked down the hall he had come from but only saw the back of the counter. I looked at the dead guy and got an idea. I picked the guy up and put his arm over my shoulder. I slipped a knife just inside each of my sleeves to keep them out of sight.

I walked him into the vault with me. All three of them turned to look at me, but horror crossed their faces. I pointed at the dead guy and than at the end of the hall where I killed him. None of them knew what to think of what they were seeing. I just kept pointing, hoping that they would either go look at what I was pointing at or something other than shooting me.

"What happened? Quit pointing and tell me," one of them demanded.

I just kept pointing at the hall. I dropped the dead guy and pointed at the knife and then back at the hall. The knife got their attention well enough for the one who hadn't said anything to walk out into the hall. No sooner had he turned the corner than I let the knife slip into my left hand. I never looked at the guy in the room, but I still hit him in his throat. I looked back at his dead body and then at the manager. I put my fingers to my lips and ran out the vault door. I started jumping up and down to get the guys attention. He looked at me and immediately aimed at me with his gun. I held my hands up in the no don't gesture and then started pointing in the vault and jumping up and down again. He walked over to the opening but never took his gun off of me. He got too close and put the gun right up to my chest when he took a look inside. I swatted his gun away and jabbed the knife into his throat. I pushed him into the vault and pointed at the manager. I pulled the knife across my throat, without touching myself, to make her think that I'd kill her too if she moved.

I went back down the hall and got down to crawl to the lobby. I stuck my head up and looked around to see how many more I had to kill. A few of the hostages saw me, but every one of them had tape on their mouths so they couldn't rat me out. I pulled out my last three knives and worked out how to kill them all without getting shot, while only having three knives. It didn't take as long as you would figure. I crawled around the counter and stood up. I brushed myself off as everyone took notice of me. The closest robber walked over to me and poked me with his gun. I looked at him as if he startled me and started to explain with motions until I spotted the gun. Then, I threw my hands up.

"Where the hell did you come from?" the robber asked.

I started pointing toward the back. I gave him directions without opening my mouth which probably confused him. He gave me one of those "what the hell" looks and put the gun to my chin and pushed up. I immediately threw my hands back up and did the gulp thing.

"You better speak up before I put a bullet in your head," the robber demanded.

The clown suit was starting to irritate me. It was itching like crazy and I was starting to sweat. I hadn't said anything for over an hour and that didn't sit well with me. The hand gestures were starting to bother me, and I was getting tired of acting. Who knew acting could be so much work. I decided it was time to finish this.

I swiped the gun away with my right and elbowed him, giving me an open shot at the partner that was behind him. I nailed him in the forehead. I grabbed his head and slammed it into the counter and stepped behind him to cross over as I launch knife number two at the guy that was behind me. His gun went of as he fell backwards. I pulled the guy up and in front of me as his last partner by the door opened fire. I used him to block his partner's shot. I grabbed my last knife and launched it at the last guy, dropping him before he could get another shot off. I slammed him into the counter again. I looked around and decided to do it twice more for good measure. After the fourth time his head bounced off the counter, I threw him to the ground.

I looked at all of the scared hostages that I just saved. I decided that it would be funny, so I waved at all of them as if I were a real clown and then walked back behind the counter. I gave the manager thumbs up as I passed the vault and went back into the bathroom. I climbed back into the sewer. I decided to head to where I parked rather than back the way I came in. I moved what I thought was the closest manhole, but it turned out that I was parked over it. To some extent it worked out better that way, but I felt that it was a tight fit. I got out of the clown suit before rolling out from under the truck. There was a guy walking by who started staring.

"Oil leak," I said with a shrug.

I got in my truck and went home. I jumped in the shower and burned the clown suit. I was pretty sure I just ruined the circus for a lot of people. I got out of the shower and started cooking something for lunch. The phone started ringing as I was pulling the food out of the oven. It was my former boss calling.

("Charles, I want you to come back to work for me. This new guy isn't as talented as you. I only have half the customer satisfaction rate that I had when you were the designer. What do you say?") He asked.

"Mr. Dufton, I have a family now. I'm getting married in just over a year. I need to stay closer to home," I explained.

("I can increase your pay,") Mr. Dufton offered.

"The money isn't the problem. I still have a large chunk of what I earned. I just need to be here more than on the road," I stated.

("Alright, how about this? You design the homes and we'll let Ted design the industrial buildings. I only have the manpower to build one thing at a time, so you'll only be on the road three to six months out of the year. And, you'll be bringing in twenty to forty thousand a year, depending on how much time your on call,") Mr. Dufton proposed.

"That is actually a very generous offer. I'll talk it over with the future wife and let you know something tomorrow," I decided.

("I look forward to it,") Mr. Dufton agreed.

That night I made dinner. Jessy was happy to see dinner ready when she got home. I knew she was enjoying the life of a working woman. I decided to talk to her after we got done eating and cleaning. She didn't give me the chance I was looking for.

"Mr. Dufton called me today," Jessy opened.

"He doesn't leave much to chance. Did he explain everything?" I asked.

"You know you'll probably be on the road six months," Jessy stated.

"I could guess that much. I told him I'd talk to you," I informed her.

"Yes, I think you should. At least now I shouldn't have to worry about you," Jessy said with a displeased tone.

"Ok, what is it that's bothering you?" I inquired.

"Did you burn the clown suit when you were done killing the bank robbers?" Jessy asked.

"Yes," I said before taking another bite.

"Please tell me you're almost done," Jessy begged.

"I can't say that I won't occasionally do something like this. It's second nature for me. But going out of my way to handle people like that, that's what stops. I'm not the avenger anymore. I'm a father and most importantly, I'm in love with you," I promised the best I could.

"I know. I love you too," Jessy replied.

24

The next year went by faster than I thought. Samuel's fifth birthday was a blast. I have to admit that I wasn't happy when they gave me a surprise party for my thirtieth birthday. Everyone was there. Judy and her bunch were late, but David was even later. I didn't get much, but that didn't bother me. I was happy for the first time ever. This was all I ever wanted, and it was enough to stop the killing. I pulled Judy to the side before she left to pass her my weapons.

"Judy, it's time for me to stop. I want you to hold onto these. They won't be doing me any good. Tell the others that they are welcome to come by anytime, but I'm out," I said as I handed her the suitcase full of my weapons.

"What about Adam and Eve?" Judy asked as they were the only unfinished business left.

"They've been quiet. I think they did what John and Mary did. I think they settled down to live life. I think we all should, for awhile at least. Wouldn't want to forget why we were fighting," I suggested.

"Charles, you were the only one who didn't have the

life to fight for. Now you do. I want you to enjoy it. If you need me, call me," Judy demanded.

She gave me hug and then hauled the suitcase to her car. I watched as they drove away. I could feel the burden being lifted as they got further and further away. I turned to go back inside, but David was standing there, blocking the door. He took a step forward and looked at me with a smile on his face.

"You're a far better man than I could ever be," David stated.

"No, David, I'm a smarter man, but nowhere near a better man. I've killed so many. A better man wouldn't have killed to make the world better. He could have done it without violence. Killing was the only way I could get the job done. You may not have been smart when you borrowed money, but you didn't kill for any reason. You started a family and lived a good life. Don't ever believe otherwise. Now get going before you're late getting home to the wife," I said, patting his shoulder as I walked into the house.

Jessy was waiting for me on the couch. I walked over and sat down. I put my arm around her as she curled into my chest. I laid my head on hers. We sat there just staring off into space. I didn't know what she was thinking about, but I was lost in the life I finally had. Thinking back, I would have never had the chance to meet Jessy if I hadn't become a killer. I would have continued to take crap from everyone, and never had anything to call my own. I would have continued to have people taking advantage of me. That's all over. I am the man I was meant to be all along. I was going to grow old with the most beautiful woman I had ever met. She would be my strength. She would be my wife.

We woke up still sitting on the couch the next morning. Samuel was already up getting ready for school on his own. He was advancing much faster than any of the teachers could have believed. I got up and finished getting him ready. Jessy went and got ready for our long day of errands. The wedding was only three months away and I couldn't wait. Jessy took Samuel to school while I got in the shower. Jessy was just walking though the door when I got finished getting dressed. We stopped and got breakfast before continuing to the bank to set up a joint account.

The bank seemed busier than usual. There were four guys that didn't seem to be doing much more than standing around. I pulled out my phone and typed in nine-one-one, just incase. I put it back in my pocket and continued to wait in line with Jessy. At nine o'clock exactly, the four men and one of the tellers, pulled guns and each let off two rounds. I hit the call button on my phone so the police would be able to hear what was going on. The robbers started collecting everybody's cell phones. I slipped mine into a trash can so they wouldn't find it.

They forced us all to line up against the windows, to block anyone from seeing what was going on inside. They pushed the manager into the vault, just like to robbery I stopped over a year ago. The other three men stayed in the lobby with us to keep an eye on things. It was all starting to make sense now. One of the robbers escaped that day. He started a new crew and revised his plan. I could only stand there and watch, hoping that the police figured out what was going on thanks to my phone call.

It was about twenty minutes later when the cops showed up. Considering they were there in full force, I could assume that they got my call. One of the robbers stepped into the vault to let the other two know that the cops had arrived. If they did like they did the last time, they would use us to keep the cops at bay while they got what they wanted.

I looked over at Jessy. She was scared. I put my arm around her to comfort her, which got the attention of one of the robbers. He looked at Jessy for a minute or two and then walked over to us. He jabbed me in the chest with his gun.

"Take your hand off of her," He ordered.

"I'm trying to comfort my wife," I stated firmly.

"I can comfort her right in front of you. Now take your hand off of her," He threatened.

I pulled my hand back to my side. The robber grabbed Jessy and started to pull her away from me. I took one step forward, but was stopped by the sound of breaking glass. The robber who grabbed Jessy went down. I darted toward Jessy and wrapped my arms around her, trying to shield her from any gunfire that might ensue. I looked up just in time to see the other robber go down as a second bullet shattered the already cracked window. I looked at the counter to see two of the other three run out to the counter. They didn't even take aim as they moved their guns and opened fire. I spun around putting me between them and Jessy. Two more shots came in and killed them both, but not before they each let off three rounds. I watched two hostages go down. One had to be dead, while the other was shot in the shoulder. I dropped to my knee and started gasping for breath.

It didn't hit me at first, but then a sharp pain shot through my chest. My back was on fire as I forced myself to fight back the pain. My body began to shake as shock tried to set in. I fought it, but then I saw something that broke me. Jessy was screaming as tears ran down her face. She was doing everything she could to keep me from falling back. After seeing her tears, I couldn't fight. My body went limp. Blood started closing up my windpipe. I coughed and blood shot out onto the floor.

The police started charging in. I could see the paramedics waiting for the all clear. Everything started to blur. I looked at Jessy, refusing to look anywhere else. She was the only one I wanted to see as I died. She was the one who saved me from the fate of a killer. I slowly reached out and touched her face. "Clear," the police called as they spread out into the bank. I smiled as the last bit of light faded away.

I can only imagine that most people can only see darkness when the light fades, but I wasn't like anyone else. I burned Jessy's face into my vision before the light went out. My body seemed to wash away, but still I refused to look away from her face. Then, the most important thing of all happened. I heard her. I heard her voice one last time. It made me sad to hear those words, knowing that I wouldn't be there anymore. But at the same time, I was thrilled to know that we were stronger than ever. Jessy whispered, "I'm pregnant." Those were the last words I ever heard, and then everything was gone.

I miss him so much. Beth was at the hospital and didn't leave my side the whole time. Judy and David were back before I even had time to call them. The three of them and a mysterious couple helped me with everything. I wish that we had put off the bank trip, but I know that Charles wouldn't have changed what happened. The police pulled his phone out of the trash and said that he was the one who alerted them to the robbery. "He was a hero," they all said. No one knew anything about what he did for all those years, but the one time he couldn't kill, he died defending everyone.

Today has to be the hardest, because this was the day we were suppose to get married. I woke up, praying that it was all just a bad dream and that today was the happiest day of my life. But reality sets in as I roll over to find no one laying there next to me. I loved Charles since the first time I saw him, that will never change.

I watch Samuel as he becomes more and more like his father everyday. It scares me, but I know in my heart that he will be just fine. Even if he follows in his father's footsteps, he will have a team to guide him. I can only hope that Samuel and his brother Charles Jr. will be able to change the world the way Charles wished he could have. Maybe one day the world will have someone who can keep it out of the darkness.

About the Author

I am a young writer who simply wants to share my imagination with the world. My real name is not my reality, so as an author I am Thomas Blood. I currently reside in Alabama, but you never know where the world will take you. I am single, but I've come to accept that it is better this way. I'll admit that as a child I hated reading, because I was always moving and couldn't sit still long enough to get into a book. Now, I've grown to love books. I'm a writer because I love to tell stories, and until my imagination fades, I won't stop writing.